MYTHIC UPRISING

Mythic Uprising

A Fantastical Sci-Fi Drama

JUSTIN K. NUCKLES

Contents

vi ~ Contents

For Claire:
My Sammy

Chapter 1

I threw myself behind one of the huge Ponderosa pines, swallowing hard and sucking in air through my mouth. My left arm hung useless at my side as I grimaced, my teeth squeaking as they ground over each other. The bullet had hit just inside of my shoulder, and it hurt. Bad. I listened as bullets sprayed the other side of the tree and whizzed past, thwacking faintly as they buried themselves into the trees behind me.

Heretic's voice came over the speakers within my helmet. "James, you've got to focus. You'll never come out of this unscathed unless you can calm your mind and focus! Remember, you're looking for Flow."

I mentally cursed the android but made no verbal reply. *Let's see you focus while bullets are flying around you like bees!* I closed my eyes and took a few more breaths, trying to make them deep ones. My chest shook as I forced it to expand while fighting the urge to exhale quickly. *Three, four.* I let myself breathe out, controlling it to release it slowly. *Two, three, four.* I repeated it a couple more times.

The bullets had stopped. That probably meant that the shooters were changing position, most likely trying to flank me on either side and catch me in their crossfire. It's what I would do.

Trying not to imagine how I would look through another person's rifle sights, I forced myself to think. *How am I going to get out of this?* I needed more time. I looked down at my hands; nothing yet. I closed my eyes, took several additional deep breaths, and imagined myself squeezing through a hole the size of a tennis ball in the air above my left palm.

My heart wasn't beating quite as quickly as it had been, and my hands weren't shaking quite as much. It seemed like my body was finally getting the message that my brain had been trying to send it. After another moment with my eyes closed, I realized that I could hear my heartbeat. The rest of the world had gone silent around me.

I opened my eyes to the now-familiar scape of my own private pocket dimension. There was no ground, no sky, no floor, no ceiling, no walls. Simply bluish-grayish fog as far as the eye could see. In the area immediately around me hovered three familiar swirling masses suspended in the air: two large ones and another much smaller. The small one was the converted antimatter atoms that made up a pacifier, a baby blanket, and a small baby beanie. I'd absorbed them in a fit of newborn rage. The second and third mass, with their unique swirling golden lights, rather than just flat blue swirl, I still had trouble looking at.

One was what was left of Linda Benson, a nurse who had been conducting a routine medical procedure that I'd... reacted poorly to, also as a newborn. The third mass was the remains of Julian Danton, the man who'd ordered the murder of my parents and father to the Danton children, Jessica, Steven, Elizabeth, and Mary.

Thinking of them jogged me out of my reverie. They were the reason I was in my current situation. I shook my head and probed my shoulder gingerly. *How was I going to get out of this?*

From tests I'd done with Heretic, I knew that time wasn't passing outside the pocket dimension. Or, at least, it was passing so slowly that I couldn't even measure its passing. I tried to imagine the situation as I'd left it.

I was being flanked. Before long, the bullets that had been peppering the Ponderosas would be tearing into *me*. I had to do something, and it had to be something unexpected. *Be creative.*

Beyond the three masses closest to me, swirled a growing collection of shifting masses of various sizes. I'd done a lot of practicing, but I by no means had this ability mastered yet. *Focus!*

The easiest thing would be to absorb the tree in front of me and hope that the surprise gave me enough time to run the gauntlet between the two shooters and hopefully get to my objective before being drilled by bullets. Simple, and probably ineffective.

I needed to do something unexpected. Something I hadn't tried before.

I had an idea, but I wasn't sure how it would pan out. Only one way to know for sure. I closed my eyes again and imagined going out of that tennis-ball sized hole again.

I knew when I heard the wind blowing through the pines that I was back. There wasn't time to waste. I directed my palms toward each other, wincing at the pain in my left arm. A blinding flash lit up the trees around me as I directed a single antimatter atom from my left hand to collide with a single atom from my right. Almost as good as a flashbang. Before the flash had even finished fading, I stepped around the tree and pointed both palms down at my feet. Widening my stance and squaring my shoulders, I closed my eyes and mentally crossed my fingers. A larger and significantly louder bang sounded right beneath my feet, and I was blasted into the air. This was another fact we'd verified through rigorous testing: I was immune to the energy of these blasts. I was apparently built to withstand them with no ill effects.

Fortunately, I maintained enough presence of mind not to yell throughout the duration of my ungraceful flight, at least preserving my surprise. Now, I just had to make it down to the ground in one piece. I had just enough time to absorb the branches that would have broken bones or worse as I flew through the air. Unfortunately, that meant that my flight was a perfect, uninterrupted parabola, and I rushed toward the ground with increasing speed. Out of instinct, I pointed both palms toward the ground and directed a couple of blasts there. I slowed, but not enough. I crashed to the ground, managing a clumsy, badly executed half-roll that saved my legs from breaking. Instead, my right shoulder and side crashed heavily into the ground, leaving me wincing in pain and breathless on the forest floor. Looking down at my feet, I realized that, although I was immune to the energy of my blasts, my clothing was definitely not. My boots were shreds of rubber and leather, held together by some melted lace. Maybe this wasn't a great tactic, after all.

Pat and Clara Walker, co-directors of Safeguard, came stumbling out of the trees, both still rubbing their eyes and blinking furiously, rifles slung over their shoulders.

"James? Was that crunch you, man? You got us with the flashbang. I can't see anything behind this glare!" Pat blinked harder, like he thought he could *will* his eyes to regain their vision faster.

Clara swore. "What was that?"

I stood up gingerly. "I think I flew?"

Pat hooted in disbelief, cackling. "You can fly? This is crazy, man! It's like there isn't anything you can't do with these abilities!"

Clara stepped to my side, her eyes simply closed as she waited for the glare to fade. She put a hand on my shoulder. "You okay? Where'd we hit you earlier?"

"Shoulder," I said, as I did a check-in on the rest of my body to see whether anything hurt more than anything else. Luckily, the liquid armor that was standard issue among those who served with Safeguard, the organization dedicated to the relocating and managing of Mythic children, had done its job well. Beyond a bruise that I was sure would be the size of a softball on my shoulder that I'd get in the coming days, my shoulder would be just fine. The bruise would be right at home among the many others I had across my body.

"You okay?" Clara repeated.

"I'll be all right," I said.

"James, that was a foolish risk to take." Heretic stepped out of the woods, his dark clothing providing him a surprising amount of camouflage effect.

I took a step and winced as one of my ankles buckled weakly. I may have lightly sprained it.

"You're the one always pushing me to be creative, to try things I haven't done yet!"

The android was inscrutable, as always, behind his face-covering and goggles. Not that the video screen hidden behind them was any better. I still wasn't sure which I preferred. The screen, when utilized, displayed images of my parents' faces, when they were the uploaded personalities speaking through the android. Long before they'd died, they'd created Heretic to do what they felt like they couldn't at the time. He'd worked counter to the aims of Safeguard for years, finding the Mythic children who Safeguard Swept, Bitted, and Hosted and taking them to his own compound to restore their memories, unlock their abilities and raise until they were old enough to look after themselves and return to their own families.

"Creative, yes. Reckless, no." It was completely Heretic at the controls now; his bland, almost lazy tone was entirely his own, and fit his personality perfectly.

"Isn't that the point of these live exercises?" I countered. "To force us to improvise against each other and push the boundaries of what we know about my powers? Every time I try something new, I learn to master my abilities a little bit more. Every time I do that, we learn a little bit more about what Caine is capable of, and Clara and Pat can learn to adapt to and anticipate it."

Heretic didn't move, facing me. He didn't say anything for an uncomfortably long time.

"Did you guys leave? You still here?" Pat piped up, still blinded from the flash-bang effect. Pat abhorred silences.

"Be more careful." Heretic turned and walked back toward the vehicle. "Let's go. I want to get back to the home in time for dinner."

Pat whispered to us behind Heretic's back. "Why? He doesn't eat."

Heretic glanced back and shouted, "I heard that!"

Clara took Pat by the elbow. Apparently, her vision had cleared quicker. "C'mon," she said, offering me an arm as well.

I waved it away as I limped after Heretic.

Pat sniffed slightly and said, "Hey, does anyone else think these trees smell like Neapolitan ice cream?"

Clara affectionately punched him in the gut.

***

"How'd things go out there today?" Rachel Kline, my biological mother, jumped nimbly over the gap between the boulders then stopped and waited for me to follow.

It was tricky with my ankle, but I managed to cross it with the help of a stick I'd picked up at the beginning of our daily short hike.

"Not bad. I think I'm getting a better feel for the balance between my hands. The blasts feel more consistent, somehow, than they did when we started. I think I'm starting to get the hang of it."

She nodded and smiled encouragingly. "Well, that's good."

I squinted. "Yeah. I still just have a hard time getting into it. It isn't easy to lose yourself in something when you have bullets flying all around you."

She laughed. "I can't imagine why that might be." She rolled her eyes.

"Good point." I tapped my walking stick on a large red boulder with a crack down the middle.

Rachel sat down on another rock and looked back toward the home.

Located on a remote corner of a Navajo reservation in the American southwest, the home was a huge Earthship: a structure essentially built from earth, used tires, and old bottles to be entirely self-sufficient and self-sustaining. There were twenty-seven children living there, in total. There used to be twenty-eight, but the oldest, Shanice Turman, had recently gone back to her family in Georgia. I was equal parts disappointed and relieved about that. Shanice and I had parted ways as significantly less than friends. I'd tricked her into helping me leave the old home in California with the Danton children. She'd never really forgiven me, not even a year later. I still had scars from the first time I'd seen her after that, and she'd had a flock of birds dive-bomb me. Shanice was a Tamer.

Because this home wasn't a House of Bricks like the last one, children all over the place were doing all sorts of things normal children just didn't do.

I watched in amusement and amazement as two Tank teen boys jousted with entire fallen trees, a third girl looking on in feigned disgust. The trees shattered as they hit each other, and the boys collapsed on the ground, laughing. Some of the shattering tree debris had hit the girl, and she flicked a boulder the size of a toaster oven at them in annoyance.

Two Tamer boys ran laughing among several coyotes that barked and whined in pleasure while three Tamer girls sat petting a veritable menagerie of desert wildlife: I saw several hawks, a crow or two, several lizards, and a large skunk which had curled up contentedly in one of the girls' laps.

I wasn't sure what was going on between the two little girls and four boys sitting in a circle but based on the fact that one of them was walking around the outside of the circle, putting his hands on either side of one of their heads every so often, at which they would burst out laughing, I knew these were the Thinkers.

I could imagine that the Tinkers and Techs were inside, probably passing most closely for normal children, either controlling electronics or building some contraption together.

"I love it here." Rachel sighed, and rested her chin in her hand, a smile playing with the corners of her mouth.

"Really? It's so hot and dusty," I pointed out, stamping my foot and raising a small red cloud to demonstrate.

"Not *here*, here." She waved her finger in a wide circle around her head. She pointed down the hill back at the home and all the children. "Here."

I smiled. The equivalent of a lifetime ago, I'd been an Assistant Director in a university childcare facility. I came by my interests honestly, it seemed.

I smiled teasingly. "I know."

Rachel glanced at me and smiled.

"So, what's next? Do you have a timeframe for when you're going to move against Caine?"

I shook my head gently. "Nothing concrete." I started absently peeling bark from the stick. It was sticky with resin. Pine. I brought it to my nose and took a deep breath in. Pat was right: there was a faint hint of something like vanilla.

Rachel furrowed her brows, tucking her chin toward her throat. "What are you doing?"

I held the stick out to her. "Pat said these pines smell like ice cream earlier. He's not wrong."

"What? Get outta' here. Lemme' see." She took the stick and held it a few inches from her nose. She sniffed gingerly. "Huh." She brought it closer and breathed deeper. "Weird."

"I know, right? Who knew?" I took it back when she offered it and sniffed one more time myself before laughing and going back to watching the kids around the home.

I cleared my throat. "Hey, there was something I've been meaning to ask you."

Rachel ran a hand absently through her pixie-cut hair, nodding for me to go on. This had become a normal part of our routine, getting to know one another, and asking questions about each other's lives.

"What can you tell me about my dad?"

Rachel nodded gently and looked back at the home. "Yeah, I've been waiting for this." She leaned back, resting her palms on the ground behind her and putting one knee up on the other as she stared up into the sky.

"Your dad: my husband. His name was Joseph Kline. He was a wonderful, wonderful man." Her eyes closed somewhat and lost their focus. She was remembering something vividly. "I remember how we were both devastated at the thought that we'd lost you. When

I told him I'd lost the baby, he was just absolutely crushed. He was so tender with Raven, too, throughout that time." She shifted, sitting forward again and rubbing a pebble she'd picked up absently between her fingers. "And he was so patient with me. We hung in for five years after we lost you. Those were hard years. Even when I started to fall apart, he was still there, still trying to help me through it, trying to bring me back from it."

The skin around Rachel's eyes grew tight and lined, as her eyes slowly filled with tears. "I left *them*. Your parents, Jared and Deby, had Swept you from my mind, but I lost Raven and Joseph on my own. All those years, I was so high, so drunk, that I lost everything, not just what was taken from me."

I shifted, uncomfortable with the pain I'd caused her with my question. "Have you ever thought about looking him up again? Finding them?"

Rachel quickly shook her head. "No. I always figured that they were better off without me. No use reopening wounds that old."

"I don't know; it seems to be working out for us pretty good."

That brought her up short. "That's true. I have no complaints about what's happened with us."

I thought briefly about what I knew of Heretic, and my suspicions that there was a fourth personality buried in his programming, in addition to my adoptive parents. I hadn't been able to get him to outright confirm it yet, but I suspected that Heretic also had an upload of my sister somewhere in his neural circuits. I'd gathered that Rachel didn't know anything about this, so I'd decided not to say anything.

"So, what's on the books for tomorrow? More training, I assume?" Rachel changed the subject.

"As far as I know. I don't know what Heretic wants from us." I twisted my grip on the branch and pounded the end of it into the ground. "He tells me to be creative, but then tells me off for trying anything new."

Rachel laughed. "James, you've been a caregiver; think back to when you were responsible for those kids in your classrooms. That's just the way it is with people we care about: we want them to excel, but we'd also do anything to keep them from getting hurt. Life is about finding a way to balance between the two."

"I guess that's true, but we've got a lot more at stake than social skills and macaroni necklaces."

"And yet," Rachel countered gently, "The principle remains the same. You're no good to anyone if you wind up dead. There are a lot of people hanging in the balance. If this Caine person is as hell-bent on the elimination of Mythics as he seems to be, you're one of the few people who can truly stand against him."

I simply nodded. There wasn't a lot of room to argue a statement like that.

Chapter 2

That night, back in the house, when the whispers and giggles that naturally accompany the sharing of sleeping space by twenty-seven young people finally quieted and stilled, I resumed my training.

I sat on my hammock at the top of the atrium in the greenhouse and kicked with my foot to set myself swinging gently. I checked my watch: 11:37. I laid back, closed my eyes, and took a few deep breaths. I opened them again. I was getting faster at entering and exiting my Space. "Pocket dimension" took too much effort to say, so I'd started just referring to it as my Space when talking to the team about it. Pat had snorted water the first time I'd called it that but wouldn't tell me why it was funny.

I dropped to the ground. I'd learned that I have total control over what happened in here. The mists and vapors that filled the Space responded to my every mental wish. If I wanted gravity, suddenly I was walking on a firm surface. If I wanted trees and forest, an ethereal grove sprang up around me. Nothing created in the Space could be taken outside, but while here, I could create literally anything and interact with it for as long as I stayed.

I blinked; the exact scenario I'd been in this afternoon materialized from the mist. The large tree in front of me, trees all around, and I could just make out two forms slinking through the trees trying to flank me.

I blinked again and breathed out slowly, rolling my shoulders and wrists. I stepped from behind the tree and blasted from my palms toward my feet. I overdid it. I blasted backward, right into the side of the tree, which caught me smoothly, enveloping me in mist and letting me fall gently down to the ground. I stood up and blinked again, and the situation had reset, tree again in front of me, and twin slinking forms in the distance.

Well, that didn't work.

I repeated the sequence over and over, flicking my hands back and forth and up and down until I finally figured out where I needed to point them so that I flew mostly up, rather than sideways into things. It felt like hours. I'd lost count of how many times I blinked the setting into reset.

I looked down at my hands and flicked them one more time. I flew smoothly upward with a blast and landed unsteadily on a tree limb roughly three stories off the ground. I leaned back against the tree trunk and found the shapes of my mist-opponents creeping toward the base of my tree. I pointed my hands, and the figure on the right disappeared in a staggering flash of light as that area exploded. I did the same thing to the one on the left.

I smiled, despite how tired I was. I held up two fingers like a smoking gun and blew imaginary smoke from their tips. *I did it. One more thing I can do with these abilities.*

I closed my eyes and took a deep breath in and let it out slowly. One more breath in, and the sound of my lungs filling with air faded into the background noise of a sleeping, crowded household.

I checked my watch again: 11:37. As usual, it was as if I'd never even been gone. I snuggled down into my blanket in the hammock and closed my eyes, more confident than when I'd climbed in.

***

My late-night training session paid off. We were back in the woods, and again, Clara and Pat were hunting me.

I dropped down into the deep plunge pool of the dry riverbed, pressing my back against the smooth rock. It was cold underneath my fingertips and the meaty part of my palms. I held my breath, listening for any indication of where Pat and Clara were, above me. My heartbeat echoed loudly in my ears as I put a finger to my lips, physically and mentally willing them to stay closed and silent. Finally, I heard a rock clatter some-where above me, and I saw a brief shadow rise from that of the embankment above. Taking one step out from the depression cut into the sand and stones of the riverbed, I blasted into the air, turning myself to face back up the wash as I flew upward twenty feet. I locked eyes with Pat, whose mouth hung slack in disbelief. Clara, however, wasn't as easily impressed and shocked into immobility. Her rifle, pressed against her shoulder, coughed once, and the suppressor flared as a bullet slammed into my calf.

It was too late: my hands were already facing them, and I blasted them off their perch, a flash of light and a wave of energy reaching me just before the sound of the blast. It knocked me backward, but I managed to correct myself with another small blast, holding my hands almost together and below waist level to counter my spinning from the original blast. Falling now, I directed one more blast downward, just enough to slow my fall and allow me to plan my landing, hitting my feet and immediately dropping down into a clumsy roll. Once again, my boots were in tatters. Flying like this would need to be a last resort unless I wanted to spend a fortune on footwear.

My calf was numb where my liquid armor had stopped the bullet, but I'd won the round. I turned back to look up at the top of the dry waterfall just in time to see both Pat and Clara helping each other up, nursing cuts and scrapes, and grimacing at each other.

"Round to me?" I shouted from my spot downstream. They both checked on me, and Pat mock put his hands in the air.

"I surrender," he yelled, eyes wide and a smile playing at the corners of his lips, even as his cheek bled from a rough scrape.

"You've been practicing," Clara spat through gritted teeth. It wasn't a question.

I nodded. "A little."

She returned her own nod, sharp and slight. "Good."

"I think I managed to get that whole thing on video." Heretic spoke up with my adopted mother, Deby's, voice. Her face shone on the video screen that served as Heretic's "face" when he wanted it, as he stepped out from the surrounding trees.

Clara groaned slightly. Pat raised a finger. "Can I get a copy of that?"

Deby—Mom—laughed. "Sure."

"How was that?" I asked.

Mom smiled. "Much better. I could stand to watch this one. That first flight yesterday was cringeworthy: really, really rough."

I nodded, self-satisfied. "I practiced last night."

Pat was nodding. "It shows."

Clara winced in pain.

I clambered back over the rocks of the dry creek and heaved myself up the dry waterfall. "Clara, you okay?"

"Yeah, just really banged my left arm good." She felt her arm gingerly, pushing on different bits and wincing anytime she pressed on the middle of her forearm.

"May I examine it?" Heretic spoke up, his screen blank. Having the screen uncovered was wonderfully helpful: the speaker, whether it was Mom, Dad, or Heretic, was reflected on the screen. I'd noticed that the fourth personality, whom I suspected was my sister, Raven Kline, had been conspicuously silent since he'd taken to displaying the screen. I still didn't know why, though.

Clara's lips pursed slightly, but she nodded. After many years of viewing Heretic as the enemy that plagued Safeguard's every move, I could see it was still difficult for her to see him as an ally. And yet, she managed to do so with only the occasional visible grimace. She must have been in a *lot* of pain.

I echoed her grimace and hissed in through my teeth. "Clara, I'm so sorry! I shouldn't have—"

Clara waved a hand, cutting off any further apology. "Don't worry about it. This is the job." I saw the muscles in her jaw bulge as she clenched it.

Heretic stepped quickly over to our huddle and gently took her arm, maneuvering it into several different positions. Each time he paused I could hear a faint click somewhere inside his skull.

When he was finished, he gently released Clara's arm, then said, "You have a small hairline fracture in your left ulna." As he spoke, the screen lit with x-ray images of Clara's arm. Sure enough, on the pinkie side of her arm, the image showed a small, faint, yet unmistakable crack in the bone.

"You do x-rays, too? So freaking cool!" Pat spoke up with his usual enthusiasm. His smile faded after a moment. "Wait... Do you—" his hands crept to cover his groin. "You don't ever take pictures, do you?"

"You do know how x-rays actually work, don't you?" Heretic's blank screen turned to regard Pat.

"Well, yeah, but I've read the comic books, too, man." Pat arranged his hands more forcefully around his midsection, shuffling from foot to foot.

Heretic turned to face Clara again and said, in a very different tone, "How old is he?"

Clara smiled. "Eternally youthful. I love it."

Pat grinned.

Heretic looked from one to the other, then made a gagging noise.

***

Pat, Clara, and I rode together in mostly silence, Clara reaching awkwardly across her lap to clasp Pat's right hand over the shifter knob with her unbroken right arm. They held hands over the center console every time they rode in the car together. Clara hissed or inhaled sharply with every bump in the road, and Pat muttered what I assumed were words of apology, comfort, and commiseration under his breath toward her.

Heretic had ridden ahead on his electric superbike to prepare for Clara; there was a veritable infirmary at the home. It was an absolute must with so many young children running around with superpowers.

Pat drove the SUV around the final corner, coming up the rise to the home nestled against the red rocks. "Something's wrong." Clara let go of Pat's hand and used her right hand to push herself up in her seat.

Heretic sat on the steps leading to the door on the

side of the structure, his helmeted head sagging in his gloved hands. I'd never seen him like this. There were no lights on in the greenhouse or in the living quarters beyond, and I couldn't see any children running around anywhere.

My heart started hammering in my chest, and my breath caught in my throat. *No. Where are they? Please, God, let nothing have happened. Where's Rachel?*

Before the SUV had even fully stopped, I had the door open and was running for the steps. Heretic raised his head, but his hands slumped down in between his legs, dejected.

"Heretic! What—" I began.

"Don't bother." For the first time, it was a young woman's voice coming from Heretic's body. Previously, Heretic had let slip that he housed not two, but three personality uploads. My sister, if that was who it was, had always used Heretic's highly electronic and modified voice to speak before. This was clearly a woman's voice. "They're all gone."

"Gone?" I stammered, staring wildly into the greenhouse, willing lights to come on and Rachel to come walking around one of the many entrances into the greenhouse atrium. "No, that can't be. Gone how? Where?"

Heretic, in the woman's voice, said simply, "Caine."

The bottom fell out of my stomach. "Caine?"

Heretic nodded once.

I looked around in disbelief. The last time Caine had crossed our paths a few months ago, he'd completely leveled the Safeguard complex with a nuclear blast, then forced the Danton children, Jessica, Steven, Elizabeth, and Mary, to use their control of air, fire, water, and earth to completely remove any evidence that the base had ever existed.

"But—" I pointed at the structure behind him, clearly intact and unharmed.

"He didn't need to destroy them quickly like he did the Safeguard base. They were children." The woman's voice from Heretic went quiet, nearly a whisper. "With the Danton children to boost his ability, who knows? Maybe he was able to absorb them all at once."

I shook my head, heart hammering and breaths surging in and out. "They— I—Rachel?" I asked.

Heretic looked up, and I could clearly see my face, wide-eyed and drawn, reflected in his video screen.

"I'm sorry," the woman's voice whispered. Heretic stood up and started walking away, back toward the superbike. "We need to leave. This is my fault. I should have known that he would find us outside a House of Bricks. We should have gone back to California as soon as the Safeguard base was destroyed."

I grabbed the robot's arm, squeezing as tightly as I could, knowing that it wouldn't hurt, and glad to have something to pour my panic into. "Stop! What do you mean, this is your fault?"

Pat was helping Clara out of the SUV, holding the door for her and shutting it with his hip when he had her out of the car. He shouted from where he was, obviously confused by my aggressive grab at Heretic. "Hey, what's goin' on?"

I shouted back without looking away from Heretic. "They're gone. Everyone's gone. Heretic says it was Caine, and that it's his fault." I lowered my voice and asked, "Why is it your fault? What aren't you telling us?" I let go of his arm and asked, "Who are you?"

He didn't answer. I pressed harder.

"You aren't Heretic, and you're not my Mom or Dad."

I waited. The robot shuffled slightly, kicking at a rock on the ground.

"Raven?" I whispered.

Heretic looked up and nodded slightly.

My throat tightened up. I was right!

"How do you know so much about Caine? What aren't you telling us?"

Heretic's shoulders slumped, and he looked down at the ground.

Pat and Clara had made their way over to us. Clara pointed to her arm. "Can we have this conversation while someone casts my arm?"

Heretic nodded and turned back toward the house.

We all gathered in the infirmary, Clara sitting on the raised table, Heretic wrapping her arm with wet plaster bandage, while Pat paced the room and I stood tensely in the corner, arms folded across my chest and biting both lips between my teeth.

Heretic spoke in the woman's— Raven's— voice.

"My name is Raven Kline. Rachel is my mother, and James is my brother."

Pat and Clara stared open-mouthed at the robot, then at me for confirmation. I nodded.

"What? When were you going to share this little tidbit?" Pat asked, looking at me.

"I've suspected it since the day Heretic rescued me from Danton and Sammy." I glanced down at my boots and shuffled slightly, then looked back at Pat. "He let slip that day that there were three personality uploads in his memory banks, and the rest I pieced together." I nodded at Heretic, who was clicking as he took a few more x-rays of Clara's arm. "This is the first time Raven has surfaced completely like this."

I stepped around Pat and leaned down on the other end of the table, a few feet behind Clara, staring at Heretic. "I want to know why you said this is your fault, and how you know so much about Caine."

Heretic put the last touches on Clara's cast, apparently satisfied that the bone had been set properly, and put away the supplies he'd used in the cupboard along the wall.

He paused, audibly sighed—which I found oddly amusing at the moment, considering he had no need to breathe—and then Raven spoke.

"Because I'm—the real me—is helping him." Heretic turned to face us, his video screen still blank. "James, he's our father."

Chapter 3

In a flash, Clara had drawn her pistol from where it sat attached to her hip via her suit's smart magnets, and taken three steps back from Heretic, barrel trained squarely on the robot's head. "You lying son of a—"

"Clara, just wait for a minute—" Pat began.

"No! I knew it, dammit!" Clara's eyes were wild.

"Clara, you were the one who convinced me to trust them, remember?" Pat's voice was surprisingly calm.

Heretic stood very still, hands held out away from his body, emphasizing the fact that they were empty. Slowly, the screen lit up and Mom's face was anxious, looking out at everybody.

"Clara, would it be helpful for me to explain at this point?"

Clara's one hand holding the gun shook, and she yelled, "No! Stop it! How are we supposed to know it's even you?"

"Did you already forget what I told you back in the trailer that day? What about the Fourth of—"

"Screw the Fourth of July! Maybe the place was

bugged! You're gonna give me one good reason, or I'm gonna blow your stupid robot head clean off!"

The screen went white, and a young woman's face showed on it. She looked to be a few years older than me and had quick, intelligent brown eyes. This was what my sister, Raven, looked like.

"I wasn't sure if I should show you what I look like." She brushed back Heretic's hood, almost as if she were smoothing hair out of the way. "I—she—" She paused. She looked down at the ground, then up at me. "How should I refer to the real me? The one with Caine? I? She? What makes it least confusing?"

Pat snorted. "Confusing? I don't know why anyone would be confused. We're listening to a robot who's really a copy of the woman who may have betrayed us all to a psychopath who wants us all dead talk about the said woman in the third person." His eyes widened, and he frowned and shrugged. "I don't know why that would be confusing."

"Just say 'she'," I suggested, anxious to hear the truth at last.

Raven nodded. "Right. She isn't helping Caine because she wants to. She's helping him so that she can keep tabs on him. She helped your adoptive parents," she looked at me again, "to build me so that her knowledge could be on the outside without being detected."

I was still reeling. "Hang on. Is Caine really our father? How is that even possible? Did Rachel know?"

Raven was shaking her head. "Rachel didn't know. When she met him, he was calling himself Joseph Kline, and he was a good man. Seemed to be, anyway."

Clara still had her pistol trained on Heretic's head.

"Why should we believe anything that comes out of this thing's speakers? I'm still waiting for that good reason. How do we know that it wasn't him that told Caine how to find us? Do we actually know what he's been doing with all of the kids he's taken from Safeguard all these past years?"

I spoke up. "I've seen people leave. Shanice: she was a girl who was here with the group previously. She left just a few months ago to go back to her family in Georgia."

"You actually saw her leave? Back with her family?" Clara's eyes hadn't left Raven's face on the video screen, and her hand was no longer shaking.

"No, but she left. Rachel saw her leave and went with her to the airport. She told me all about the trip."

Pat was rubbing his hands. "If he were human, I could just read him."

Raven looked at him. "You can! That's a great idea! Heretic isn't just a robot."

Pat nodded mockingly. "Oh, we know. He's an advanced physical representation something or other, with human symbiotic technology married to it. He told us. Several times."

Raven stared at Pat, her eyes narrowed and her mouth in a tight grimace. She shook her head slightly.

"That's not— It's— Sure. In any case, you *can* read him. He has a brain. It's how we gave him Mythic abilities."

"You did what?!" Clara shouted.

"Yeah. He has all three of our Mythic abilities: Tinker, Thinker, and Tech. Well, technically, I'm a Tink/Tech."

Pat and Clara stared. I'd never told them how Heretic had used his Thinker ability to perform a Reversal on me, allowing me to regain my Mythic abilities when he'd rescued me from Julian Danton.

Raven looked at them. "Have none of us mentioned that?"

Pat and Clara shook their heads.

"In any case, read him. Read us. See that we're telling the truth. You know all the big secrets now. There's nothing else we're holding back." Raven sat down on the table, closed her eyes, and the video screen dimmed off.

Pat, Clara, and I exchanged looks, then Pat shrugged and stepped forward, raising his hands to Heretic's temples. He closed his eyes, and I watched his eyebrows crease together as he concentrated. It wasn't but a few moments until his eyes sprang open again, eyebrows high.

"That was the weirdest thing I've ever experienced." He turned away from Heretic and shook like a dog, every joint in his body flapping. He stepped to Clara's side, stretched his neck and shook his head a few times, then said simply, "He's not lying."

Clara's gun lowered, but her face retained its steely gaze. "Speak."

The video screen lit again, and Raven's face looked around at us. "Here's the thing. If Caine knew where to find us, he can find us again. We need to leave."

"Leave? And go where?" Pat spoke up.

"The only place we'll be safe. We have to return to the House of Bricks." Raven looked at me. "I think we need to go back to your adoptive parents' house."

A shiver worked itself up my spine. "Why that one? Why not your place in California?" I hadn't been back to my childhood home since I'd left to go after the Danton children the very first time. It felt like a lifetime ago, now.

"Because the site in California doesn't have the Safeguard database servers. We still don't know how Caine found us. If he's also somehow managed to access those servers—" Raven didn't finish her sentence. She didn't need to. We all could imagine.

***

Driving across the country again allowed me time to really think about everything I'd learned from Raven in the last day.

Rachel, my birth mother, was gone, probably dead, killed by the man she'd called her husband over twenty years ago.

All the children that I'd helped Heretic to care for

and watch over for the past several months were gone, again, presumably dead.

My sister Raven, whom I'd never met, was working as a double agent with Caine, the Wolf, a Mythic who, apparently, was willing and able to completely wipe other Mythics from the face of the earth.

That same psychopath was also my father, the man who gave me the abilities that set me apart from nearly every other person on earth, even other Mythics, aside from himself.

It was a lot to think about, and I was thankful for the relative privacy of the back seat of the SUV. My eyes filled with tears and my throat tightened uncomfortably multiple times on the long drive east. I'd recently taken to journaling in a notebook to help me think through and process some of the weightier issues I'd faced in the last couple of years. The note-book was getting very full.

I took my turn alongside Clara and Pat in driving nonstop to get back to my home in Illinois. As it ended up, I took the last leg of the trip. As we crossed over the bridge that spanned the Mississippi River, I waited for that unmistakable feeling of coming home that I'd always gotten driving in this direction. It never came. The trestles of the bridge were the same. The murky, flat waters of the river were the same. Even the green wall of the trees on either side of the river was more or less the same. And yet, something was not. *I guess too much has happened. Too much has changed; I've changed too much for it to still feel like home.*

As we drove past my great-grandfather's mailbox, the decommissioned bombshell, I felt a pang of regret and an ache of loss. That feeling of "everything will be all right" I'd always gotten was absent here, too.

I'd expected the house to have fallen into disrepair; as far as I knew, no one had been living there for well over a year. I was stunned to see that the lawns were cut, the house seemed well-maintained, and there were even flowers growing in an obviously-weeded flower planter.

There's someone living here. My face and the backs of my hands flushed, getting hot, red, and prickly all over. *How can someone be living here? Surely, they would have had to try and find me in order to sell it?* Not that I'd been easy to find over the last two years.

"Someone staying here?" Pat spoke up from the back seat.

"Sure looks like it," I spat.

I *was* glad to see that Roger Caplan's red pickup was no longer parked outside the house. At least *that* reminder of the past was gone.

My eyes seemed to involuntarily seek out the two matching mounds, no longer freshly dug dirt, but still sparsely covered earth. Someone had planted some sort of vine that was just beginning to grow at the foot of each grave and had installed some sort of marker at the head. *Who would have known that my parents were buried here?*

That question was answered when the front door opened, and a wide-waisted woman wearing a faded pair of jeans and a flowery, fitted, long-sleeved blouse backed out of the screen door, carrying a large cardboard box. The woman turned around, and I gasped sharply. Pat, Clara, Heretic, and I all froze. The woman saw us and stopped herself, eyes going wide.

It was Sammy Charleston.

Sammy, the Tech who had betrayed Safeguard to Julian Danton and gotten an entire team of Mythics killed.

Sammy, the Tech who had watched as Julian Danton had tortured me, first for information, then simply for amusement, for weeks, and done nothing.

Sammy, the Tech, was living in my parents' house.

***

I wasn't sure what happened exactly next. It seemed like three things all at once. Heretic/Mom/Dad/Raven performed a flying kick into the box that started from off the porch and sent Sammy flying backward into the house. Clara fired three shots from her pistol that ricocheted off Heretic's back, and Pat simply stood there, holding a single note in a wordless yell. I could only stand there, paralyzed. After several more seconds, Pat stopped yelling to take a breath, and Clara dropped her gun back to her hip.

Heretic had darted into the house and reappeared, holding Sammy with one hand by the back of the neck, and the other holding her arm behind her back. She must have landed right on the couch directly beyond the door; she seemed miraculously unhurt, if incredibly uncomfortable.

"Ow! Let go! What the hell?!" She flinched and grimaced in Heretic's unyielding grip as he walked her down the stairs, into the yard, then let her go. The four of us stood around her, saying nothing. She looked from face to face, glancing several times at Heretic, and staunchly avoiding my gaze altogether.

Clara looked at Heretic. "She's lucky you got to her first."

Heretic returned her look. "It wasn't luck. I calculated an 87% probability that you would shoot her. She may be a traitor, but she doesn't deserve to die, and you don't deserve to live with that magnitude of guilt. I did that for you."

Clara muttered something and absently scratched at the cast on her left arm. Pat took a step over and put an arm across her shoulders, saying nothing but squeezing gently.

Sammy still wouldn't look at me. I could hardly take my eyes off her. My thoughts kept tumbling like clothing in a dryer. *She's just as beautiful as I'd thought the first time I met her, the first time we went after the Danton children. Had she already joined up with Danton and Roger Caplan when Caplan had murdered my parents? How had she had the stomach to kill in cold blood the other four members of our fireteam during that second raid on Danton's home? How could she sit by while Danton had tortured me endlessly for days at a time? Why was she so pretty?!*

It was like I couldn't hold onto any one of those thoughts long enough to get to an answer. They were like fish: I'd grab onto one just long enough for it to feel substantial, and it would wiggle away, only to be replaced by another.

I wasn't sure how many seconds had passed when I suddenly glanced around and realized that everyone was looking at me, Sammy included. As if they were all waiting on *my* reaction.

"What?" I said, before even thinking.

Pat spoke up, and his voice was uncharacteristically serious. "You were closest to most of her betrayals. What do you think we should do with her?"

I suddenly couldn't breathe. Were they asking me to pass judgment on her? No; I couldn't do that.

I looked at Sammy. Her eyes were wide, and I saw her shoulders move up and down rapidly in quick, short breaths. *She's terrified.*

I spoke, quietly. "Did you help betray my parents?"

Sammy looked at me, and her eyes filled with tears. "No! I loved your parents!"

"You had a damn funny way of showing it," Clara growled.

I looked over at the graves, at the headstone and the ivy. I looked back at Sammy and pointed with my chin at the graves. "You?"

She nodded, looking down at the ground.

I continued. "You killed four people. Jose, the others. Your own fireteam."

"I know! I—" Her voice cracked, and she put a

hand over her mouth, shoulders and hands shaking. Tears welled out at the inside corners of her eyes and dropped down her cheeks, collecting on opposite sides of her chin before dropping off into the lawn. She dropped down to her knees in the grass, one hand keeping her from falling over.

"No way! Jose?" Pat blurted. Sammy just gaped at him. Clara, Heretic, and I groaned and turned to glare at Pat. Clara whacked him with the back of her hand. Pat grimaced and sucked air through his teeth. Shaking his head, he said, "Sorry: I heard it. I heard it."

Sammy turned back to look up at me. "There isn't a single day that goes by that I don't regret that moment. I panicked!" She wiped her eyes with her thumb, smearing mascara across her lower eyelid and down her cheek. "It haunts me. I have nightmares about them. I still see Jose's face, even when I'm awake."

"Then why did you do it?" I was surprised at the volume and the anger in my voice.

"Money!" Sammy's whole posture fell. I had the impression that, if she could have, she would have simply sunk into the earth. "Danton was going to make us all rich. You heard what he had to say." She couldn't meet my gaze again. She was probably remembering the context in which I'd heard Danton's plans: locked in a basement closet, on the receiving end of Danton's ability to cause and cure physical illness.

"I have student loans. A lot of student loans. I hadn't found a job. I was terrified. With Safeguard, none of that was going away. Danton was going to be rich. He promised to take care of me if only I'd help him find his kids."

"Julian Danton was a textbook narcissist. He manipulated everyone around him with exactly what they wanted to hear in order to get what *he* wanted out of them." Heretic spoke up quietly, without passion.

Sammy just nodded, looking back at the ground. "Yeah," she whispered "I found that out later. By the time the op to take him down came around, he said he'd kill me if I didn't take care of the lead team before they could reach him. I believed him."

"Why come back here?" I asked, gesturing around us toward the farm.

"I don't know. It seemed the safest place. I figured, if anyone came after me, at least we would be on equal footing here."

"All right, but really, what are we going to do with her?" Pat spoke up again.

I looked at Sammy, studying her. "We can put her in the cellar."

I had a sudden realization, and I turned to look at Heretic in equal disbelief and dismay. "I don't have the wristband! We can't get into the record room or my parents' Closet!"

Sammy turned to look at me, her eyes wide. "Your wristband? Like, the one that kept you invulnerable to Mythic abilities?"

I nodded, distracted. The last time I'd seen the wristband, Julian Danton had been putting it into his sportscoat waist pocket. Had I absorbed it when I'd accidentally absorbed Danton?

Sammy put her hands out to stand up, and Clara immediately had her pistol up and trained on her.

Sammy raised her hands and looked at me. "I have your wristband. It's right here." She looked pointedly at Clara, who narrowed her eyes suspiciously and nodded slightly.

"Slowly," Clara grated out between clenched teeth.

Sammy slowly pulled back the cuff of her long-sleeve shirt and removed my wristband from her wrist. It slipped off easily.

"Here," she said, holding it out without looking at me. Her cheeks were red.

"Why did you keep it?" I asked, taking it from her.

Sammy didn't answer.

"Oh, come on!" Pat yelled. "James, are you freaking kidding me? It's because she's low-key into you, man!"

It was my turn to blush and staunchly avoid looking at Sammy.

Clara still held her pistol in her hand, but lowered, at the ready. "Again, she's got a funny way of showing it."

Pat wrapped his arms around Clara's good arm, and underneath the armpit of her bad arm in what looked to be a very awkward hug. In a low, husky voice, he said, not quietly, "Well, not everyone can have what we have, baby." He chomped his teeth in her ear, then bit his lower lip and looked at her with narrowed eyes.

"Stop! You're gonna shoot yourself in the foot," Clara said in protest, looking pointedly down at her pistol.

"Doesn't matter. So long as I don't cut off my nose to spite my beautiful face." Pat gave Clara a quick peck on the cheek but released her. Clara shook her head slightly, but I also saw her stifle a smile.

Heretic spoke up, saving Sammy and me from having to say anything to pull the conversation out of the awkward nose-dive it was in.

"James, if you have the wristband, I suggest we head inside and do what we came here to do."

Clara half-raised the pistol, supporting her shooting hand with the one in the cast. "I'll take care of Sammy. Where's this cellar?"

I looked long and hard at Clara.

She rolled her eyes. "I'm not going to shoot her, James. Just tell me where the cellar is. Does it lock?"

I pointed toward the workshop, shaking my head. "It doesn't. Not from the outside, at least. There's a bar on the inside, but not outside. You'll have to put something heavy on it."

"We'll figure it out," Pat volunteered, drawing his own weapon and gesturing to Sammy to stand up. She stood, and with one last quick glance toward me, walked slowly toward the workshop, followed by both Pat and Clara.

Chapter 4

I led the way into my parents' Closet: I opened the safe in the walk-in closet, used the wristband to open the false back, slid down the short ladder, then opened the biometric scanner lock. It was just as I'd left it, the stark white and stainless-steel surfaces gleaming. As the lights faded up, I looked to Heretic for direction.

The android walked immediately to the bank that had a security camera etched into the metal and pulled out the rolling kiosk that slid neatly into the walls. The huge screen immediately turned on, and Heretic went to work. He adjusted the keyboard and selected an icon on the screen which brought up a password box. Mom's voice came from Heretic's speakers:

"Ahem?" she said expectantly.

"Seriously?" I asked. "We're still pretending like you need passwords around me?"

"Boundaries are important, Jamie."

Can you maintain boundaries with a dead person? It struck me what an odd situation all of this continued to be. I never thought that was a question I'd be asking myself, let alone in earnest.

Heretic's gloved fingers flew over the keyboard, and the computer beeped softly as he inputted the password. A moment later, a window opened with a few text boxes for things like first and last name, ability, region, and Host.

Search field parameters. I heard Mom grunt, then Heretic removed the right glove from his hand, revealing a hand covered in skin. That surprised me. I'm not sure why; he'd told us all multiple times that he was "a complex artificial intelligence being suspended in a vehicle that represents the symbiotic marriage of a proximal replication of human tissue and transhumanist techno-physiological advancement, additionally housing not merely one but three unique and complete human personality constructs." I had the line memorized by then. But, up until that point, I'd never actually seen anything beneath the clothing and helmet that he always wore.

As I watched, he removed the tip of his middle finger, revealing a USB drive insert, which he rotated a half-turn, to allow him to insert it, palm-up, into the port at the side of the keyboard. I stared at him, and he turned his face screen to look at me.

"Well, you didn't think I was just all skin and bones, did you?"

"Honestly, you keep surprising me," I said.

He nodded. "Good."

He turned back toward the database, which now

was flashing through individual files, faster than I could process them. Photos of faces on one side, demographics and details on the other, raced across the screen in a dizzying blur.

"Hmm."

"What?"

"It doesn't seem that anyone has accessed these files since the time of your parents' deaths."

"Huh. Not even after that, when Pat and Clara were running things?"

Heretic shook his head. "These files, even though they're backed up via our private network, are only accessible via this terminal. Pat and Clara didn't have access to them."

"If they're only accessible from this terminal, why are we checking to see whether anyone has accessed them?"

It was Raven's voice that responded in a mutter. "I'd have found a way..."

"Hallo the hole!" Pat's voice came echoing down the access tunnel before his feet dropped heavily to the bottom.

I heard him say something up to Clara, who must have been right above him. She said something back, short and curt. He replied with a few clucking noises and, "ope... oh..."

"Babe, just get out of the way!"

Clara slid quickly and smoothly down, clasping the ladder with both insteps and her one good hand.

I looked away as I heard Pat apologize quietly. "I was just trying to help."

"I know. There are a lot of things that are still just easier to do on my own."

When they walked over, they were holding hands.

"What do we know?" Clara asked. Always to the point.

Heretic finally removed his finger drive from the computer, replaced the fleshy cap with fingernail and all, and put back on the glove.

"Nobody's accessed the database."

"Not at all, huh? Well, that's good news." Clara picked at her cast.

"It is, and it isn't."

Pat groaned. "Ugh! Am I the only one who hears this guy? Enough with all the mysticism and woo-woo, man!"

Clara raised an eyebrow at Pat. "Seriously? Some of the puns you use, and you're gonna go after him for that?" Pat muttered but smiled slightly.

"As I was saying, it both is, and it isn't." Heretic took a step back from the computer bank, crossing his arms. "It means that we still don't know what means Caine is using to track and find Mythics, because it certainly isn't digital."

"You mean not via the database?" I asked, confused.

"No, I mean not digital. I wasn't just searching the database. While I was plugged in, I ran a search for my —Raven's—electronic signature anywhere on the web.

She hasn't been active for days, and nothing related to finding Mythics."

"Well, couldn't she have just masked her signature?" I asked. "Doesn't that just make good sense if they're trying to stay hidden? Like clearing your browsing history?"

Pat chuckled, but it died and became a clearing of his throat when Clara turned to glare at him.

"No, I—it just makes sense." Pat stumbled.

"She could, but she wouldn't. Not from me." Heretic countered. "Don't forget that she's on our side."

"Okay," I said slowly. "So where does that leave us?"

"Now we wait." Heretic's voice was firm, and his slight head nod seemed emphatic.

"Wait?!" Clara's voice shook. "Wait for what, exactly? There's some super-powered and super-charged psychopath out there hunting down Mythics, and your solution is simply to wait?"

Heretic turned to face Clara, and this time Raven's face lit up the screen. "Yes. I've been waiting for a true opportunity to take down Caine for years." Her eyes flicked at me. "James is our first chance to actually do that."

"How wonderful for you," Clara snapped. Pat reached out a hand to touch her elbow, but she shrugged him off. "No, I'm done just taking her word for things. We deserve more information than what she's strung us along with."

Raven straightened, and she flicked her head as if

she were flicking hair out of her face. I guess these uploads were pretty complete; even a person's unconscious tendencies came with it.

"First, we wait for my web alerts to start working. While I was hooked into the system, I took the liberty of creating alerts for each and every individual in the system, for both real name and Hosted alias, along with geographic tags for their area. If Mythics in the system start going missing, we'll know about it as soon as anyone reports it, or it gets featured in the news."

She raised a gloved hand and held up two fingers. "Second, we wait until we have a real plan for how to take Caine down. It's not as simple as literally stabbing him in the back."

Clara took a step back, clearly deflated. "That... that wouldn't work?"

"No! Don't you think that if it did, I would have done it by now?" Raven was shouting.

Clara obviously didn't take kindly to being yelled at. She recovered her step forward and shouted, "Only if you were actually trying to kill him, and not working for him!"

"Are you kidding?!" Raven raised her hands to her head as if she were trying to pull her own hair and seemed even angrier when there was nothing there. She balled up her fists and groaned in frustration. "You know what happened the first time I saw someone get a knife in him?"

My own eyes widened in shock. "The first time?" I echoed. Pat paled, and even Clara seemed to hesitate.

"The first time! It was in England: he was after some punk kid who was hiring out his Tank abilities to local organized crime. Small-time stuff, mostly; the kid was just the muscle behind some break-ins, thefts, and things like that. Caine found him, and the kid pulled a knife unexpectedly."

Raven broke off, her eyes on the screen losing their focus, and it seemed she was remembering. She focused again, looking right at Clara. "It was a big knife. I'm no doctor, but it sure seemed like it should have taken out his heart. Anyone else, it would have killed them, no question."

Her voice got quiet. "The kid just left it in, he was so surprised that Caine didn't drop. Caine took the knife out, then shook. Like a dog. That was all it took, then he dropped the knife and dusted the kid right there in the street."

Pat raised a finger to his throat. "You mean like..." He drew it across.

"No. Like..." Raven pointed to me. "Dusted."

"So, am I invulnerable, too?" I asked, trying to process what Raven was telling us. "Wait, no I'm not. I sprained my ankle, remember?"

"You've absorbed two people."

I shuddered in revulsion. They'd both been accidents, and I still felt keenly guilty about them.

"Caine has been doing this for years."

Clara spoke up again, apparently okay with letting go and changing the subject. "How long, exactly?"

Raven shook her head. "I don't even know. I joined

up with him after several years in the foster system. He found me when I was ten. But he's been going for a helluva lot longer than that."

"How do you know?" Clara asked.

"He has a place. In Paris." Raven offered.

"You mean like a house?" Pat clarified.

"No, more like a workspace," Raven said.

Pat's eyes got big. "Dude has a lair?"

Clara elbowed him sharply. "What about it?"

Raven closed her eyes and paused. "It's like the catacombs."

"He has a lair decorated with human skulls?!" Pat's eyes were huge. "He's a bona fide villain, and I'm not allowed to get excited?"

"So, how old are the catacombs?" Clara asked, continuing to ignore Pat.

"The ones the world knows about?" Raven clarified. "The late 1700's, I think. These are... considerably older."

"How do you know that?" I asked, genuinely curious.

"Hang on, homeboy is *several hundred years old*?!" Pat cried out.

Raven managed to ignore him. "Because some of the skulls have dates on them. The earliest I noticed started about 525 AD."

Pat stepped into the space between all of us and held his hands up, forming a T. "Time the freak out! This guy Caine has been disappearing Mythics since 525 A.D.?!" He looked from face to face.

I looked at the floor, attempting to digest the information myself. I couldn't make my head fully wrap around the implications. I just blindly accepted it, the same way you accept a credit card bill: at this point, these were just numbers. The real emotion of dealing with it would come later.

Clara whispered to no one in particular, "The better part of two thousand years?"

"This guy is like a freaking vampire! Are we sure he isn't straight-up immortal?" Pat was still standing in the space between us all, and I saw him look at me out of the corner of his eye and slightly edge away from me.

"The short answer?" Raven asked. "No. Those are just the skulls that are there, in the crypt. I have no idea whether that's when he started taking down Mythics, or just when he started keeping track."

No one said anything for another several seconds. I didn't know what was going on in everyone else's heads, but I was struggling to deal with the idea that my biological father was some sort of immortal super-powered psychopath who'd been killing people for longer than most recorded history.

"So, we wait," Clara spoke up quietly. "For what, though? You know who he is and where he is. What are we waiting for?"

"We need him to come to us. Here. In a House of Bricks."

Pat lifted his eyes from the floor. "But I thought you said that James was our best chance at defeating him? If we're in the Brick, James' powers won't work, either."

Raven nodded. "Right. James is our insurance. Think of it like world politics: you don't immediately go after the first guy to develop Weapons of Mass Destruction. First, you've gotta have your own to be taken seriously, then you take care of his Weapons of Mass Destruction. Notice that we still aren't dead by Nuclear Holocaust; it's because everyone knows that nothing good comes of just attacking the other guy with everything you've got in the open." Raven shook her head. "No, you go after the guy in secret and try to take out his weapons. After that, he becomes vulnerable, and you have the upper hand."

"Does he know about me?" I asked. My stomach felt tight and I was having a hard time getting enough air.

Raven turned to me and shook her head. "I don't think so. I don't know how he could, yet. You haven't done anything to be in the public eye, and we haven't come in contact with any of his people."

"That you know of," Clara chimed in.

"I'd know." Raven's eyes on the video screen narrowed, and I even saw her jaw muscles tighten in the image. "Raven is his second-in-command."

Clara swore and blinked down at the ground while Pat groaned, running his hands through his hair and looking up at the ceiling. I just stared at Raven, saying nothing.

After another moment of silence, I spoke up again. "So, when do we let him know about me, then? In your analogy, you said it depends on the other guy knowing you've got your own weapons, right? What's that called, again?"

"Mutually-assured destruction," Pat piped up.

Everyone looked at him in surprise.

"What?" He smiled. "I read. Besides, I always thought it seemed just like relationships. You know: you don't tickle me, I won't tickle you. Mutually-assured destruction!"

Clara's head sunk, and she raised her eyebrows at Pat in what I could only assume was disbelief.

"What?" Pat protested. "What else would you call it?"

Clara smiled and shook her head. "Trust?"

Pat squinted and flashed his own smile. "All right, I can see how you got there. I've heard it both ways."

I glanced back to Raven, who was simply staring at Pat, brow furrowed, and her mouth hanging open on the screen.

"We wait until we figure out how he's finding Mythics now and disrupt it. I used to be his eyes; we monitored news and social media just like Safeguard did. He isn't using that anymore, that I can see. We wait to let him know we're here and just how big a threat we are until we can send him a message that fits."

"Until then, we just wait for him to kill more Mythics." Clara scratched harder at her cast and finally slapped it, wincing immediately after.

Raven turned to face her. "I've done what I can. I

took a moment to put out on the Safeguard servers and frequencies a black-out order, telling everyone to stay put, stay quiet, and not attract any attention. This is what you do, right? Hide from the rest of the world? I assume that that's something they can do, and do well? I mean that in the best way possible right now."

"You did?" Clara blinked and her face softened. She hesitated for a moment, then said quietly, "Thank you. I was worried about them."

Raven nodded, smiled slightly, and said, "I figured."

I spoke up. "So, now we wait?"

Raven nodded. "Now, we wait."

***

I was back in my old room. It felt like some things would never change. It seemed forever ago that I'd been here with the Danton kids. I'd taken my old room then, as well. The familiar queen size bed, the small black desk with the retro lamp that looked like an old oil lamp. Nothing had changed since I left for college several years ago. Most of the posters were gone, but the furniture was all the same, even down to the dark navy sheets on the bed. The skeleton was the same, but the life I'd lived in it seemed a million miles away now.

I lay quietly in the dark, my hands behind my head, listening to the sounds of the house in the night. I heard the familiar click, then the whir as the air conditioning kicked on. I instinctively adjusted so that my face hit the pillow directly where the bulk of the cool air from the ceiling vent hit. I closed my eyes as the cool, dry air created the familiar and frustrating contrast between my face and the rest of me, still slightly sticky with humidity and summer heat.

I lay there until the AC rattled off several minutes later. I lay without moving for a few minutes more, my eyes closed, but my mind racing in my skull. I considered entering my Space to train with my abilities but gave up on that quickly. It wasn't only that I couldn't think of anything specific to train in; I didn't think I could get into it, with as distracted and scattered as my thoughts were right now. Then I remembered where I was, and that I couldn't get in even if I wanted to under the Brick.

I sat up and twisted to put my feet on the ground. The old, compacted and worn carpet had almost no cushion left, and I could feel the wood of the floor underneath clearly. I rubbed my eyes, gently massaging around the sockets. Sleep was a long way off. I quietly slipped on my socks and shoes, picked up the con gun from my nightstand, then let myself out into the hall and slowly crept out to the back door.

I had no destination in mind as I closed the door behind me. I stood for a moment on the patio, staring up at the clear, darkened sky and listening to the muted sounds of night in the woods. I walked, my pace slow and meandering, as I took in the property by night. I walked past the long clothesline, toward the animal pens. The goat pen was empty. I wondered idly where they'd gone. Their distinctive sweet and sour odor still lingered in the yard. I walked past the enclosure that Mr. Urnck, my family's sour old hog, had inhabited. The gate was open; he too was gone. The chicken run and coop was an identical story: door open, residents conspicuously absent. I noticed these details but didn't really stop to dwell on them. I kept walking, my eyes taking in only the next six to eight feet around me.

I stopped. Without meaning to, I'd ended up right outside my dad's workshop. I opened the door and stepped inside, shutting the door quietly behind me.

Pat and Clara had done their job well. They'd rolled my father's huge tool chest right over the top of the trap door that led to my great-grandfather's secret cellar; the cellar where Sammy was being held captive. I got down on my hands and knees to peer beneath the chest. I could see the trap door propped slightly open, a wooden toy block wedged between the door and the frame. Light spilled out of the opening. Sammy was still awake, then.

I was just about to stand up and quietly leave when Sammy's bang-covered forehead and blue eyes popped up into view.

"Hello?" She peered out of the gap, eyes darting around. "Who's there?"

I realized that with the workshop in darkness, she must not have been able to see me in the small amount of light that escaped from the cellar. I held my breath, watching her for a moment.

Her eyes didn't focus on anything in particular. "Hello? Are you going to feed me? Let me use the bathroom? What's the plan here?"

I didn't say anything, instead going back to my original plan. I stood up as quietly as I could and tip-toed to the door, opening and closing it behind me without letting the latch click.

"What did she have to say?"

I jumped at Heretic's voice behind me. I instinctively pushed out against him, but he didn't even move. He stood uncomfortably close to me in the darkness, silently looking up at my face.

"What? Nothing. I didn't talk to her."

Heretic tilted his head fractionally. He reminded me of a puppy. "Then why go in?"

I turned away from him and marched toward the house, relieved he couldn't see my face reddening in the dark. "I just wanted to make sure she was locked up for the night."

I stopped and turned around to face him, again shocked to find him closer behind me than I'd expected. "What are you doing out here?" I shot at him.

"Keeping watch. It seems only logical that, as the only non-biological member of our party, I take on the responsibilities of watching over the property as everyone else sleeps."

"Oh. Right." I was more than a little ashamed. I

hadn't even thought about setting a guard before I'd gone to bed. "Don't you ever have to... recharge or something?"

"Oh, no. My power source comes from a combination of solar cells, kinetic energy capacitors, and a microreactor; I'm quite energy efficient. Thank you for asking." He was entirely Heretic right now, with none of the ameliorating influences of the other personalities he stored.

"...Got it. Hey, can I talk to Raven?"

Heretic's screen lit up and Raven's face slowly came into focus.

"What is it, James?" Everything she said just always sounded so intense.

"Nothing, really; I just wanted to talk."

She looked around as if checking in on what was going on around her. She nodded toward the shop. "She really didn't say anything?"

I shook my head. "Not really. She asked for food and to go to the bathroom. Other than that, I didn't even talk to her."

"Mmm." She didn't say anything more about it. "What did you want to talk to me about?"

I pursed my lips and frowned for a moment. "Caine?"

She nodded slowly, looking down at the ground. "What do you want to know?"

I shrugged, despite the darkness. "Anything you can tell me, really. I mean, he's my father, he's apparently immortal, and you're convinced I need to face him and kill him. Start anywhere you want!"

"There isn't a whole lot more that I know. When he was still calling himself Joseph Kline, He was kind. Sad, but kind." She looked up at me. "You know he was still around when they took you, right? I mean, he was away on a work trip, but he was still with us. Still involved." She rubbed her fingers together absently. "They tried to make it work, for a few years. Rachel left after a few years. Losing you, her leaving, it broke him. He abandoned me for a few years. I wound up in the foster system for a while, until I was about ten. It was around then that he showed back up and took me with him to Europe. I didn't know it at the time, but he went completely bat-shit crazy. Went on a Mythic killing spree. He didn't invite me into his 'work' for several more years. Long enough for me to know better by then."

"But you're still helping him." The words were out of my mouth before I realized I was saying them out loud. I cringed and gritted my teeth.

She nodded, almost imperceptible in the dark. "Do you know who Mark Felt was?"

It didn't ring any bells. I shook my head.

"Ever heard of Deep Throat, in connection to Watergate?"

That, I'd heard of. "Yeah, the informant, right? Leaked the information to the press?"

"Think of me as your Mark Felt. I stay so that I can take him down. He needs to be stopped."

That made sense, I suppose. "Why does he do it?" I whispered.

She shrugged, turning to look back across the property. "I still don't really know. I've never been able to get him to talk about his life before us. I've only pieced together that it's most likely him who's been killing for this long because of what I saw that time he got stabbed in London."

"Shouldn't we find out more about him?" I asked.

She scoffed. "I've been around him almost my entire life. You don't think I've tried?"

"Right, but maybe that's the problem. I mean, maybe you've been too close to him. You haven't really been able to do any searching where he isn't."

She turned to look at me, her eyes wide. She gestured from her neck down to her feet. "What do you think was the point of all of this?"

"Oh, right." It was sometimes easy to forget that somewhere out in the world was a Raven Kline whom I had never met. This was only an approximation of her stored on an android's hard drive.

"Yeah. Right." She reached up and brushed a hand across her forehead, again as if she were pushing a lock of hair back from her face.

"In any case, we'll stop him," I offered. I had another question I wanted to ask, but I was afraid of the answer. "Do—do you think there's any chance Rachel is still alive?"

Raven sighed. "I don't know." She paused. "I've

never seen him take prisoners, but she was his wife; he had to have recognized her.”

I nodded and swallowed with difficulty, not looking at her and glad for the darkness. “One last question.”

The android shifted in the dark.

I took that as assent.

“Why didn’t you tell me before that I was like him? When you first did the Reversal on me? You lied. You made it sound like you didn’t know anything about it.”

Raven folded her arms. “I kept a lot of things to myself. I reached out to your parents with my plans for the Heretic android several years ago. They were looking for a way to bring down Safeguard, I didn’t disagree. I didn’t tell them my ultimate reason for reaching out.”

I waited, but she didn’t say anything. “Which was?” I prompted.

“You. I needed to know that you would be safe from Caine. Your parents forgot about me that day, in the hospital. They missed me. Forgot about me, in their rush. I never forgot what I saw, what I knew about my baby brother. I never stopped looking for you. When I found Deby and Jared, they initially thought I was a threat, but I was able to convince them I was on their side. Like I said, they felt strongly enough about Safeguard that, in their minds, I didn’t need any more reason to be involved than that.”

It was my turn to shift from foot to foot in the shadows. “Why not tell them about Caine, though?”

"I'd hoped to be able to bring him down my-self. That was the goal. I hoped that I could search, dig out something—anything—that would help me to learn more about and stop Caine without involving you." She brushed at the android's blank face again. "That obviously didn't work out. I wanted you safe, above all."

My hand went to my wrist with a sudden thought. "The wristband? Was that you?"

She shook her head. "Jared found the loop when he was excavating for the basement years before. It was only by accident that he realized the effect that it had on your powers, and through you, others. I still have no idea where it came from, or what, if anything, it has to do with Caine."

We both stood, not speaking, for several more seconds. Finally, she spoke up again. "We good? Her-etic's protocols are driving me crazy with his need to patrol."

I nodded, then cleared my throat. "Yeah. Thanks."

The android didn't say anything, simply walked away into the dark, leaving me alone with my thoughts.

Chapter 5

"There has been another incident." Heretic walked into the kitchen and gestured for us to follow him. Clara was the first up from the breakfast table and down the hallway toward my parents' bedroom.

"Who now?" Clara bent over the console, peering at the details on the screen. A news article on the monitor offered information about a family in Boston who had gone missing without a trace. No signs of broken entry, no witnesses who saw anything out of the ordinary, and no clues as to what might have happened.

"Jason and Melissa Metcalf, and their daughter Amy." Heretic switched the open window, displaying a Safeguard file. "Host family for the last six years."

"That makes seven," Clara spat through gritted teeth.

"And continues to follow the trend we've noted previously," Heretic said, nodding. "They're being targeted geographically."

The android brought up yet another window and displayed a map of the eastern United States, with seven points on the map highlighted.

"Okay," Pat offered. "So, now we do what we talked about; we figure out who's next on his list and set a trap for him."

"You are correct; we have talked about that course of action, and it is a poor one. The probability of significant collateral damage and loss of civilian life in the event of a direct confrontation with Caine is .97." Heretic's normally detached voice had a touch of what I thought was probably annoyance.

"You keep saying that!" Clara burst out. "What's your alternative? We can't just keep letting him hunt these families down one by one unopposed!"

"We still need more information. As I have said before, we need to understand how he is finding these individuals in the first place. Before we can adequately protect them, we must know how they're being put at risk in the first place. It's painful and unfair, but it's the truth."

"Then we'll do recon," I ventured. "If he really is finding them in order geographically, then *we* have the advantage. We know who the next family is already. He still has to find them. We can do a stakeout. Watch and wait to see how it happens."

Pat and Clara were nodding, and they turned to look at Heretic.

Heretic spoke. "You assume that he isn't working from a list. He may simply be efficient."

I frowned at the blank face screen. "Wasn't it you who said that *no one* had accessed the Safeguard database? What other list could there be?"

The robot paused for a moment, then joined Clara and Pat in nodding. "I accept your alternative solution."

"But we get the family out. We stake out the house, but the family gets moved somewhere else." Clara put both hands on her hips, the hand in the cast awkward, but still able to communicate her resolve.

Heretic sighed. "It changes the equation too significantly. By artificially changing the variables, the outcome becomes too unpredictable—"

"No. These are people. They aren't 'variables'." I saw a glint of light in the corner of Clara's right eye, but no tear made it out. "These are families who love each other, and we *will not* just sit by and watch them be murdered."

Pat put a hand on her shoulder, and Clara raised her own to touch his, squeezing.

"So, who stays behind with Sammy?" I asked. I avoided making eye contact with Pat. Even in the corner of my eyes, I could see him craning his head at me, his scalp wiggling as he raised his eyebrows repeatedly and grinned at me.

"Me." Clara raised her good arm, then elbowed Pat sharply.

"Ow! What? No! Babe, you know I'm no good at these things. Stakeouts? Me? Hardly a perfect fit."

"I'm no good in the field right now." Clara waggled the casted arm. "Not off-Brick. You don't need a Tinker out there. You need a Thinker, an android, and a –" she looked at me.

I shrugged, shaking my head.

"A whatever?" Pat grinned, looking back and forth between us.

I frowned. "A whatever?"

Pat stared. "Oh, come on! You've never seen any of the Muppet movies? A whatever, like Gonzo?"

I just looked at him. "Why are you the way that you are?"

It was his turn to shrug.

****

I climbed out of the white SUV and stretched, yawning loudly. I flinched slightly as my knee popped audibly.

Pat turned around in the driver's seat to look back at Heretic on the bench behind. "Maybe you should wait in the car. We try to situate our Host families in pretty normal neighborhoods; you might be a little conspicuous."

Mom's face lit up the view screen, and she gave Pat a scathing look. "Yes, Pat, I know. I'm the one who signed off on this location."

Pat grinned sheepishly. "Right. Sorry." He looked at me. "It really is easy to forget who he's got in there, isn't it?"

"Would you please just go talk to the family?" Mom's voice called from the back seat.

Pat stepped out and closed the door, then opened

it up again. I heard him say, quietly, "You need me to leave a window down or something?"

"Pat!"

Pat came to stand next to me; he was grinning. I snorted and shook my head, smiling. The man was incorrigible.

"I just like to push his buttons."

"I hadn't noticed," I said.

Together we walked up the sidewalk to the door of the house. It was a simple single-story, the door in the middle of the structure, symmetrical windows, and those faux-window attic things. It was unremarkable, in an unremarkable neighborhood. I never would have guessed that a family of Mythics lived here. Which, really, was the whole idea, so: mission accomplished.

"Let me do the talking," Pat said out of the corner of his mouth.

"Yeah, I wasn't really planning on saying anything. I don't know these people at all."

"Oh." Pat looked a little deflated. I got the impression he'd been hoping for more of an argument from me. "Well, that's for the best. As the ranking member of Safeguard, I have a certain feel for these kinds of things."

I rolled my eyes. "Whatever you say, Pat."

I watched as Pat took in a breath and squared his shoulders, standing up as straight as he could. He knocked, and I stood a couple of steps behind him, turning perpendicular to the door to make myself as small and non-threatening as I could manage.

A balding man with round plastic-framed glasses, a white collared shirt, and gray slacks opened the door. "Hello? Can I help you?"

"Larry? Larry Woodward?" Pat didn't move, just stood there with his hands on either side of his waist.

"Yes; who are you? What's this about?" I noticed the man visibly tense and close the door a few inches. I heard a shuffle of footsteps in the hallway behind him.

"Sir, I'm going to ask that we take this inside; never know who might be watching." I winced as the words came out of Pat's mouth. That was his best "feel" for it?

I spoke up from behind Pat, quietly. "We're with Safeguard."

The man narrowed his eyes. "I'm sorry. I don't know what that is."

I put my hand on Pat's shoulder. "Is there some sort of old-school greeting or code or something?"

Pat shifted from foot to foot. "Not that I've ever heard of. Here, may I?" He held out his hand to Larry as if to shake hands.

Larry Woodward turned his head fractionally to one side, but slowly extended his own hand. Pat took it and shook it. Larry's body visibly relaxed, and he turned to say something to someone behind the door as he dropped Pat's hand.

"Director! Sorry about that; we've never met or spoken in person, so I didn't recognize you. This is a surprise! You should have let us know you were coming; we could have had something ready."

Pat's chest had swelled again when Larry had called him "Director". "Yeah, we would have, but un-fortunately, this isn't a standard visit. Can we come inside?"

Larry stepped aside and opened the door all the way, gesturing into his home. "Please!"

Pat swept in, and I stepped inside, my shoulders hunched and my head down, still trying to appear as a non-threat.

A woman, presumably Larry's wife, stood in the living room off the hallway behind the front door, a short-barreled shotgun still held against her shoulder, but lowered to the floor. The combined diameter of the barrel— clearly a 12-gauge—, her grip, stance, and posture told me that this was not a woman to mess with; she clearly knew what she was doing.

Larry closed the door behind us and followed us into the living room. Pat was holding his hands up, simply staring wide-eyed at the woman and her shotgun.

"It's all right, Caroline. I read him just like he read me. This is Co-Director Walker." Larry gestured for her to put down the gun.

"And him?" Caroline gestured to me with her chin, both hands still holding her shotty.

"I—" Larry blinked and looked at me, then at Pat.

"My name is James Strader." I decided to speak up, holding my hands out from my sides to show they were empty.

"Strader?" Caroline's scowl softened. "Any relation to the former Directors?"

I nodded once. "They were my parents." I intentionally left off "adoptive" parents. No need to complicate things.

She finally unshouldered the shotgun, putting on the safety and carefully setting the gun on a side table.

"I met them once. They were good people. I'm sorry for your loss."

I nodded in thanks, not feeling like telling her, *"Oh, it's fine; they're actually still sort of around, inside of an android."* My life was definitely more complicated than it had once seemed.

"So, what's the surprise visit for?" Larry asked, inviting us to sit. "Can I get you anything? Water? Coffee? Something stronger?"

Pat held up a hand. "We don't really have time. We're here because there's every chance that you and your family could be in danger." I guess we weren't beating around the bush.

"Does this have to do with the disappearance of the Metcalfs?" Larry asked, going to stand by his wife.

I nodded, and Pat said, "Exactly. Someone is hunting Mythics."

Larry swore under his breath, and Caroline's face went white. Larry put his arm around his wife's shoulder and said, "You think we're next." It wasn't a question. "Where do we go?"

"We want you to stay at a hotel. Somewhere local, where you can be back home quickly. We think you might be next, but we hope to be able to stake out your house and observe the person after you. We know who it is, we just don't know how they're finding everyone."

Pat's face had a frown etched between his eyebrows, and for the first time, I realized how heavily this wore on him. Through all his wisecracks, all his jokes, and poorly timed humor, I hadn't been able to see how he really felt about it all. Here, away from Clara, as a leader of the crippled Safeguard, I could see the weight of all that had happened resting on Pat's shoulders for the very first time.

"You know who's doing it?" Caroline spoke up. "Is it Heretic? I heard last year that we knew where he was hiding out. Why don't we just go after him and blow him to hell?"

"Oh, uh..." Pat raised a hand to the back of his neck. "No, it isn't Heretic. It's someone much worse. But it *is* the same person who was responsible for the training facility bombing."

Larry swore again. "Is that what happened?" he spoke up. "We never heard for sure. I mean, it made the news, the whole compound just disappearing without a trace like that, but we never heard from anyone exactly what happened. There was a lot of speculation, but nothing solid. Just gossip from some of the folks locally that we managed to meet up with."

"Yeah," Pat said quietly. Again, I was surprised at the pain I saw briefly cross Pat's face as he stared blankly at nothing.

"How soon can you be ready to go?" I asked, trying to take some of the weight off Pat.

"Twenty minutes?" Larry said, looking at his wife for confirmation. She nodded. "Just long enough to throw some things in the car and unplug Spencer from his video games." I saw Larry grimace as he said that last part.

Gamer kid. When's the last time I was worried about nothing more important than video games?

"Good," Pat said, clearing his throat. "We already made a reservation for you at the hotel over on Main and Pinewood Avenue. Under the name Frank Williams. We already paid; you just need to check in."

Caroline stood up without even saying goodbye, just simply going to work, sweeping up her shotgun as she passed it.

Larry walked Pat and me to the door. I shook his hand, and he smiled at me, a thin, tight smile. I pursed my own lips in reply. When he shook Pat's hand, he pressed it with both of his own. "Director—" Looking Pat straight in the eyes, he said, "Thank you."

"Hey, this is what we do, right?" Pat replied.

We walked down the sidewalk and climbed back into the SUV. Heretic spoke up from the floor, where he was laying impossibly contorted, presumably to keep out of sight. I thought it was a pretty good call.

"How did it go?" he asked without getting up.

"I thought it went pretty well," I said, looking at Pat.

"Fine. They're getting ready to leave," Pat agreed.

Pat and I watched a few minutes later as the garage door opened, and Larry and Caroline pulled out in a green sedan, a sandy-haired teenage boy in the back seat. Larry gave us a single-finger wave from the steering wheel as they pulled out of the driveway and drove away up the street.

"Was that them? May I get up now?" Heretic spoke up, still contorted between the front and middle seats.

"Nah, you better hang out for another little while," Pat said, glancing at me and smiling.

"Your tone suggests otherwise," Heretic said, unfolding.

"Nailed it, Heretic," I said.

The android sat up on the bench seat, looking up the street in the direction that the Woodwards had disappeared. "What now?"

"Now," I said, "We wait."

Chapter 6

Stakeouts with an android on your side turned out to be pretty lowkey. Anytime Pat or I needed a break, we could depend on Heretic to keep watch without so much as a word of complaint. Being a Mythic in the real world also had a lot of... perks... that a significant part of me found ethically and morally questionable.

We had the police called on us a couple of times during that first afternoon and several times that night. Each time, Pat managed to touch the officer's hand in some way, and they would shortly realize their mistake, and move on.

When we got hungry, Pat walked down the street to Wendy's and picked us up food. Both times, he made an exaggerated point of leaving his wallet on the center console of the car and made a show of being surprised when he said that the manager had given him our food for free.

"Pat, that's stealing, plain and simple, man. You're nothing but a common thief!" I said, after the second run.

"No. I'm basically Robin Hood. I'm just taking from the 'Have's' and giving to the 'Have-not's'. In this case, us!" He dug into his burger, and the rest of the conversation was lost on him.

In the early predawn hours of the following morning, there had still been no sign of anyone coming or going from the Woodwards' that we had seen.

"I'm gonna go check the house really quick, see if anyone's been inside that we haven't noticed," I volunteered, anxious to get out and stretch my legs.

"All right, just shout if anything looks out of the ordinary. I haven't felt any other Mythics around, but we *are* at the very edge of my ability to sense them. Doesn't hurt to check." Pat nodded, blinking rapidly, and holding his eyes closed for several seconds as he spoke.

I nodded, then opened the car door and slid out of the SUV to the ground. The street was lit only by a few streetlights halfway through each block. The result was a lot of darkness; only a few of the houses had left their porch or outside lights on throughout the night. I tried to stay in the light as much as possible. If anyone was watching from inside the houses, I wanted to appear as inconspicuous as possible. Sticking to the shadows felt too much like something illegal and questionable.

Once I reached the Woodwards' house, I walked straight up the sidewalk and knocked on the door, trying to see through the windows on either side of it. I couldn't see anything out of place in the house, and when I tried the door handle, it was still locked. I might as well check the back door, too.

I started around the house, my feet leaving distinct marks in the grass where I'd knocked down the thick dew. I rounded the corner into the backyard, making my way through a gate in the fence, past a trampoline, and a huge tree with a rope swing hanging from one of the upper branches. I stopped. In the grass, leading from the rear fence that separated the yard from a back alley up to the back door, were spots in the grass, similar to my own footprints left in the heavy dew. I crouched down next to them, looking closely. They were obviously footprints, based on their position and spacing relative to each other. But, as I turned around to look at my own, they were significantly different. Mine were much longer than they were wide, with a clear footprint. The other marks, in contrast, were roughly circular. The shape made me think of an animal's paw, but the size was huge; I'd not seen any-thing with a paw that big, myself. I figured a bear or something similar might make a mark that big, but I didn't think it likely that they had bears in town around here. The tracks clearly made a line from the fence to the door and back.

I stood up and made sure the door was still locked: it was. Nothing I could see inside looked out of place or disturbed. I walked back to the car, frowning slightly as I thought.

"What's up?" Pat asked as I climbed in.

"James, you look upset, was everything all right with the house?" Heretic asked.

I nodded a few times. "The house looks fine. Doors are locked, and everything inside looks fine."

"Then what is the problem?" Heretic pressed.

"There were some tracks leading from the back alley up to the back door, then back out again."

Pat sat up straighter and whipped his head around to face me. "Footprints? That's not good!"

I shook my head. "No, not footprints. That's what I was afraid of, too. But they were the wrong shape. They almost looked like animal tracks."

Pat visibly relaxed. "Oh, so you mean like a cat or something?"

Again, I shook my head. "Not unless this cat was a lion. They were really big."

"How big?" Heretic asked. His face screen suddenly lit up with a small oval. "Say stop when the oval reaches the approximate size of the tracks you saw."

The oval started slowly growing. I waited until it expanded to be roughly how big I remembered the tracks in the backyard. "Stop."

The screen went slowly dark again, and Heretic spoke. "This is puzzling. Were there any additional details you could discern from these tracks?"

"No; they were just in the dew on the grass, so it's not like I could see claw marks or individual toes or anything. Why?"

Heretic's head tilted to the side slightly. "Well,

without any additional identifying details, the indicated parameters are highly unlikely, unless there's a zoo nearby that has lost one of its occupants. A footprint this size has equivalents only in the big cats of Africa and Asia."

Pat frowned and squinted. "Anyone know if Caine has a pet tiger or lion?" He turned around to look at Heretic. "Raven?"

The face screen lit up and Raven's face appeared. "No, he doesn't. At least, not that I've ever known of."

"All right, this is still too big a coincidence to be nothing. Let's check in with the Woodwards." Pat started the car, and we started rolling forward down the street in the direction of Main Street.

A few minutes later, Pat pulled into the parking lot and found a spot near the back of the building. "Can you get us in the door?" he asked Heretic.

Heretic stared at Pat. "I assume that was a rhetorical question and not a genuine inquiry as to the extent of my abilities?" I'm pretty sure that he would have "harumphed" if he had known how to.

Pat screwed up his face and mouthed a mocking mimicry of Heretic's reply. I threw an empty burger carton at him.

"What?" Pat climbed out, and I followed, easing the door closed in the stillness of the early morning. The sun hadn't even risen yet.

Heretic led the way across the parking lot and up the short sidewalk to the rear entrance of the hotel. He hardly even paused at the door, only long enough to run a hand past the card reader, which emitted a quiet beep and a small green light. He pulled open the door and held it for both Pat and me.

"Which room?" I asked.

Pat closed his eyes, and his eyebrows creased. He turned around to look at Heretic again.

"Oh, for heaven's sake!" the android hissed. He paused a moment.

"You can't feel them?" I whispered to Pat.

"No, but it can be finicky like that. Kind of like a radio signal, sometimes different buildings and stuff in the way can cause interference."

"I accessed the housekeeping program via the Wi-Fi; they're in room 221," Heretic whispered.

Pat led the way to the door marked "Stairwell" and waited for Heretic to beep us in, then held the door for everyone.

Leaving the stairwell on the second floor, I saw Pat stiffen.

"Something's wrong. Did anyone happen to look for their car in the parking lot downstairs?"

I nodded. "I saw it. You still don't feel them, do you?"

Pat's face was white. He shook his head.

We all raced down the hall. At room 221, Pat gave a few short, rapid knocks, whisper-yelling, "Larry? Caroline?" He knocked a few more times, slapping his hand against the door frame after.

My own heart was racing. I flashed between alternately flexing and clenching my fingers, bouncing on the balls of my feet. *Please let them just be asleep. Let them be sleeping!*

Heretic slid his hands across the key mechanism, and the tone and green light ushered us into the room. Pat eased the door open just a crack and light from inside lit up the edges of the frame.

Pat and I both swore loudly, and he shoved the door the rest of the way open.

The room appeared as if the Woodwards had simply stepped out momentarily for something. If they had left the room at an ungodly early hour, left their car, and forgotten the keys, wallet, phones, purse, and two pistols that were placed strategically on the nightstands.

"How the hell is he doing it?" I spoke aloud.

Pat was holding his head, breathing heavily, pacing rapidly back and forth between the beds, the same curse tumbling over and over from his mouth.

"There isn't even anything out of place!" I marveled. "They didn't even have time to go for their guns! How is he doing it? How did he find them?" It was too much; I didn't let myself reflect on the Woodwards. *Focus on the problem.*

"Would you shut up?!" Pat snapped.

I blinked, shaking my head and drawing my chin to my throat. "Sorry?"

"The Woodwards are gone! They're dead, and you're fangirling over their killer like a psychopath!" Pat took several steps toward me, his fists balled and raising up from his sides.

"I'm not fangirling! I'm trying to do what we came here to do: figure out how Caine is doing this so that we can stop him!" I was yelling.

"You both need to shut up. And don't touch anything." Heretic grabbed us both by our wrists and began pulling us out of the room.

"Don't touch me!" Pat yelled, trying to rip his arm from Heretic's grip and failing. I didn't try; I knew by now from long experience that Heretic's strength was nothing to fight against. Not for me, at least.

"Shut up. This room just became a crime scene. When the Woodwards are reported and discovered missing, the police will be all over this hotel room. We need to get out of here, and now. Before you wake anyone else up and we leave witnesses that can't be wiped off a server."

Neither Pat nor I offered any further resistance to the android. He was right. We exited the room and hustled down the hall back to the stairwell. As we left the building, Heretic said quietly, "I'll drive. Give me the keys."

Pat offered them up without a word. Heretic climbed into the driver's seat, I slipped into shotgun, and Pat slammed the rear door behind him, sliding across the bench to sit behind me.

No one said a word while Heretic drove to the freeway and started west. We'd gone several miles in silence before Heretic said quietly, "I corrupted the video footage at the hotel before we left. They'll have no video of us when they check it."

"Wait, what about Caine?" I asked. "Couldn't we have checked the footage before you erased it?"

"I did check. There was no footage of Caine or anything else out of place on the security footage."

I looked at Heretic, my mouth falling open. He glanced in my direction.

"You seem to forget that I am essentially a living super-computer with the Mythic abilities of a Thinker, a Tinker, and a Tech. I accessed the security footage to search for clues the moment we were close enough for me to access the Wi-Fi."

"Right," I whispered.

The SUV went quiet again.

Several miles later, Pat said, "I need a bathroom. Take this rest area exit."

Heretic pulled off the freeway and drove down the nearly empty parking lot toward the building. Several semi-trucks with trailers formed a looming wall between us and the freeway, and the yellow-orange lights of the rest stop contrasted starkly with the blue-grey of the lightening sky.

Pat had the door open and was stepping out of the car before it even stopped moving. Heretic turned off the engine and I undid my seat belt, unsure whether I should follow Pat or not. I kind of had to go myself, but I wasn't about to follow Pat in. I'd never seen him that way before. Never seen him yell, much less filled with rage. Since I couldn't decide whether I should go in, I simply sat, sharing silence with Heretic. He seemed far less bothered by it than I did.

Several minutes passed; I knew because I kept checking my watch, trying to gauge just how long I should give Pat before going in after him, and how much longer I thought I could hold it.

"Screw it." I opened the car door and fast-walked up the sidewalk to the square, metal-roofed building. I pushed open the bathroom door, bracing myself for a tense encounter with Pat. He wasn't visible anywhere, so I went to one of the urinals and took care of my business. I finished and washed my hands. Still no sign of Pat. I looked at the stalls, bending over just enough to check for feet, while pointedly avoiding the awkward "stall gap". No feet.

"Pat?" I called out. No one answered.

My heartbeat quickened. *Did Caine somehow find him, too?*

"Pat!" I yelled louder. I ran outside the bathroom and went to the back entrance of the rest stop building. There were woods several hundred feet from the back of the building. I went through the back doors and looked around. I swept the empty parking lot; no other cars, no one in sight. The streetlights audibly clicked off as I jerked my head back and forth. There were several picnic structures around the property. I studied each one I could see from where I stood. I could just barely see the toes of a pair of shoes sticking out from behind one of the walls. I sprinted for the shelter, my heart hammering in my ears. *Please don't be dead, please don't be dead!*

I came around the corner, and Pat raised his head

from his arms, where he was crouched on the ground, arms wrapped around his knees.

"It's my fault." His voice was hoarse, and it broke more than once during that short confession.

"What?"

"It's my fault. It was my op, I told them where to go, and I was in charge. It's my fault they're gone." He swallowed with visible difficulty and let his head drop back down onto his arms.

I could think of a thousand reasons why that wasn't true. A thousand different arguments made it one hundred percent *not Pat's fault.*

I didn't make any of them. Instead, I sat down, scooted my back against the wall next to Pat's, put my hand on his shoulder, and kept my justifications to myself.

Chapter 7

The Woodwards hit the local news the following day. Heretic had driven us through the night back to my family's home in Illinois, and we were gathered in the Closet, reviewing the situation on the wall monitor.

"It's being considered another missing person case, at this point. No indication of foul play, no risk factors in immediate relationships, they're just presumed to have up and left their life without a trace for some unknown reason." Clara shook her head, her mouth pulled down into a tight frown.

Pat stood slightly away from the rest of us, leaning against the wall, his arms folded, with one foot pulled up flat against the wall. Classic aloof bad-boy pose. *I wonder if he's talked to Clara about how he took what happened?*

"We know the police won't solve anything," Heretic chimed in. "There's nothing *to* solve. There will never be any bodies, no further developments. For them, the trail only grows colder from here on in."

"So, where does that leave us?" I wondered aloud.

Even though Pat clearly felt responsible for what had happened to the Woodwards, I was becoming increasingly frustrated with the one person who could actually do anything about what was happening: me.

I hadn't spoken to anyone about it since Rachel had disappeared, but I kept remembering what Heretic had said to me the day the Safeguard compound had been destroyed: *We expect you to save them, James Strader. Mythics everywhere are in peril.*

They certainly were. We'd been watching the pattern unfold for the last several weeks. Eight families, including the Woodwards, were all gone in the blink of an eye.

"Here's what we know," Heretic said, reaching up to touch the screen. A large map of the United States appeared. Eight red dots along the Eastern seaboard blinked into being, followed by several hundred green dots scattered across the remaining bulk of the country.

"These are the Safeguard Host family sites throughout the United States. The red dots: the families he's already taken. The green: those still remaining." He pushed something else, and a blue line began tracing between the dots, working south from the Northeast, then ping-ponging up and down in a slow track west. "This line represents my best calculation as to the potential order of his future attacks. These are estimates given travel efficiency, based on the patterns of his past attacks. However, since we still don't know for certain how exactly it is that he's finding the families, there is a significant probability that there could be some variation between the projection and his actual route."

"We get it, Heretic," Clara blurted. "We don't actually know jack about where he'll be." Her voice trailed off until the last few words were barely above a whisper.

"Okay, but we can do something about it. We can get them all to safety." I tried to smile, but it died on my lips, looking around the room.

"Because it worked super well last time," Pat spoke up without looking at me or anyone, his eyes not leaving the floor.

"The Woodwards were basically down the street from their house. What if we had them all come here?"

Clara looked up. "To the Brick?"

I nodded, emboldened by the hope I thought I heard in her voice. "Exactly."

"That *would* solve the issue of their being absorbed by Caine. However, we still don't know how he's finding them, whether Mythic-based or otherwise," Heretic said, one hand cupping his chin. Sometimes he did an excellent job of appearing human. "If it is some conventional means that we simply haven't identified yet, they would still be susceptible to physical violence once found, *and*," he paused. "They would all be in one place, making it simpler for Caine to fulfill his objective of total Mythic elimination."

"Come on," I said, turning to face Heretic directly.

"Raven, isn't there something you can do to find out how he's doing it? I thought that's the whole reason you were staying on the inside, was to inform on Caine. Wouldn't the method he's using to track down and destroy Mythics count as important information?"

"Your argument is not without merit—" Heretic started speaking, then stopped as the face-screen lit up. Raven's face appeared.

"Hi, yeah, no. It definitely does, but I don't think you understand what I'm working up against on the inside. I'm his top Tech, but not the only one, by any means. It's no simple thing to leave a message for someone outside his organization where someone on the inside won't find it. It took me ten years working with Deby and Jared to develop and construct the Heretic android without being detected. The idea of Raven being able to communicate something as significant as that in just a few months without being discovered is almost laughable."

"Okay, so Raven can't help us on this one. Not directly, at least. I'm sure she's doing what she can from the inside without putting herself in more danger." I nodded at android Raven, to reassure her that I trusted the real Raven implicitly. "But let's revisit the whole Mythic evacuation idea, can we?"

Clara shook her head. "It's just not feasible, James. Your parents sheltered a few kids at a time here. It wasn't designed to host thousands. That's what we'd be talking about, literal thousands of Mythics; it would be a logistical nightmare."

"All right, then what's your suggestion?" I shot back. "We can't just sit around and do nothing."

Clara shook her head. "I don't know. I honestly don't know."

"Okay, so are we back to considering a full-on assault against Caine? I mean, we know who he is, there's a good chance we could find out where he is—" I held up my hands as if offering the idea to Pat and Clara.

Heretic was back. "No. This is still not a good option. Although regrettable, Caine seems only to be interested in Mythics. He doesn't seem interested in harming the rest of the population. Antagonizing him with a full-on assault, especially including a Mythic such as yourself, James, who is probably impervious to his assaults? It could escalate the situation to a degree that we should not be comfortable considering."

I dug the heels of my hands into my eyes and groaned. "Then what are we supposed to do? Does he just win? We just wait here alone, until everyone else is gone, and he finds us, too? Just sit back and watch all the other Mythics be killed? Is *that* your answer? And what about the Danton children?" My stomach clenched. If I was being honest, it had been a while since I had thought about the Dantons, myself. The guilt I felt over what they were probably being forced to do for Caine made me shudder, sending goose bumps cascading up and down my arms.

Clara stood taller and squared up with me, her eyes hard and narrowed to slits. "You know better. If there were anything we *could* do, we *would.*"

I scoffed. "So, that's it, then? We do nothing while consoling ourselves with the rationalization that nothing is all we can do. That we *would* do something but don't?"

Pat heaved himself away from the wall, going to stand by his wife. "Don't talk to her that way, James. You know her better than that."

Clara shrugged off his hand, stepping away from him. "I can stand up for myself, Pat."

"No, I know, I just—" Pat trailed off, his shoulders dropping and gripping one elbow across his chest.

Heretic shut down the monitor and pushed the computer bank back into its slot in the wall. "I think perhaps we need to take a break."

I folded my arms and stayed where I was, glaring at the other three as they filed out of the room and climbed the ladder out.

When I was alone in the Closet, I went to the door and pulled it closed, sealing the room. As soon as I heard the bolts slide into place and the room pressurized, I sucked in a deep breath and yelled. No words, just rage. I yelled until my vocal cords stung, and my hands shook from the effort of forcing the very last shred of air from my lungs. When I was done, I stood in the center of the room, sucking air and shaking.

A quiet beep took me by surprise. A faint red glow emitted from the security console. I slid the bank out from the wall, and the monitor faded to life, just in time for me to see the rear end of a black sedan roll into the long driveway. The screen switched as another camera activated, revealing the front of the car, a BMW, headed for the house.

"We've got—" I started yelling, then remembered I'd sealed the room. I slid out my mother's armory bank, grabbed her con gun from the rack, and ran to the door, pulling the handle on the inside that disengaged the locks. As soon as it was open, I sprang up the ladder and bounded out of the safe with the false back that hid the entrance to my parents' Closet. "We've got company!" I yelled, unsure where everyone else had gone.

I made it to the front door just as the BMW rolled to a stop in the graveled parking area. I stepped to the edge of the porch and put one hand up on the railing, the other I held in what I thought might pass for a casual position slightly behind my back, holding tight to the grip of the con gun.

One of the back doors of the BMW opened, and a well-dressed, clean-shaven middle-aged man with white streaks at the temples of his otherwise-black hair stepped out.

"James?" he asked, catching me completely off-guard. "James Strader?"

My eyes narrowed suspiciously. "Can I help you?"

The man reached into the waistcoat pocket of his three-piece suit and pulled out a slip of paper. "My name is Henry Hoover. I have a message from Raven."

***

After Heretic rode outside the Brick with Henry so that he could verify that he wasn't in the service or employ of Caine, we invited him inside to give us his message.

"So, who are you, exactly?" I asked.

"I'm a business owner from Utah," he said.

"Uh-huh. Obviously, a pretty successful one," Clara said, her arms folded.

Henry smiled and tilted his head to the side. "I do all right for myself," he said.

"Apparently," Clara growled.

"How do you know Raven?" I asked, wanting to bring the conversation back to the point.

"That's the funny thing," Henry said, shrugging. "I don't."

I blinked several times, and Pat chuckled dryly, shaking his head.

"So..." I prompted.

"Well, the other day, I was in a meeting with a potential client, and my secretary came in and said that there was a woman outside who said she needed to speak with me." He laughed as he recalled. "I wouldn't have even bothered, except that she said this woman kept saying repeatedly that she needed to talk to me about my gift."

"Your gift? What gift?" I asked, puzzled.

"Well, I—" Henry began.

"Tech, or Tinker?" Clara asked.

"Excuse me?" Henry asked, turning to look at her. I could see confusion in his eyes.

"Are you a Tech or a Tinker?" Clara repeated.

"I don't know what that means," Henry shook his head.

"It's not rocket science," Pat said, his voice short and curt. "Do you build things, or do you control technology?"

"I—both, I guess. How did you know?"

Pat blew a sarcastic raspberry. "Well, you don't smell like a Tamer, and you're definitely better dressed than any Tank would bother with. We Thinkers typically have too much empathy to do well in business, so it was either Tech or Tinker. Figures that you're both," Pat spat.

Henry seemed genuinely taken aback. "I... apologize if I did anything to offend you—"

I snapped my fingers a few times in front of Henry's eyes. "Ignore them. I'm assuming this woman outside your office had a message from Raven. What was it?"

Henry shifted on his chair. I could tell he wasn't used to being the one on the receiving end of so much impatience. "Well, it was strange. She seemed distracted. Dazed, almost. She told me that someone named Raven Kline knew who and what I was, exactly how I'd been able to build up my business, and that there were other people like me who needed my help. Then, she handed me this slip of paper, and she simply walked away." He held out the paper, a 3x5 card, and I took it. Written on it were just a few lines of text. My name, followed by my family's home address, and three words at the bottom: "New aberration: Lycaon"

I stared at the three words, my stomach twisting. A new Aberration. Caine had used the Danton children to create a new Aberration. The only question was, "Who or what is a Ly-kay-on?"

Henry spoke up. "I looked that up. Apparently, he's some mythological king of Arcadia who tried to feed Zeus his own cooked son, and Zeus turned him into a wolf for it."

My mouth dropped, and I looked at Pat. He turned to look at me at the same time. Out loud, we both whispered, "Wolf?" The tracks outside the Woodwards.

"Hold on," I said, shaking my head. "Caine has a werewolf working for him now? Werewolves are now a thing?"

"All legend has its basis in fact," Heretic said. "It shouldn't surprise us that there's truth in this one."

Henry held up a hand. "Would someone please explain to me what's going on?"

Clara pushed his hand down. "What do you drink, Mr. Chairman of the Board? This is gonna be easier for you a few drinks in."

"I don't drink." Henry's eyes were wide.

Pat rolled his eyes. "Oh, one of *those* Utahns, huh? Then this is gonna be *really* interesting."

Chapter 8

Several hours later, Henry leaned back in his chair at the kitchen table, his herbal tea long since forgotten and cold. I laughed as I took in his slack jaw, slightly glazed eyes, and long exhale. I'd felt the same way when I was learning about this world of Mythics and abilities.

"This is... something else," he muttered.

"So, you didn't know about Mythics before today?" I asked.

Henry shook his head.

"What did you think your abilities were?" I couldn't believe that he'd never thought about it before.

"Well, it sounds really stupid to say it now, but my parents used to just tell me that I was special, but that I had to dial back how special. They used to tell me my fifty percent was the same as everyone else's hundred and ten percent. It always made me really uncomfortable, but now—" He scratched at his jawline. "Does it make me conceited to say that, now it makes a lot of sense?"

I saw Clara shrug. "It is what is. Why do you think Safeguard never found you?"

"Probably because of my parents, honestly. They were pretty adamant that I never show the world the entirety of what I can do. They always encouraged me to excel, but just a little bit more than normal." He laughed. "They used to tell me, 'Henry, just find the smartest kid in the room, and only beat him by a little bit.'"

"Yeah, you're the pinnacle of humility and grace in success," Pat shot from where he was making himself a sandwich.

Henry looked at Pat, then leaned in toward me, glancing at Clara as he did so. "Okay, between you and me, what's that guy's problem?" he whispered

I winced and shook my head once or twice. "You caught him at a really bad time. Pat's usually a really funny, friendly guy. He—" I hesitated, unsure exactly what to say. "He's lost some people. Feels like it's his fault."

Henry was nodding. "Survivor's guilt."

I looked at him in surprise, thinking. "Yeah, I guess that would be pretty accurate."

Henry shook his head. "That's a shame." He noticed my stare and said, "I've had Army guys recruiting me for years. Most of them have become friends. They talk, I listen."

Clara folded her hands on the table. "We've spilled our guts; your turn. Why did Raven send *you*? How can you help us?"

I turned my chair to more directly face Henry. I was anxious to hear his thoughts on this, as well.

"Honestly, I don't know. I'm not sure how she even knew about me."

"She's a Tink/Tech, too," I said. "She must have recognized something familiar in you."

"Huh," Henry said. He folded his arms. "So, you mentioned this Caine guy. And he's literally hunting people like us? That wasn't exaggeration or sensationalism at all?"

Clara stared at him. "Do I look like someone prone to exaggerating or sensationalizing?"

Henry paused, and I watched him size Clara up. He pursed his lips and shook his head slowly. "No, you do not." He broke off looking at Clara and looked around the room at all of us. "Okay, so what do you need?"

Pat laughed. "You think you're just going to sidle in here and solve all of our problems with a wave of your hand?" He scoffed. "Savior complex much?"

"Maybe, maybe not. What do you need?" Henry took time to make eye contact with each one of us around the room.

No one else said anything, so I took the opportunity to speak up. "We're not really sure, at this point. Thanks to your message from Raven, we now know how Caine's been finding Mythics." I blinked and blew air through my nose. "A freaking werewolf. The good news is that, because we know it's a Mythic ability, a House of Bricks could help keep them from being detected. The bad news is that we couldn't support them all in one place, logistically. We've got here and Heretic's old place in California, but neither place is situated to be able to support the kind of numbers we're talking about. We're talking literal thousands."

"Yeah, that House of Bricks, you mentioned that before; that's what you call this place? The quiet?" The corners of Henry's mouth had started turning upward.

"The Brick; it negates all Mythic abilities, yes." Clara leaned forward in her seat. "You didn't seem surprised by it when we took you off to let Heretic read you."

Henry was full-on smiling now. He looked at Pat. "I'm about to wave my hand and solve all your problems."

Pat frowned and blinked a few times. Then he blew a low raspberry and turned back to his sandwich, muttering.

I scooted forward, only partially resting on my seat now. "What does that mean?"

Henry laughed. "I believe everything happens for a reason. I don't think it's a coincidence that Raven, wherever she is, found a way to reach out to me, of all people."

"Please, skip to the part where you solve all our problems." Heretic had been largely quiet up to this point in the conversation.

Henry nodded. "Long story short, I have a ranch up in the Uinta mountains of Utah. It was originally established as a campground for young people, but after speaking there at a camp one year and feeling that sense of quiet, I had to have it." Henry's smile widened. "So, I bought it."

"Wait," I started blurting. "You have a Brick?"

"So, we're just gonna ignore the part where he bought a youth camp right out from under them? I'm pretty sure that makes him the low-budget film bad guy. Did anybody else watch 'Ernest Goes to Camp?'" came Pat's voice from behind us. We all ignored him.

Henry nodded again, his excitement matching my own.

"A Brick that used to be a campground or something?"

"Think more low-scale resort, but yes. I've since made my own upgrades and additions to it. I thought I might use it to host my own conferences and retreats from time to time."

Clara broke in, her own voice quick and filled with energy. "How many people can it accommodate?"

Henry was grinning now. "Literal thousands."

Behind us at the counter, Pat swore loudly. We all turned to look at him. He stood, still leaning heavily against the counter on both hands, his head sagging, to the point that we almost couldn't see it above his shoulders. Without warning, he spun on his heel and held his hand out to Henry. "Welcome to the team," he said. He wasn't smiling, but I thought I could see the old twinkle back in his eye.

Henry accepted the hand without making any disparaging remarks or belittling Pat's abrupt change in attitude. I liked and respected him all the more for it.

Henry stood up. "I'd better go. I'll let you folks get on with notifying all of these people—Mythics, our people—" his eyes lost focus for a moment. He blinked and seemed to come back from somewhere in his head. "And letting them know that there's a place for them in Utah."

Before any of the rest of us had said anything, he stood up, gathered his suit coat from the back of the couch where he'd set it, and was halfway to the door.

"Wait!" I said, standing up. "Don't we need to figure out logistics? An address, all that?"

Henry stopped at the door, his hand already on the knob. "I assume you have email?"

I nodded sheepishly.

"Then I'll find you," he said with a smile. "Remember, Tinker Tech."

"It's just, 'tink/tech'," Pat said quietly. "No -er. Just like, a hyphen... or something." He trailed off because Clara and I were both glaring at him.

Henry grinned one last time, pulled the front door open, and swept out into the driveway. His driver opened the rear door. Before he disappeared inside, Henry put one hand on top of the car and looked back at the rest of us: me, Clara, Pat, and Heretic, all standing quietly on the porch. "I'll send a plane when you're ready," he called out to us. Then he disappeared into the BMW, the driver lowered himself in and flew the car out of the driveway and out onto the road. And just like that, Henry Hoover was gone. The man certainly knew how to make an entrance and exit.

***

Late that night, Clara, Pat, and I sat around the kitchen table, saying hardly anything as we studied the glasses on the table in front of us.

I broke the silence. "Is this gonna work?"

Pat sniffed and lifted his eyes up to the ceiling, resting his head on the back of his chair. "They'll at least be safe. And we'll have a chance. Without powers, it's just a numbers game, right? We'll have thousands to his... insane death cult." He jerked his head up. "Has Raven said how many followers Caine actually has?"

I shook my head, thinking. "I don't think so."

"Well, in any case, he can't have more than all of the Safeguard Host network."

Clara nodded. "I like our chances, anyway. We told everyone in the message we sent out to meet us in Utah and to come ready for a fight. That means we'll have a small army, not counting the kids, to back us up. I truly like our odds in that regard. The only thing that worries me is that we'll be painting ourselves into a corner. It'll basically be an old-school siege. If we get all dug in at this camp, all Caine has to do is starve us out. He can wreak havoc on our supply lines from the outside, and just wait for us to die or surrender."

"Still, it's the only fighting chance we have," I said. "Otherwise, it's everyone just waiting to be picked off, one by one. This at least gets us all together where we have the strength in numbers and buys us time to figure out our next move."

Clara nodded then yawned, leaning her head down onto Pat's shoulder and closing her eyes.

I watched Pat smile, then he shifted, turned his body toward Clara and adjusted her head onto his chest, and put one arm around her shoulders. "C'mon, let's get you to bed," he said gently, then planted a kiss on the top of Clara's head.

Clara inhaled deeply and opened her eyes, sitting up again, then stood up and stumbled toward the hall, muttering "G'night," as she went.

Pat stood up, clapped me once on the shoulder, and followed her down the dark hallway. I sat at the table as I listened to their bedroom door click closed.

I sat there for a moment, as the familiar sounds of my parents' house rose to fill the silence. The A/C clicked off just a moment later, allowing me to hear the crickets outside being accompanied by the staccato beat of the clock hanging on the kitchen wall. At that moment, I was thinking about my parents. It seemed appropriate, sitting in their kitchen, in their house, holding one of their dishes in my hands. Pat and Clara reminded me of them. The way that they were with each other. Their gentle teasing, but the all-smiles teasing, the kind where you could still see the love around the edges, not the kind born from irritation and resentment. I sat at my parents' table, and I remembered them and what they had, what they'd taught me over the years, through their quiet examples.

I sat there, ticking off the beats of the clock until my heartbeat slowed even past the rhythmic tapping of the timepiece. Then I stood up. I wanted to check in with Heretic before I went to bed.

I found him out near my dad's workshop again, a single light on inside the building.

"Everything okay out here?" I asked, going up to stand next to him in the relative darkness.

The android nodded but didn't say anything, his arms folded, and his head slightly bowed as he leaned against the side of the workshop.

"You okay?" I asked out of habit. Once the words were out of my mouth, I felt ridiculous. Heretic was a robot. It wasn't as if he could feel "not okay".

"The woods are quieter tonight," he said in a whisper.

I shivered involuntarily. "That may be the creepiest thing I've ever heard you say!" I swore.

"Was it? I apologize. I was only stating an observation in what I thought to be an appropriate volume, given our circumstances. I will adjust." He shifted, standing more upright and unfolding his arms. "The woods are indeed quieter this evening. I need to investigate. Will you take charge of Samantha?" He began walking slowly away without waiting for an answer, leaving me standing at the door to the workshop.

"Sure, I'll just be right here. Take your time!" I

shouted at his back. He didn't reply, only disappeared into the dark beneath the trees.

I stepped inside the workshop. I leaned down to peer beneath the tool chest at the trapdoor. It was closed. Sammy must have long since given up peering out at whoever was out here. I stood there, debating with myself for a moment. Finally, I gave in and pushed the big rolling chest aside. I stood on top of what I knew to be the trap door, my feet on either side of the single hole that functioned as a finger hold to get the door open. There was light coming through the hole; I knew Sammy was awake.

"Sammy?" I called. "I'm opening the door. I need you to stand back."

There was no reply. I drew the con gun from where I still had it magnetically holstered on my thigh and raised the door. Light flooded out, but no one came rushing the door, as I'd half-expected.

"I'm gonna come down, okay?" Again, no response.

I stood back from the trap door and could just barely make out a pair of feet, drawn up onto one of the bunks against the wall. I stepped slowly down into the bunker, the con gun held close and ready.

Sammy sat with her back against the flat rear wall of the bunker, the wall that I knew opened up to reveal the former records room of the Safeguard organization, which opened with the wristband on my arm. Since it didn't make a difference in my ability to use my powers inside the Brick, I'd taken to wearing it again. I slipped it off my wrist and into my pants pocket. No harm in being careful.

"Really?" Sammy said, her arms resting lightly on her knees at the elbow. She looked pointedly at the gun and raised her eyebrows.

I lowered the gun but didn't holster it. "You almost killed me once."

She shook her head. "Never did. See, I know how to work a safety. That trigger wasn't being pulled the instant I had the rifle on you."

"You let a madman torture me for weeks and didn't do anything to stop him."

She said nothing, just looked away. I found myself admiring her profile, appreciating the slight upturn at the end of her nose, the way her bangs directed my gaze to her eyes, and that high, reddish-brown pony-tail. I noticed that she had a small scar on the side of her neck and found myself wondering how she got it. *Focus!*

"You could have stopped him," I continued.

She scoffed and glared at me from beneath her bangs. "And how would I have done that?"

"Anything: helped me escape, called the police?"

"What good would the police have been against Julian Danton, James? He repeatedly held his own against multiple trained Safeguard agents—"

"You betrayed us to him!" I interrupted. "Don't pretend that the strike team was ineffective. If it was, it was only because you'd engineered it to be so."

She looked down at her hands and I heard her exhale a deep breath.

"You're right." It was barely above a whisper. "I was afraid." She looked up again, putting her head back against the wall as she turned to look at me. Her eyes looked wet. "I'd made a deal with Danton, and I was terrified of what would happen if I broke it. By that time, I'd seen what he could do to people. And after watching what he did to you?" She shook her head. "He was a psychopath. I had no choice but to switch out the cable and sabotage the team."

That's how she was able to use her powers while we'd been cabled together! I'd wondered all this time. "And you didn't do anything to stop him, or to help me." It came out with far more bitterness than I'd intended. I regretted it the moment I'd said it.

Sammy pulled her knees up even closer to her chest and rested her head against them, wrapping her arms around her shins. I was distracted for a moment by the pleasant bulge of her belly under her shirt, pushed to the sides by her thighs, forming small ridges and rolls that pushed against the fabric. With her face hidden, she whispered, "You really were unconscious after his sessions, weren't you? It wasn't an act."

It was my turn to avoid looking at her. I squeezed the grip of the con gun. I chose not to answer.

"I came to you each time, after. Stopped the bleeding, gave you things for the pain, did whatever I could to fix the damage he'd done to you." She wrung her hands in front of her, fingers rubbing each other frantically. "When Danton found out, he sent me away. That was the last time; when I came back after that, he was gone, and you were nowhere to be found. I was terrified; I didn't know what had happened to either of you. I took off and came here."

The last time. The time that I'd absorbed Danton unconsciously in self-preservation. Somehow, I'd known. Even though I was unconscious, some part of me must have known that that time was different. I'd absorbed him because some part of me recognized that Sammy wasn't around to care for me that time. The threat had been great enough that, even unconscious, some part of me had recognized it and reacted.

"What did happen that day?" Sammy asked.

I realized she still didn't know. Didn't know about me, about my powers, about what I could do. I ignored her question.

"Are you getting enough to eat and drink? Do you need anything else?"

She sighed and nodded briefly.

I turned around and climbed back up the steep stairs out of the cellar. She didn't know what had happened to Julian Danton, and I wasn't sure I wanted her to.

Chapter 9

I tried to steady my shaky breaths and willed my heart to still its erratic beat. I pushed the tool chest back across the trap door and squatted down on my heels, my back against the tool bench along the opposite wall. I wiped one hand down my face as if I were trying to wring it out from my nose to my chin. I only had a chance to take a few more deep breaths before I heard a scuffle of footsteps and loud grunts from outside.

I came up to a squat, lifting my head only just enough to see out the window, the con gun held at the ready in both hands. Out the window, I could only just barely see movement in the dark, with occasional flashes of bare skin, confusingly enough.

I crept to the door and flicked on the switch for the floodlight on the outside of the workshop. Even with the garish light, it took several moments for my brain to really make sense of what my eyes were seeing. Heretic was outside, scrambling around on the ground, grappling a man who was, inexplicably, completely naked. The man was significantly taller and heavier than Heretic, but the smaller android, in addition to having a strength belied by his small frame, also moved skillfully, using what I assumed to be Jiujitsu or something similar in manipulating and maintaining a shocking level of control over his massive opponent.

With a startling twist, Heretic rolled the man to his front, face down in the dirt and grass of the yard, with one arm contorted strangely behind him. The man let out one seething hiss and went still, all his muscles contorted and tense. He spat a single phrase of some foreign language I couldn't understand; it sounded like Russian, or something else Slavic. I was no linguist.

Heretic replied in what I assumed was the same language, and the man nodded, his mouth full of dust and grass. Heretic released the pressure he was holding on the arm, and the man's body relaxed, sinking down to the ground.

Embarrassed for him, I went into the back of the shop and retrieved one of the ragged, stained towels my dad kept in there for rags. I stepped outside and tossed it over to the man. He looked at me, nodded, and drew it around his midsection. As he pushed himself up onto one knee, Heretic barked something at him, and the man glared at him. Heretic took several steps back, saying, "James, put your gun on him. If he moves, don't hesitate to take him down."

I brought the con gun up obediently.

The man had tattoos everywhere. I couldn't begin

to fathom their meaning. There were skulls, daggers, and eight-pointed stars in abundance, in various configurations and arrangements across his body.

A single snarling wolf head adorned the space between his shoulder blades. I didn't know a lot about tattoos, but this one definitely looked newer; the ink of all the others was faded and blurred gray, while this one was still vibrantly black, and the lines were still crisp.

"Who the heck is he?" I asked out loud.

Heretic blurted another line in the language, I assumed asking his name.

The man said nothing, but I saw his jaw muscle clench, and he lifted his chin, staring up into the dark sky without answering.

Heretic repeated the question, sharper.

The man's eyes narrowed, but he again said nothing.

"Why the hell is he naked?" I asked. Something clicked. I looked the man in the face. "You're the Aberration."

His eyes darted to meet mine for a split second, then returned to their defiant staring.

"Yeah, he recognized that word, at least, if he doesn't speak English. He's our werewolf; that's why he's naked."

At the word "werewolf", the man slowly dropped his gaze to meet mine, and he smiled. It may just have been the most evil-looking smile I'd ever seen. Then, he raised his face to the sky again and howled, long and high.

When he finished, he returned to his blank stare at the sky, thick arms relaxed as he held the towel around his waist. It was as if he wasn't even bothered that beneath it, he was completely naked, indeed, had been bare and buck-naked only moments before.

Clara and Pat burst out of the front door, Clara sweeping the area with a rifle held tentatively on top of her casted left arm. Pat was still pulling on his shirt, his eyes heavy and wrinkled from sleep. *How had he even had time to fall asleep?*

Both of them stopped when they saw the nearly-nude giant standing proudly in the driveway.

Pat's mouth dropped open and his eyebrows kissed his hairline in a perfect mirror of my own initial confusion. "What the—"

"Okay..." Clara said, the rifle maintaining its single-eyed glare at the man.

Hearing her speak, the man dropped his gaze again and looked at Clara. I saw him wink, then he made a single kissing noise with his lips.

Pat reached for Clara's rifle. "All right, shoot first, ask questions later."

Clara twisted away from his reach and kept hold of the weapon. She walked toward the man while looking at Pat.

"Pat, it's fine. Don't worry about it. He's our prisoner." Clara turned back around to face the towering foreigner. "He's just forgotten how prisoners get treated, is all." She made a show of looking the man up and down slowly.

The man leered, smiling that sickening smile again, then resumed his upward, aloof stare, though this time he flexed visibly, displaying veins and muscle groups that I'd only seen on men's fitness magazine covers.

Clara continued a slow walk behind the man. "He's forgotten that prisoners have no DIGNITY!" The last word was a roar as she struck the back of one of the man's knees with the butt of the rifle, sending him staggering to his knees. She wrenched the towel away with her left hand, the rifle still ready in her right.

"Whoa!" Pat and I shared equal cries of protest.

I turned my attention squarely to Clara. Her eyes were slits, and they didn't deviate from the back of the man's head. I saw the man in my peripheral vision turn to glare at her, and she smiled.

"What's the matter?" she asked quietly. "You were the one who asked me to dance. It's not my fault you didn't know the steps."

I turned my attention back to the man, following Clara's example in keeping my gaze squarely on his face. For the first time, there was a break in his cool, calm exterior. He said something short in his language.

"Does anybody know what he said?" Clara asked.

"I don't care to repeat it," Heretic said.

Clara's smile widened. "Good. Then it seems we understand one another just fine, don't we?"

Pat was still standing just off the porch, hands on his hips, looking up at the night sky and repeatedly blinking his eyes. "Not gonna get that outta' my head any time soon, am I? You know, Heretic, you're a Thinker, too, right? I'm gonna need you to un-sear something from my eyeballs next time we leave the Brick."

Clara beckoned us all over to her with her chin. When we were all close enough, she whispered, "Any idea who he is, besides Eastern European?"

"I'm pretty sure he's Caine's werewolf," I offered.

Clara nodded. "I'd buy that. He made a killer a better killer. Makes sense."

"Killer?" I asked.

"There's a good possibility she's right," Heretic offered. "I have analyzed his tattoos, and most of them are at least loosely affiliated with multiple Eastern European organized crime syndicates. The profusion of skulls and daggers symbolizes death and murder, probably his role, and the subpar quality, condition, and execution of the tattoos indicate they were probably applied in prison. My guess is that he is a repeat offender, probably from a very early age."

"How'd he find us here?" Pat asked. "I thought he was working his way up the East coast?"

"Followed stink!" the man called from where he'd stood up again, this time covering as much of his midsection as he could with his hands.

"So, you do speak English?" Clara replied, tightening up her stance and aiming at the man.

He nodded once.

"What's your name, my nudey-dudey?" Pat shouted, picking up the towel from where Clara had dropped it and flinging it back at the man, who caught it.

"Vasily. Novikov." The man held the towel tightly, shifting from foot to foot, his eyes darting back and forth from Pat, whom he'd addressed, to Clara, at whom he glared.

"So, he literally tracked us by our scent, if we're to believe him?" Pat whispered out the side of his mouth. "He must have, what? Caught it when we were trying to save the Woodwards?"

"And followed it all the way to Illinois," I finished, horrified and impressed all at once.

I had a terrible realization. "We need to leave. Now!" I started walking away from the group, toward the house.

"Whoa, what's the rush?" Pat asked.

"If he's here, Caine isn't going to be far behind, if he isn't here already."

Clara swore. She walked up to Vasily, stopping several paces from him. She re-centered the rifle on his chest. "How long do we have?"

Vasily sneered, but his smile wasn't as broad as before. "Death here for you. He come now."

Pat swore loudly. He ran his hands through his hair and down his cheeks, squeezing them together. "So, do we try and outrun him, or do we wait him out? It looks like we're testing our theory early. Also, is no one else in the least bit distracted by the fact that this man is naked?" He looked around.

Clara and I exchanged glances, but Pat just threw up his hands and blew another raspberry.

I looked around the circle of light created by the floods on the workshop wall.

"Where's Heretic?"

Suddenly Vasily leaped at Clara. I winced involuntarily as the rifle fired, two loud cracks. I drew my con gun. Clara and Vasily tussled, and it didn't take long for the huge European to wrestle away the rifle and throw Clara to the ground.

I was waiting for him. The con-gun *whumph*-ed in my hands and Vasily went flying, hitting the ground heavily and sliding, then rolling, for several feet before he stopped, limp and unconscious.

Clara pushed herself up on her elbows and nodded her thanks to me. I nodded in return.

"Pat," I called, jogging over to Vasily, "grab some zip ties out of the workshop. Cabinet to the right of the door, middle shelf, blue bin."

Keeping the con gun pointed straight at the still, naked form, I swept the rifle behind me, then bent and picked it up, slinging it across my shoulder.

Pat came out of the shop carrying an entire handful of thick zip ties. He came to stand next to me, staring at Vasily. "You think he's actually..."

"Not sure," I said. "This is only my second time shooting someone with this."

"This is your second time shooting someone with that thing?!" he hollered. "I've been a Safeguard field agent my entire life, and I've never shot anybody!"

I stared at him. "Are you serious?"

He shrugged. "Well, yeah. I mean, I'm mostly a clean-up guy, you know? I like to think of myself as a field support specialist."

"Guys!" Clara pulled us back to the precariousness of the current moment.

"Right." Pat crept jerkily to Vasily's side. He used his foot to prod one of the man's hands, which rolled limply in the grass. Pat knelt down and proceeded to pull Vasily's wrists together behind his back and zipped them together. He did the same to his ankles, then I helped him roll the big man onto his side and used a couple of zip ties together to attach the loop on his wrists to the one on his ankles.

When we were finished, Pat held up one more zip tie. "Hey, you know how, on dogs and cats and stuff they used to just take the rubber band and—zzzhip!" He mimed zipping the tie closed holding one hand up in the air, as if full.

I stared at him in disgust.

"He threatened Clara, man. I don't like that."

I said nothing, walking away and shaking my head.

"Oh, come on. It was a joke! I wouldn't actually do it." He chased after me.

Heretic emerged from the shadows of the trees, coming from the direction of the driveway. He held something up. "I found this."

Pat, Clara, and I gathered around him. It was a backpack with the shoulder straps loosened as far as they would go.

"I found a cell phone and a few other things inside. While outside the effect of the House of Bricks, I searched it. The good news is, I think we are safe for the moment."

Clara held her hand out for the backpack, and Heretic handed it to her. "How did you know he had one?"

"I didn't. I left to perform a search of our perimeter for Caine. I didn't find him, but I did find the backpack. It must have fallen off Vasily when he entered the House of Bricks and changed, and he didn't notice."

"What makes you say we're safe?" I asked.

Heretic pointed at the phone. "The cell phone is how Vasily communicates with Caine. There are text messages between Vasily and another number—Caine, I presume—giving the locations of all of the Host families who have been attacked."

"How does that make us safe?" Clara asked.

"Because the last several texts have all been from the other phone number, asking for updates and locations. Vasily hasn't answered any of them. He isn't following Caine's protocol, and Caine doesn't know where he is. If I know Raven, she's most likely scrambled his phone signal so that it can't be tracked, as much for Caine's protection as ours. That means we have enough room to breathe for at least a little while longer."

I took a deep breath in and held it for a moment, then breathed out, and felt my limbs turn to jelly. For the time being, at least, Caine still didn't know where we were. That left us with the question, what next?

Chapter 10

"It's simple: we kill him." Clara folded her arms across her chest, settling deeper into her chair in the Closet. It was the next morning. We'd begun the discussion in earnest as soon as we'd all met in the kitchen after a few hours of pretending to sleep.

"Are you serious?" Pat stared at his wife. "Who are you? What happened to the sweet ex-soldier I married?"

"I agree with Clara." Heretic spoke from where he stood in front of the computer terminal, hands held together behind his back.

"Oh, now you have the vote of the psychotic robot. Well, in that case..." Pat blew one of his now signature raspberries.

Heretic turned to face him. "I thought we were developing our friendship quite nicely?"

Pat rolled his eyes and pointed with both hands toward Clara. In a hoarse whisper, he said, "We are, Harry. It's not personal, I'm just trying to make a point, all right?"

Clara and I exchanged glances.

"Harry?" I asked, trying not to laugh.

"Heretic just seems rude. Can we please stay on topic? Don't be immature." Pat crossed his own arms and raised his eyebrows, what seemed to be his best attempt at appearing mature.

"James? What's your vote?" Clara spun on her chair to face me, unfolding her arms and leaning down on her knees.

I sighed heavily. "I don't know. I'm on the fence. I'm not thrilled with the idea of our killing people indiscriminately; that's exactly what we're trying to stop." I picked at a seam in the metal of the folding table we'd pulled out of the wall to sit around. "At the same time, this is how Caine is locating Mythics. That being the case, it seems like, if we have the chance, we should take him off the board."

Pat stared at me. "Take him off the board? I'm sorry, when did we become the freaking Gestapo?"

Clara slammed her good hand down on the table. "Caine changed the game! We're not playing hide and seek with the world anymore, Pat! This is survival, pure and simple. I know that's not who you are, but it's who we have to become, like it or not!"

Pat blinked and took a step back as if Clara had just physically punched him in the face.

No one said anything for a moment, and the silence stretched into something tangible.

"Umm, this is weird. Can I go back to that outside cellar?" Sammy spoke up from her chair in the corner, her hands zip-tied to the legs of the chair.

"I don't think that advisable at the moment; Vasily is a very dangerous man." Heretic spoke without looking away from the monitor.

"Yeah, I'd still prefer that to this," Sammy muttered.

I didn't like seeing Pat and Clara like this. This was a bigger rupture than anything else I'd seen between them in the whole time I'd known them. "Hey, Pat, what she's trying to say—"

Pat held up his hand. He shifted his stance to fully face Clara, who wouldn't look at him. "She's very good at saying exactly what she means, James. It's always been something I love about her."

Without saying anything else, Pat left the Closet, climbing up the ladder and out of the room.

I watched him go and turned to Clara as his feet disappeared from view. She shook her head, without looking at the door and the stairway where he'd gone.

When Pat's receding footsteps faded, Clara spoke. "So, we're all in agreement, then? The werewolf dies?"

I looked around, suddenly uncomfortable. Clara's face was steely and staring at nothing, her jaw flexed. Heretic's face screen was blank, and he said nothing. I made brief eye contact with Sammy, simply because she was there, and she hastily said, "Hey, don't look at me; I would rather be literally anywhere other than here."

"Shut up." Clara had apparently reached the end of whatever patience she had.

"Uhh..." I began, having a sudden thought. "Do we

even know if we *can* kill a werewolf? How many silver bullets do you have?" I asked, only half-joking.

Clara glared at me. "Those are legends. This is reality. I'm happy to try my luck."

Suddenly, Heretic made a sound like a clearing throat. "I'm not sure we should kill him."

Clara threw her hands up. "Of course. The robot gets cold feet!"

Heretic turned to her and turned his head slightly. "I'm not certain what my feet have to do with this, but I am having second thoughts."

He put his hands behind his back again and walked toward the rest of us, away from the monitor. "What were the chances that Caine, in his mission to eradicate Mythics, should get his hands on a set of Elementals, who, it just so happens, have the strange and unprecedented side-effect of creating Aberrations from the people around them? Further, what were the chances that, after the death of the children's father, the original Aberration, the next manifestation would turn out to be a Werewolf, some sort of apex predator with unparalleled tracking abilities?"

"We aren't machines, we don't know the chances. If it's important, why don't you just tell us?" Clara asked loudly.

"My point is, Caine obviously understands far more about Elementals and Aberrations than we do. The question must be posed, what if he simply creates another? Will we have accomplished anything?"

I rubbed my forehead, squeezing my eyes shut. "You think he can predict the form of the Aberration?"

"Predict... Control... at this point, who knows? I've examined all of Raven's latent memories contained within my memory banks, and there's no information on this topic more detailed than what we've learned up to this point by accident."

I watched Clara chew the inside of her lip. "So, what you aren't saying is that, holding Vasily here, where he can't be of use to Caine, but isn't dead, so can't be replaced, might just be the most effective thing we can do to throw Caine off his game?"

Heretic nodded. "I came to a similar conclusion."

Clara smiled, but it was thin, artificial. "Pat will like that." She turned toward the stairs, then glanced at Heretic. "You couldn't have brought this up before I went full homicidal in front of my husband?"

"I was—" he had just started to reply when Sammy let out a loud curse.

"Your husband just got cold-clocked by your other prisoner." She nodded at the monitor, which displayed the security cameras around the property. Vasily was just visible on one, with Pat thrown over his shoulder like a dummy, running awkwardly yet surprisingly fast down the driveway.

Clara's own curse echoed around the Closet as she, Heretic, and I rushed toward the door, trying not to fight each other up the ladder. We ran down the hallway, Clara in the lead. She swept up the rifle that she kept near the door and threw the door open, fumbling with the knob with her casted hand. She dropped immediately to one knee on the porch, resting the foregrip of the rifle on the handrail, her broken arm resting on top of it. I stared down the long driveway at the form of the big, naked man carrying a flopping Pat across his back. I waited for the familiar cough of the rifle, but it never came. I looked down at Clara, confused.

"Clara—"

"I can't get a clean shot," she said, through audibly gritted teeth.

The driveway was several hundred yards long. They were almost to the mailbox, beyond which the effect of the Brick only lasted a few dozen feet.

Clara swore. "Where are the keys? I'll go after them."

I raced back inside and grabbed the keys to the white SUV, but Heretic stopped me.

"Look."

We all looked back up the driveway. Even from this distance, it was evident that Vasily was growing, which was terrifying in and of itself. His skin darkened to a deep grey, mottled color. The hair on his head grew longer and mane-like. His ears grew longer and deeper, standing up off his head, then laying down slightly. He turned, briefly, to look back down the driveway. Looking back at us with a face that was no longer human, I assume he saw us on the porch because he took Pat off his shoulder and dangled him by the arm in one huge hand, careful to keep Pat between him and us. He threw his head back and a deep, snarling howl reached our ears. Then he turned and loped across the road, disappearing into the woods.

"Give me the keys." Clara's voice was a low hiss.

"Clara, did you see him? You can't go after that—"

She spun around and my jaw exploded in agony; I fell backward against the house, my vision swimming. I felt Clara's fingers pry the keys from my hand, and heard her steps move away, down the stairs of the porch, and across the gravel of the driveway. I stood up to the sound of the engine turning over, and the SUV spinning out in reverse, throwing gravel at the house. I threw my hand up and turned my head as several rocks bounced off my arm, neck, and chest. There was a roar, more gravel, and I turned to see the red tail lights of the SUV speed down the driveway through a cloud of dust. She barely slowed when she hit the road, and the SUV listed dangerously as she took the turn. There was a loud squeal of tires, then she was gone, leaving the dust to settle nervously as rays of hesitant sunlight poked through the canopy of the trees.

＊

With Clara and Pat gone, Heretic and I didn't know what else to do, so we defaulted to our original plan of leaving the farm ASAP. We packed what we could, trying to strike some semblance of balance between what we thought we could use, what we thought we would need, what we couldn't bear the thought of leaving behind, and what we actually had room to take. The result was a growing pile of suitcases, bins, and weapon cases in the front room. By evening, we had gone through the house and the workshop and put everything irreplaceable but nonessential into either the workshop cellar or the Closet. After that, we had nothing to do but wait and hope that Clara came back and that she'd somehow manage to bring Pat with her.

Clara didn't come back until late that night. Heretic was the first to hear the SUV and lifted a few of the blinds to check who it was.

"It's Clara," he said flatly.

I stood up from the table where I'd been staying awake with a fresh pot of coffee and followed the android to the front door. We stood on the porch and waited for Clara to come up. The SUV had turned off, but the door didn't open. We waited and waited, but nothing happened. Suddenly nervous, I realized my hand had dropped to the con gun at my thigh. I stepped off the porch and walked slowly to the driver's side, trying in vain to see through the windows to the inside of the vehicle.

I opened it, keeping myself out of a direct line with the driver's seat, uncertain about what I would find. The interior light came on, illuminating Clara, sitting in the seat, seatbelt still buckled, hands still on the wheel.

Her eyes were swollen and red-rimmed. There was

dirt smeared across her cheeks just below her eyes. Her hands were covered in mud, fragments of leaves, scratches, and small amounts of blood from the cuts, as were her clothes. Her face was devoid of expression of any kind, her eyes unseeing, unfocused. The only thing that even proclaimed her living was her breath, which was shallow and rapid.

"Clara?" I whispered. She didn't even blink. "Clara... did—Is..." I couldn't even think what to say, how to staunchly avoid, and yet get an answer to the awful question I couldn't bring myself to ask.

Clara blinked, and her gaze slowly dropped from the distance to the steering wheel in front of her, then slowly rotated to fall on me. The bottom lids of her eyes puddled with fresh tears, and she whispered one word.

"Pat."

She collapsed onto the steering wheel in front of her. When I pulled her toward the door, trying to urge her to get out of the car, she simply fell toward me, limp and weeping. The seat belt and I were able to keep her from falling completely out of the vehicle. I got my arms where I could support her, then reached blindly around to try and undo the seat belt. She fell into my arms and I heaved to get her better situated, then staggered toward the house. Heretic was at my side in an instant, closing the SUV door, opening the front door, and pulling out a chair at the table for me to set Clara into.

She sat down, supporting her head heavily in her hands.

Unsure what I could say, I started babbling. "We went back and reviewed the footage. Vasily must have been able to break the zip ties somehow, then he just pushed the tool chest off the trap door. He basically just squatted the weight of the tool chest, until it overbalanced and fell over. We had no idea he was that strong."

Heretic put a hand on my shoulder. I looked at him, and it was my mom, Deby's face that looked out at me from the screen. "She's in shock."

Showing Mom's face, Heretic gently took one of Clara's hands and guided her out of the chair. Clara followed her guiding hand robotically. The juxtaposition of what I was witnessing struck me for a moment —the robot empathetically guiding the human— as Mom put a hand gently under Clara's shoulder blade and guided her toward the hall. I followed, not knowing what else to do. Mom took Clara to her and Pat's room, where she helped her take off her liquid armor. I stood in the doorway, feeling useless and awkward. I ducked my head out of the room when Mom started to help Clara with her pants.

When I glanced back after a count of ten, Clara was beneath the sheets and blanket of the bed, her eyes staring straight up at the ceiling. Mom adjusted a couple of pillows underneath Clara's legs and tucked the blanket in. As she straightened to leave, Clara put her hand out, fumbling for Mom's gloved hand;

her eyes never left the ceiling. Mom leaned back in, then sat down on the edge of the bed. She looked at me and motioned with her chin for me to leave. I pulled the door closed and turned off the light in the hall, wondering, *what is Clara going through that she reached out to Heretic for comfort?* Something told me it was going to be yet another long night.

Chapter 11

The following morning, I got a call from Henry Hoover. The call on my phone was from a restricted number, which I'd gotten used to associating with Henry. We'd spoken several times already, coordinating our departure from the Brick.

"Hello?"

"James? Henry Hoover here. Listen, I got your message yesterday; I'm sorry to hear about Pat. I got the feeling he didn't like me very much, but even more so that he was going through something difficult at the time. I'm sorry to hear that. How's Clara? Was she able to find him?"

"She's—" I paused. I hadn't seen Clara or Heretic all morning. It was eleven o'clock already. "It's hard to say," I said honestly with a sigh. "She didn't get in until late—well, early this morning, technically. She still hasn't come out of their room."

Henry echoed my sigh on the other end of the phone. "That's rough. Really rough. Are you still going to be able to meet my jet out of St. Louis this evening? Or shall I tell them to postpone for a few days?"

"Honestly? I don't think we have that kind of time. Especially now that Vasily escaped and knows exactly where we are? I think we're living on borrowed time as it is." I didn't say that I'd already loaded the SUV with as much of our gear as would fit while still leaving us adequate seats, strapped the rest to the roof, and was only waiting for Clara and Heretic to reemerge so that we could leave.

"No, I get it." Henry went quiet for a minute. "All right, if you think you'll still be able to make it, I'll go ahead and let the order stand. Once you get into Salt Lake, I'll have a couple of cars waiting for you. I'm assuming you have quite a bit of gear, correct?"

I laughed. "Just a little bit."

"I'd expect nothing less from an operation like yours. We'll get you here just fine. Travel safe, brother."

"Thanks."

I hung up the phone. *Now, the only thing left is to get us all to St. Louis.*

I crept down the hall and knocked as lightly as I could on the bedroom door. I waited several seconds, counting my breaths in the quiet. ...seven...eight...

The door opened, and Clara stood in the opening. She was dressed, and her liquid armor was back in place, but her eyes were bloodshot and the hand holding the door open tremored noticeably. Clara was up, but she was not doing well.

I couldn't think of any greeting or well-wishing that didn't feel like it made light of the horror of the day before, so I just asked, "What do you need from me to be ready to go?"

Clara didn't answer, just hefted a large duffel onto her shoulder and pushed past me into the hall.

Heretic came out of the room after her, his screen dark and his head down.

Clara paused in the now-empty living room, then looked out the window at the loaded SUV. Without a word, she went through the front door and loaded her duffel into the back seat, climbed in next to it, and shut the door behind her.

I looked at Heretic. "How's she doing?"

The android shook his head again. "Not well. I've tried to engage her in conversation multiple times this morning, and she won't say a word. I'm worried for her."

"That definitely makes two of us," I mumbled. "I loaded everything we decided on yesterday, and everything is all locked up around the property. The only thing left is Sammy. I'm still not sure what to do about her."

"She's coming with us," Heretic said. I thought I detected a bit of indignation in his tone.

"No, right, I know that; I'm just not sure about the 'how' part of it all. Did I tell you what happened the last time I rode in a car with a Tech as my prisoner?" The memory of how Roger Caplan had taken control of the vehicle around me and effectively kidnapped me and the Danton children, all while essentially paralyzed and bound and gagged in the back of the vehicle still sent shivers up my spine.

"As much as it galls me to say it, I think our best option will be if I Sweep and Bit her, much the same as Safeguard used to do to the children they abducted." Heretic said it quietly as if he didn't want anyone but me to hear.

"Oh." I hadn't considered that option until now. I was surprised at how my gut tightened and my jaw clenched when Heretic suggested it. "For how long?" I had a hard time wishing that on anyone, even Sammy.

"We don't need to decide that now. Perhaps, indefinitely. She did betray all of Safeguard, and personally murdered an entire fireteam with the exception of you." Heretic was sometimes too direct.

"I remember; I was there." I folded my arms, staring out the window at where I imagined Clara's head would be in the SUV.

I exhaled. "All right, we'll do it, but we *will* talk about this later."

Heretic nodded and retreated down the hallway, toward the master bedroom and my parents' Closet, where Sammy was still being held. I followed close on his heels.

Sammy was stretching her neck as I walked through the safe room door. She glanced at me, then staunchly away, avoiding making eye contact with me.

"Time to go?" she asked.

I nodded.

"Finally. My butt's been asleep for like an hour."

Great. Now I have to try not to think about her butt.

I dug into my pocket for my knife and put my-self behind her chair, where hopefully my face wasn't going red, or that, if it was, Sammy wouldn't see it. I cut the ties that held her to the chair, and she stood up quickly. I jumped up in response, one hand darting out to grab one of her wrists, the other holding the knife away from her, ready. Her wrist was slim, but her forearm was just a little bit squishy under my fingers, and her skin was smooth and soft.

"I'm just sore," she said, trying to pull her wrist away. I held on.

"James," Heretic said from the end of the room.

I looked, and he tossed me a pair of handcuffs from the arms rack on my dad's side of the room. I caught them and clacked one cuff around the wrist I was holding.

Sammy swore as I clicked the other one around her opposite wrist. She addressed Heretic. "Are you serious? Handcuffs? Like I'm not just as eager as the rest of you to get out of here? I saw that thing too, you know. If you think I want to be anywhere in the world but safe on Hoover's magical dude ranch, you're insane."

I looked up at Heretic. I hadn't thought about it from her perspective before. I'd only considered her our prisoner, and therefore we had to take precautions to keep her under our control and take her where we wanted her. I hadn't considered that just maybe what she wanted was the exact same thing that we did and that she'd come willingly.

Heretic shook his head at me as if he knew what I was thinking. I nodded, hoping to muster some resolve. I didn't say anything to Sammy, and she said nothing more, either. She walked to the ladder, but then held out her hands. "I can't climb wearing these."

I hadn't thought of that. I felt my face get hot again. I wasn't sure what to do. It felt foolish to take her cuffs off when I'd only just put them on. I didn't want to take them off and look like an idiot. But she also very clearly couldn't climb the ladder wearing them, either.

Heretic walked over and took her elbow, guiding her closer to the ladder, then said, "Stay straight."

"Stay straight?" Sammy repeated, obviously confused.

Heretic placed a hand on either side of Sammy's thick waist and suddenly heaved her into the air. Sammy screamed, but to her credit, managed to stay straight and stiff as Heretic caught her feet in his hands and pressed her upwards, just like a male cheerleader, her feet just a few rungs below the top of the ladder.

I watched Sammy disappear as she stepped unsteadily off Heretic's hands with first one foot, then the other. Her curses echoed loudly down the shaft.

Heretic turned to me, and Raven's face illuminated the screen.

"I know we're not close; we barely even know each

other at this point. But, please, as your sister, let me give you some advice: get it together with this girl. She's not your girlfriend, she's not your crush, she's our prisoner, and she's hurt people. Hell, she's killed people."

"I—She's not—we aren't..." I stuttered, not having the slightest clue, myself, how any of those statements were supposed to end.

"You're right; she isn't, and you're not. Get it together." She turned and climbed up the ladder.

When Heretic disappeared, I leaned against the side of the shaft, hitting my head against the metal. "This is a nightmare," I muttered. "An absolute, total nightmare." I pulled the thick door closed, sealed it, and climbed up the ladder after Heretic and Sammy.

We were all loaded into the SUV just a minute or two later. I drove, Sammy rode shotgun, Heretic behind her, and Clara sat behind me. I still hadn't heard her say anything yet.

I looked at the house, at the workshop, took in the porch, with its rocking chairs, hanging potted plants, and painted railings. Glanced back toward the empty animal pens and the empty cords of the clothesline. More than any other time in the last few years, this felt like "goodbye".

I backed the car around and directed it down the driveway. At the road, I rolled the window down and put one hand gently on the decommissioned bomb mailbox. Then I put my blinker on and rolled out of the driveway to the right.

Several yards later, the interior of the car erupted into chaos.

"No!" Sammy screamed, as she sank against the dashboard of the car, trying to disappear into the space for the passenger's legs. "I knew you were going to try this, dammit!"

Heretic's arms were flailing, trying to reach Sammy's head. I heard the motors of the passenger side seat, raising the seatback more upright and lifting it, creating less space for Heretic to fit through.

Heretic went to the side, going around the seat entirely, and bumped me heavily. "Hey!" I shouted. I pushed him back, hard, toward his seat. I pulled the car over to the side of the road, slamming on the brakes and sending Heretic careening back up into the front. Throwing the car into Park, I grabbed the android by both shoulders and heaved him back into the back seat. I undid my seat belt and turned.

I glanced at Clara just long enough to see that she just sat there, watching expressionless and motionless. I turned my full attention to Heretic.

"James, we agreed this was necessary. Why are you hindering me?" He again reached forward. I shoved him back down. He might be strong, but I still outweighed him, although I didn't know by how much.

"Just stop! Both of you, stop!" I held hands out toward each of them, not touching, but ready. Both Heretic and Sammy stopped flailing and visibly relaxed.

Raven's face appeared on Heretic's screen. "This

is exactly what I was talking about, James. She's not your friend."

"Just listen!" I interrupted. "If she'd wanted to escape, she could have used her ability a hundred different ways to take over the car and do just that as soon as we were out from under the Brick." I looked at Sammy directly in her wide, frightened eyes. "She didn't."

"Raven, you're not used to trusting people very much; I get it. You've essentially been undercover for the last dozen years. But here, our goals are aligned. I'm not asking us to trust her with participating in a mission or anything. You heard her earlier: she wants to be safe just as badly as the rest of us do. I think we can leave her the dignity of her mind long enough to get her under lock and key again."

Raven sighed and shook her head.

"Besides," I added, "if she does try anything, you'll be right there to stop her, and we can Sweep and Bit her then. For now, just read her enough to know that she's telling us the truth."

I looked between the two of them. Sammy nodded and tentatively held out both hands, still handcuffed together, which Raven grabbed roughly and squeezed. I saw Sammy wince, but it only lasted a moment. Raven threw her hand away and settled into the seat again.

"She's telling the truth, for now."

I nodded, taking a second to look at everyone in

the vehicle one more time. Clara stared out the window, entirely detached from the drama that had just occurred.

Sammy straightened in her seat, again avoiding looking at me.

I signaled and drove the car back out onto the road.

After a few minutes of silence, Sammy whispered, "Thank you."

"Let's just be clear: that wasn't for you. I still don't trust you. I just happen to feel very strongly about the whole Sweeping and Bitting thing. You need to know that if you try anything, I'll let Heretic rewrite your entire existence. He'll bury your mind so deep... you'll..." I faded out, unsure how to finish the threat. *Ugh. I'm an idiot.*

I saw Sammy nod, looking out the windshield.

No one said anything for the rest of the nearly two hours it took us to drive to St. Louis. The silence pressed down on me like a weighted vest. I kept wondering what each of the others was thinking. I tried to imagine the agony Clara must have been in and felt like I might have a better idea of what she was going through than I first realized. That kind of loss didn't heal overnight.

With four personalities inside of Heretic's head, I didn't have the foggiest notion of what silence was like for him/them. Was there ever such a thing as silence for them?

What I kept coming back to, though, throughout

the two hours, was what Sammy was thinking. It bothered me that, of everything going on in the car, she was where my mind kept drifting back to.

I gripped the steering wheel tighter and gritted my teeth. *I really don't like her.*

Chapter 12

Following Henry's instructions, I drove to a charter jet hangar at Lambert International Airport. A man wearing a pilot's uniform walked outside to greet us.

I glanced at Sammy, beckoning for her to move her hands toward me so I could unlock the cuffs.

"They stay on," Raven spoke from the back seat. I turned to look at her. The goggles and face covering that Heretic used to wear regularly were back in place, hiding the video screen, but it was undoubtedly Raven's voice.

"What about the pilot? Do we want to create these kinds of questions?" I asked.

"I'll handle it," was all Raven said in reply. I shook my head and climbed out of the car, anxious to keep the pilot from looking inside and seeing Sammy's cuffs.

"Mr. Strader?" He extended a hand to me.

"James," I corrected briefly, taking the offered hand.

He shook it firmly, smiling cheerily all the while. He had just a bit of grey showing beneath his pilot's cap, but his eyes already had deep crow's feet at the corners. I couldn't decide how old he was.

"Tucker Wilson. I'll be your pilot this afternoon. Mr. Hoover said to get underway as soon as you're loaded. Can I help you with your gear?" He nodded behind me at the heavily loaded SUV.

"Oh. Uh, sure," I stumbled.

As Clara climbed out of the car, Tucker held his hand out again. "You must be Mrs. Walker?"

Clara didn't say anything. She didn't even glance at Tucker. She slung her duffel over her shoulder and marched up to the jet and up the protruding staircase.

"I—I'm really sorry about that. You'll have to forgive her; she just lost her husband very unexpectedly." My voice caught as the full weight of what I said washed over me. Pat.

"Oh! I'm sorry to hear that." Tucker's eyes flashed a look brimming with sympathy to the open door of the jet.

I wiped at my own eyes, not ready to bare my whole soul to this kind, yet stranger of a man. "Let's get this gear loaded."

"Of course. Hello." Tucker touched the brim of his cap to Sammy, who was just getting out of the car.

"A private jet, can you believe it?" Raven's voice was a full octave higher than it normally was as she leaped out of the car, grabbing hold of both of Sammy's hands, the long, loose sleeves of her black jacket draping down across Sammy's wrists. The old goggles and the face-covering were back in place, hiding the LCD screen that shed light on Heretic's multiple personalities. Raven let out an ear-splitting squeal, pulling Sammy along behind her toward the jet. "Come on! I can't wait to see the inside. I bet it has a TV. You think it has its own WiFi?" They both disappeared up the stairs, Sammy looking back with equal amounts of confusion and disbelief in her eyes.

"Virgins, huh?" Tucker chuckled.

"What?" I gasped, choking on my own breath.

"First-time flying private? I can always tell the ones for whom it's their first time." He laughed again, opening the back door of the SUV and stepping up to undo the straps for the rooftop carrier.

"Oh. Yeah." I closed my eyes and took in a deep breath, willing the blood to stop turning my face into a mood ring. I could tell it didn't do any good. I busied myself undoing the straps on my side, eager to have something to hide behind.

"So, what sort of convention are you folks headed to?"

"Convention?" I asked in confusion, undoing the zipper on my half of the carrier.

Tucker had already unloaded several cases. "I fly a lot of sportsmen into Utah; I know what a gun case looks like. I figured a convention based on your friend's outfit, but now I'm wondering if it's for some sort of specialty gun show?"

"Yeah, video game shooter's convention," I lied.

He'd already laid the framework for it. I just carried it home. I followed him to the jet and the gear storage compartments.

"Really? Huh. Only in Utah. We love our video games, and we love our guns. I guess it was only a matter of time." He loaded up the first two boxes and reached for mine. "You hunt, too? Or just a collector?"

"Uh, both," I said, walking back to the SUV.

"Nice," Tucker said with a smile.

We finished loading the gear, Tucker cheerful and eager to fill the silence, me equally eager to let him.

"You can park the car over there," he said when we were finished.

Once the car was moved to a corner of the hangar, I climbed the stairs into the cabin and Tucker pulled them up behind me.

"All right, folks. Make yourselves at home. We'll get going quick as we can and be in the air very soon thereafter."

"Thanks, Tucker," I replied.

He smiled and retreated into the cockpit.

I fell into the first available seat and lay my head back heavily. My muscles were screaming from being flexed. It hadn't really registered just how nervous I was about getting onto the plane with Sammy in handcuffs and all of our guns and gear. Now that we were loaded and leaving, I felt considerably better, if also considerably drained.

Heretic appeared at my elbow and squatted down in the aisle.

"Any problems?"

"Miraculously, no," I whispered, uncertain how well the sound carried down the short hallway to the open cockpit door.

"Good. Relax," he ordered. "You look like you're about to pass out."

Passing out sounded like an excellent idea. I decided then and there that Heretic could watch over everything that happened between takeoff and landing. I reclined my chair, adjusted a few times, and closed my eyes.

***

I was startled awake when the plane began descending sharply and Tucker came over the cabin speakers. "All right, folks, we're just coming into the Salt Lake valley. If this is your first time here, I'd take a good look out to the right of the plane, where you can see the Wasatch Mountains under a spectacular sunset, and the sunset itself over the Oquirrh Mountains to the left. Welcome to Salt Lake City."

I'd never been to the western United States before. The sensation of dropping down between those two ranges of mountains made me strangely claustrophobic, which was odd since I could see the lights and buildings of the city stretch far off to the very foot of the ranges, and even perch precariously along the lower slopes of the mountains themselves.

It was such a strange feeling to step off the plane, feel the dry heat of the high desert blast me in my face, and yet be able to look up at those mountains and see snow still frosting the top like a glaze on a cake. I'd seen snowcapped mountains in pictures before, but it was a confusing contradiction to feel the heat of the air around me and see the white, knowing it was snow.

"Problem?" Tucker called from behind me at the top of the stairs.

"Sorry," I muttered.

Two large black SUVs advanced to the open door of the hangar we'd taxied into, and the drivers got out, two men in suits.

"Mr. and Mrs. Walker?" one of the men asked.

I saw Clara stiffen on the tarmac ahead of me, and the knuckles of the hand holding the strap of her duffel on her shoulder went white.

"Mr. Walker... He—" I started, but Heretic cut me off, poking his head out of the open door of the plane.

"Yes, that's us. It's been a long day, please. We'd like to just get loaded and on our way."

The men just nodded and started hauling off bags and cases.

I turned and watched Heretic hand his jacket to Sammy, and arrange it over her wrists. She held it and walked without protest down the stairway and to the back of the first SUV. Heretic opened the door for her and then climbed in after her himself.

I turned to watch the men, joined by Tucker, make quick and organized work of unloading from the plane and then repacking the luggage into the two SUVs.

When they were finished, Tucker walked to me, his

hand again outstretched. "Nice to meet you, James. You folks enjoy your convention!"

"Thanks," I said, offering him a genuine smile. He smiled back and walked back to the jet.

I turned around in time to see Clara climb into the front passenger seat of the SUV that Heretic and Sammy had selected. I groaned. I now had a choice: I could either ride on my own with the driver of the other SUV, or I would have to squish into the back next to Sammy. My heart started racing and I started sweating as a cascade of thoughts ran through my head. *If I sat by her, we'd probably touch legs and shoulders.* A thrill ran up and down my spine. *This is the woman who sold me out to Julian Danton.* My stomach tightened. *What would we talk about, so close together, with everyone else around, for the car ride? Didn't Henry say that it was several hours to his ranch?* My face got hot.

In the end, the decision was taken away from me. The man in the riderless rear SUV climbed into the driver's seat while the driver of the other vehicle opened the rear door and gestured inside.

What choice did I have? To do or say anything else would just make the situation more awkward. I swallowed and nodded, then climbed into the seat next to Sammy. The instant the door closed behind me, I knew I'd made a mistake.

My long legs didn't fit behind the front seat; they only fit at an angle, which meant that they pressed right into and in front of Sammy's. Not only that, but the roof of the SUV sloped enough toward the opening of the door that my head hit, forcing me to either hold it at an uncomfortable cramped angle when sitting up straight or lean to my left, putting me inches away from Sammy. I reached for the seatbelt at my shoulder and looked for the receiving end. It wasn't even visible. I tried to scoot to the side, creating as much room as I could. No good; the buckle was still mostly beneath the curve of Sammy's backside. Internally cursing the narrowness of the middle seats, I stammered and muttered apologies as I tried to push the buckle beneath Sammy without touching her. I could tell she was trying to politely ignore what was happening by the way she stared straight ahead, with no emotion on her face, despite my apologies. My face reddened further. Finally, she leaned toward Heretic just a bit more, and I was finally able to click the seatbelt and then retreat to awkwardly staring out the window on my side.

I should have ridden in the other car.

***

At first, the driver tried asking a few questions of Clara, making polite conversation. Clara ignored him. I thought about saying something in her defense, then thought better of it for two reasons. One, I knew how Clara felt about people coming to her rescue, and two, speaking from where I had to hold my head put me very close to Sammy, and I was suddenly painfully aware of how long it had been since I'd brushed my teeth. I chose silence as the option with the fewest negative outcomes.

The blast of the air conditioning made it difficult to hear anything, anyway. I turned my attention to the outside as we drove east toward the larger mountain range. The light from the setting sun receded up the face, chased by the shadows from the other range. The result was otherworldly. A stark line between light and shadow, with the light being driven into a smaller and smaller area, until finally, before we were too close and I lost sight of the peaks, the light was all but gone, erased by shadow.

I tried not to draw parallels between this amazing sunset, my first with real mountains, and our own situation. What if we were trying to slow the inevitable? What if, by drawing all the Mythics here, we were only making a single, larger target for Caine? How long before he simply wiped us all out, erased us from existence? With the fleeing of the light, my thoughts grew only darker. Through several mountain passes that made my ears pop multiple times, hours across rolling foothills and a slow and steady climb which probably meant more mountains, I spiraled downward. Our path was lit now only by the headlights of the vehicle. They showed dirt roads pressed on either side by trees.

I thought of everyone I'd already lost. My parents, my fireteam at the Danton's, all of my peers at the Safeguard training facility, Rachel, Pat. Oh, Hell. Pat.

I squeezed my eyes shut and swallowed hard past the knot in my throat, suddenly very glad for the dark in the vehicle. I took several deep, steady breaths.

"You okay?" Sammy whispered.

Crap. She noticed.

I nodded. I wasn't sure I could say anything without making it obvious how close I was to tears.

"You sure?" she pressed.

I nodded again, lowering my head and pressing it to the window, trying and failing to create some space between us.

At that very moment, I felt the subtle but noticeable difference when we passed into the boundary of the Brick. I knew, from the way everyone else began looking around at the same time, that they'd felt it, too. *We must be close.*

It was a few minutes later that we started seeing lights that winked in and out several hundred yards ahead through the trees. Shortly after that, we passed through a large metal gate and into a clearing. A beautiful lodge, with double-story windows showcasing brilliant chandeliers staring out from the front of the building, lit up the night. I could see that the lodge nestled right up against a hillside, the front half supported on huge wooden pillars. A staircase that ran the full width of the building extended from ground level where we were up to the porch that extended from the huge windows.

I could clearly see Henry Hoover push open the double glass doors and walk out onto the porch, standing at the top of the stairs, his hands held casually in his pockets.

The car stopped and I gratefully threw open the door and climbed out, my legs protesting their long entrapment.

Henry threw his arms wide and shouted down to us from his vantage point.

"Welcome to Camp Respite!"

The man knew a thing or two about presentation.

Chapter 13

"Who's this?" Henry asked, gesturing his hands out toward Sammy. "I don't believe I've had the pleasure."

I felt a twinge in my gut and a surge of adrenaline I ignored. "Henry Hoover, Samantha Charleston."

"Are these really necessary?" Henry asked, putting a finger beneath the links connecting the cuffs and looking at me. "We're an hour by car from the nearest main road with any traffic, and I'm betting that she probably wants to be here anyway, given the circumstances. What did she do, exactly?"

"It's not really your problem," I said, turning away and feigning interest in the gearboxes I'd unloaded.

"Oh, come on, James. Where's she gonna go?" he pressed, waving off our two drivers, who'd made short work of the gear and climbed back into their SUVs, which disappeared quickly in the total darkness of the night beyond the clearing.

"Look, just drop it, okay?" I shot back.

Henry let the finger drop but kept looking at me.

"James, this is meant to be a haven for these people,

not a prison. I don't really go for the whole captive thing." He folded his arms high across his chest, one hand in his armpit, the other clasping his bicep. "If she wants to be here, that's great. If not, I refuse to be party to holding someone against their will."

My face felt hot, and my mouth was suddenly flooded with saliva. I couldn't talk, so I simply walked toward the two of them, ramming my hand into my pocket for the key and holding it out to Sammy. I couldn't bring myself to be the one to undo them. Touching her was too confusing.

I turned back to the gear and heard a few clicks as the handcuffs released. I heard Henry's smooth, low voice say behind me, quietly, "There. Much better. It's nice to meet you, Samantha. Welcome to Camp Respite."

I knew it was silly, and I knew it was temporary, but at that moment, I hated Henry Hoover. *Why does he get to be the benevolent one? I don't really want her in handcuffs, either! I know she wants to be here. I've already thought of that!*

It didn't matter. He was the one who'd requested the key. I was the one who had begrudgingly given it up.

I yanked two of the cases from the growing pile on the porch and stormed inside with them. When I came back outside, I watched Henry approach Clara, who had thrown her own duffel to the top of the stairs and reached for a few cases of her own from the shrinking pile on the ground. I simply stood there, watching.

Henry put a hand out to Clara, touching her shoulder. "Clara?" His voice carried up to the top of the porch. That stupid low, silky voice; it was like a radio host's. "I'm so sorry. What do you need?"

Clara stood there, a case on either side, the one still casted hugged awkwardly around one. She squinted up at him, her mouth turned slightly downward. "Not really a hugger." She stepped around him and trudged stoically up the stairs, passing by without even glancing at me.

I tried not to look happy. I wasn't; even now, my throat started closing up thinking about Pat, and I had to blink back tears. But, I would be lying if I said that there wasn't a small part of me that was glad that Henry was left standing alone and ignored at the bottom of the stairs. I immediately felt terrible about it. He *was* the source of our temporary salvation, after all. The man had been nothing but generous to us, virtual strangers. But he'd been deflated, and I'd been glad about it, even if only for a moment. I gathered my own armful of gear to haul inside, smug but convinced I was a terrible person.

Henry came up with the last of the gear a moment later, close behind Heretic. He set the bins down near the rest and closed the double doors.

"Again, everyone, welcome. So, this is the main lodge. The main kitchen facilities are here, along with a few conference rooms, a spa, and a full wing of guest rooms. It was intended to serve smaller groups, so you guys can stay here, and we'll put everyone else in the extended camp cabins as they arrive."

My guilt over my reaction to Henry earlier drove me to speak. "Thanks again, Henry, for doing this. It's incredibly generous of you."

He beamed. "It's my pleasure. What's the point of being a billionaire, if you can't help a few thousand people every once in a while? I'm pretty sure it'll even be a tax write-off. My accountants will be *very* happy."

I didn't even know what to say to that. Neither did anyone else, apparently. The room went silent.

He looked from face to face, and I think he realized that he'd made us uncomfortable. He cleared his throat and pointed down a hall. "The kitchen's this way. Are you all hungry? The caterers won't get here 'til we send for 'em. I asked a few different companies to be on standby when people start arriving. I figured we probably wouldn't need 'em all at once, just call 'em up as needed." He must have seen something in someone's face again, because he groaned, smiled, and said, "Sorry. Logistics. All I'm saying is, I can whip something up if you're hungry."

"I could definitely eat," I said. "I haven't had anything since breakfast."

Henry looked appalled. "Really? Oh, you guys! I'm so sorry! Yeah, let's head to the kitchen, and we'll fix you something. What are you feeling? Pasta? Sandwiches? Salad? I'm just trying to think of something quick here."

"Whatever's easiest," I said, not wanting to tax our host.

"No, I insist!" Henry chuckled. "Everyone leaves this kitchen satisfied. Those are the rules!"

Henry was true to his word. In the end, he'd cooked a delicious angel-hair pasta with spinach, sun-dried tomatoes, and sausage in light cream sauce; a wonderfully crisp chicken Caesar salad; and a fantastic sandwich stuffed with minced olives, Italian meats, and cheese. I left the kitchen considerably heavier than I'd entered.

"Everyone get enough? If you leave hungry, it's your own fault!" Henry grinned, holding open the door back out to the hallway.

"Which way are the rooms?" Sammy asked. I noticed that she stood closest to Henry, and the corners of her lips turned up in the slightest of smiles. *Ugh. She doesn't quit, does she?*

Henry held out a hand back toward the entryway and lobby area. "On the other side of the lodge. We didn't want the kitchens driving people crazy while they were trying to sleep."

"What are the sleeping assignments?" Heretic asked.

"Pretty simplistic; find a room that suits you and get some sleep." Henry grinned. *He's always got to be the funny guy, the benevolent hero.*

Henry was starting to get under my skin.

***

The next morning, I rolled out of the queen-size bed, took a quick shower, threw on some clothes, then went wandering the lodge. This side of the building housed the guest rooms on the second and third floors and a few conference rooms on the ground floor. Across the main entryway, which shone just as bright during the day as at night thanks to the huge windows and abundance of mirrors, were the spa and the kitchens. Kitchens on the ground floor, spa on the second and third. It was a great location for a retreat. I wondered at the practicality of it in housing several thousand individuals, though. How were we going to fit so many people here? Henry had mentioned "extended camp cabins", but what did that really mean? Surely, he couldn't have cabins like this for each and every individual we were hoping would arrive safely?

I decided to ask him about it at breakfast. I followed my nose to the kitchen, where I found exactly what I thought I'd been smelling for the last several minutes.

A large plate of crispy bacon and glistening sausage links was kept under a bank of warming lights, while Henry, wearing a beige apron over his white button-up shirt and slacks, piled a last few steaming, fluffy white pancakes onto a large heaping platter.

"Perfect timing! Grab the syrup and orange juice out of that fridge, will you James? Do you drink coffee? There's a machine on the back wall of the conference room. I've set us up in there for breakfast this morning." He set off across the lodge, practically bouncing out the door. I hurried to the fridge for the requested juice and syrup, then raced after him.

Henry had set up a single round table in the first conference room and brought five chairs around the outside. He'd even included one for Heretic. Setting down the platters of meat and pancakes, Henry wiped his hands on a towel dangling from a pocket of the apron and went to a large console on the wall of the conference room near the door. He pushed a couple of buttons on the LCD screen, then spoke. His voice was amplified through speakers that echoed throughout the lodge.

"Chow's on! Breakfast in Conference Room A in five minutes!"

He pushed another button, and I heard the intercom click off.

"How about that coffee? Shall I turn on the machine?" he asked, pointing with his forehead at the large commercial coffee dispenser at the back of the room.

"Might as well," I said, shrugging.

"I don't drink it myself, but I always like to have it available for those who do, if they choose to," Henry said, jogging to the machine and reaching for a switch on the back. The machine flickered on, and a minute or two later, the smell of freshly ground and brewing coffee permeated throughout the conference room.

Henry took a deep breath, closing his eyes. "Never even tasted it, but I do love the smell."

I shook my head to myself but said nothing. *This dude's weird.*

Clara walked in alone, but Sammy and Heretic weren't long behind her.

"Is there something anyone can do about this freaking robot? It was waiting literally outside my room, just waiting for me. Best part? It won't even tell me how long it was there for." Sammy stormed in and yanked a chair out across from Clara.

Clara just stared, her face expressionless, devoid of any emotion whatsoever.

"I don't trust you. Based on your past history, it seems likely that you will leverage any opportunity to align yourself with whomever you perceive to hold the most power in a given situation. Since, at the moment, that happens to be Henry Hoover, I'm not concerned." Both Henry and Sammy shifted uncomfortably as Heretic said that, and I crossed one leg over the other, impatiently. "However, since Caine's arrival is imminent, and he unequivocally holds the greatest power in our situation, I find it warranted to keep you under observation, bare minimum. Restraint is not objectionable."

"Hey, now. No restraints. My house, my rules, remember?" Henry took the opportunity to speak up. "Now that it comes to that, how about we sit down, have some breakfast, and talk about what needs doing, huh?"

Heretic considered, nodded, and sat down next to Clara.

"All right, now, I grew up in a big family, and the

only time we got any important talking done was when people's mouths were too full of food to argue. So, I figured we could have breakfast and hammer out some things regarding what's about to happen." Henry pulled out his own chair and sat down.

Who made him the boss? It rubbed me the wrong way that he should just assume leadership like that. I looked at Clara, but she only picked at a single pancake on her plate, no syrup. Heretic just sat there, and I certainly didn't want Sammy to lead out. *Why shouldn't I, if Clara isn't going to?*

"No, I've been meaning to bring that up," I started.

"Now, I have some things I have to take care of off the mountain," Henry continued, almost as if he hadn't heard me. "I won't be back until probably the day after tomorrow at the earliest, so I wanted to get some things decided now."

I spoke up, louder this time. "I think that's a good idea. Heretic, any news from folks about when they're planning on arriving here?"

Heretic shook his head. "Many people I've communicated with have been very concerned about being tracked through online or digital means. Many have said that they wouldn't be flying, but rather driving, and not in a predictable fashion."

"That sounds familiar," I muttered, remembering my time driving cross-country with the Danton kids a couple of years ago.

"That being the case, I think we'll start to see a steady flow of refugees throughout the coming week, some of the earliest arriving as early as tomorrow." Heretic nodded as an end to his statement.

"Okay!" Henry jumped in. "Now, what's the latest word on Caine himself? Anyone had any news from Raven at all?"

I looked around the table. I certainly hadn't heard from my sister. A few headshakes. Clara just stared at her pancake.

"Okay, so," Henry glanced noticeably at Clara. "I know that the werewolf escaped." He paused for a moment as if waiting to see if Clara would react in some way. She didn't. "Is it safe to assume that he's probably back with Caine by now, or back to tracking for him, at least? How long do we think we have before Caine actually shows up?" He looked at Heretic. "Any predictive models? Educated guesses? Stabs in the dark?"

"If we assume that Vasily has returned to active service of Caine, it's possible that he is already on our trail. He tracked us from the Woodwards in a day and a half. We did fly from St. Louis, which should confuse the scent somewhat, but we don't know that for sure. We have no idea just how enhanced his senses actually are. For that matter, I just realized that I have assumed that he's using natural senses. There's no reason that has to be the case. I recommend we err on the side of caution. I would assume that we have a week, as much time as it takes him to traverse the distance on foot, which it seems he does."

We all jumped when Clara tossed her fork onto her

plate, then sat back and crossed her arms. "How fast could everyone get here if they drove straight lines, directly? Their cars are faster than a wolf on foot."

Heretic nodded. "Assuming that most are coming in at least pairs, I'd say as soon as tomorrow evening, if they wanted to drive through the night in shifts, per Safeguard practice."

"Give the order," Clara said.

"Why, Clara?" Henry spoke up. "What are you thinking?"

"We get everyone here, beneath the Brick, then you send Caine a message." She looked at Heretic. "Direct to Raven, you tell him exactly where we are, exactly how to get here, exactly how many of us there are."

"Uh, are you crazy?" Sammy said.

"You don't get a say here," Clara spat.

"That does seem... counterintuitive," Henry offered carefully.

"I thought the plan was to buy us more time?" I pressed, just happy to see Clara engaging with the world again.

Clara shook her head. "Time is against us here. It's not to our advantage." She looked at Henry. "I don't care how much money you've sunk into prepping caterers, food, and water for this deal. It won't be enough. Any army is only as good as its supply line; once Caine gets here, ours is cut. Best to rip off the Band-Aid and arrange for that to be when our supplies, manpower, and morale are at their highest. It's only a downhill slide from there."

Silence settled around us as we considered her points. They didn't *not* make sense.

"You do make a sound argument so far," Henry put forth slowly. "But what about when Caine gets here? Then what? What's the plan at that point?"

Clara's eyes lost their focus as she stared at something in space only she could see. "After that, it doesn't matter."

"See?" Sammy yelled, standing up and forcing her chair back from the table. "She's freaking crazy! She's got a death wish!"

"Sammy, sit down. Please." Henry's voice was calm, frustratingly calm. I hated him for it. "It isn't a bad plan; it's just missing a few pieces." He turned to me, Heretic, and Clara. "We make the calls. Give the order, or whatever. We have two days: we come up with something or we die. It's that simple." He stood and put his fingertips on the table. "I'll keep my business to one day. I'll be back tomorrow evening. We have roughly thirty-six hours to figure out how to prevent genocide. May God bless and watch over us all." He pursed his lips into a half-smile, tapped his fingertips on the table for emphasis, and walked out of the conference room.

How does he manage that every stinking time?!

Chapter 14

Clara left the table without a word after Henry's departure, leaving me, Heretic, and Sammy. I helped myself to a few more pancakes and sausage links, thinking about what Henry had said. *Prevent genocide.* That's what we were trying to do. No pressure, right?

Heretic stood abruptly.

"Where are you going?" I asked around a mouthful of syrup-soaked sausage.

"I'd like to become familiar with the typography of our new base of operations."

I nodded. "You could say it like that." I pointed at him with my fork, a freshly-speared sausage bobbing on the end. "Or, you could just say, 'I'm gonna have a look around.'"

Heretic looked at me for a moment, then said, "I'm gonna have a look around. Keep an eye on this one." He pointed unabashedly at Sammy, then walked toward the door.

"Hold on!" I stood up. "You're not just gonna leave me with her again, are you? Really?"

Heretic didn't respond. He walked out the door and didn't reappear.

Sammy waited, watching the door, then said, "Relax, sausage man. I don't need a babysitter. You do you, I'll take care of me."

Part of me wanted nothing more than to take her up on it. There were still moments when Sammy sneered or frowned all I could see was her standing above me, a rifle pointed at my chest. Every decision I had to make where she was concerned had so many facets to consider, so many conflicting thoughts and wants. *I want her to die. I want to be close to her. I want to be anywhere but where she is. I want to keep an eye on her.* I didn't do anything but stand there as she walked to the door and peered around the jamb as if she expected Heretic to still be somewhere just outside. When she walked through, I scrambled to action, gathering up the last few links on my plate and rolling them up into the last pancake.

I jogged down the hall to catch up with Sammy, holding my pancake burrito in two hands.

"Seriously? Are you just going to do everything that split-personalitied robot tells you to do?"

"Well, like he said, we don't trust you." I licked a drip of syrup off one of my fingers.

"Fine. Then you're just going to have to keep up." She pushed open the front door and walked out onto the porch. I followed, trying my best not to notice the way her denim-covered posterior shivered side-to-side with every step. I swallowed, trying to keep my eyes high.

The air felt so different from home. This time of year, this time of day, the air would be close and thick, almost wet, and hot everywhere. But here, now, walking out of the shadow of the porch, the warmth of the sun hit my skin pleasantly, in stark contrast to the pleasantly cool surrounding air, and even more so to the marked cool of the shade.

Sammy bounded down the steps and turned right around to head back up toward the hill behind us.

I sighed. "Where are you going?"

"Where does it look like I'm going? I'm climbing to the top of this mountain behind us. It's been a long time since I've been back out West. I want to get the view from the top of a mountain."

I looked above her at the face of the rise ahead of her. "There's no path, no trail, you don't have any food, no water, no map, and no compass. That's a terrible idea."

"Come on, country boy, where's your sense of adventure?" She was baiting me.

"Adventure without preparedness is just stupidity." I mentally patted myself on the back for that one. It felt pithy and witty.

"Come on, don't be a downer. I'm just going to the top of this hill right here. What can happen?"

I shook my head, looking around for Heretic, hoping he would help me talk sense into her. Spotting no one, I had no choice but to follow after Sammy, cursing her in my head. "Wait!" She didn't.

Neither of us was wearing the right shoes for something like this. I quickly had pebbles digging into my ankles and poking into the bottoms of both feet, and I slid halfway down the length of every step upward I took. Sammy wasn't doing much better, up ahead of me. She went from tree to tree, stopping to pause and look back at me and the lodge every several yards. In no time at all, we were both gasping for air and sweating like crazy through our shirts.

By now, we were several hundred yards up the slope, but it was steep enough that we were probably a hundred feet above the lodge already, I guessed. We could only just see the shine of its blue metal roof through some of the trees.

We continued our scramble, both too out of breath to trade anything more than the occasional acknowledgment, just checking that the other person was still there and going up.

We hit a sheer granite rock face soon after that forced us into a decision: we could either start down, or we could attempt to go around and find a way upward. Sammy made a unilateral decision. Onward in pursuit of upward. I followed without comment.

Eventually, we found a place where two slopes converged, with larger rocks and freer of looser dirt and pebbles that made forward motion such a challenge. We scrambled up some waist-high drops and around some larger boulders. The crest of the hill that Sammy had originally pointed at extended in a narrow ridge down and to our right. To our left, the other slope continued its steep ascent, always upward.

Sammy turned and began to walk out toward the point, her feet slipping slightly in the scree.

"Hey, be careful," I shouted at her back. "Don't forget that we're on top of that face we had to go around now."

"Thanks, Dad!" she called back, laughing.

I shook my head. *She's an idiot.*

I picked my way carefully in that direction. The face in question had been at least a good thirty feet. I had no desire to slip down all this loose rock and go sailing out off that drop-off. We were going slightly downhill toward the point we'd seen from the ground. I looked ahead and saw that Sammy had already reached it. The loose rock and dirt ended, leaving maybe a dozen feet of bare rock, strewn with pebbles, that she was standing on. She stood there, hands on her waist, and a breeze picked up the high ponytail her hair was in, throwing it back and forth like a flag.

You've got to be kidding me.

She turned to look back at me and smiled. "It's a lot higher than it looked from the ground," she said, then took another step forward. I was only a few feet behind her at that point, so I clearly heard the crack and rumble, then saw Sammy start to lose her balance over her forward foot that was suddenly plunging down with the large chunk of granite that had just calved off from the face.

Everything from there on seemed to happen in slow motion. She turned and threw out her arm toward me, fingers splayed and reaching, her eyes and mouth gaping. Her other foot slid out from under her as she tried to draw herself back in with it, sliding uselessly on the pebbles beneath it. I caught her hand with both of mine, but her center of gravity was already headed out into empty space. I was jerked forward.

I managed to get one foot out in front of me before being pulled down to my knees. I leaned back with my hands around her wrist, trying to use my leg to leverage backward, but my hands were pulled to the edge of the cliff. I heard a heavy slap as Sammy collided with the rock face below me, then both heard and felt a pop reverberate through her arm, into my hands.

The sound I heard from Sammy at that point could only be described as a screech. There was no word, no tone to it, just a shrill grinding of her vocal cords that stabbed at my ears and echoed out across the clearing below us. I was pretty sure Sammy's shoulder had just dislocated.

My foot against the rock in front of me slid a couple of inches, sending a jolt of adrenaline-fueled tightening throughout my body.

My wrists bent awkwardly and painfully over the edge. If I couldn't find a new position soon, all of the pain so far would be for nothing, when either my grip or my footing gave.

Acting purely out of instinct, I drew my front leg behind me and laid flat on my chest, letting my torso be pulled toward the edge. Sammy screamed again, but whether from the pain I was sure she felt in her shoulder or the sensation of falling again, I wasn't sure.

"Don't let me go! Please don't let me go!" The words flew from her mouth so fast and high, that I almost didn't catch them. I didn't bother answering.

I extended my legs as far back behind me as I could. When everything stopped moving, I was lying flat on my chest, my armpits riding the edge of the cliff, my face staring down into Sammy's tear-streaming eyes.

"I need your other hand," I said quietly, through gritted teeth.

"What?!" She screamed.

"Stop moving, if you can, and give me your other hand."

She nodded, eyes closed, and mouth open in a silent cry.

She brought up her other arm, and I heard her hiss then bite back another scream. I caught her wrist with my right hand, and her fingers clamped around my wrist, nails digging painfully into the skin.

"All right," I tried to say calmly. "Look at me. Look at me!"

She managed to open her eyes.

"Is there something that you can stand on, some foothold that you can use to bear up some of your weight?"

She looked down, and I felt her body start to swing as her feet felt around the cliff face.

Suddenly the weight on my arms decreased just enough to be noticeable. Then her foot slipped, and the weight returned.

"It isn't big enough," she whimpered.

"That's okay, just enough to give us a chance. Use it." I forced myself to speak slowly, injecting a calm I wasn't feeling into the words.

She nodded. A smaller portion of the weight lifted.

"Heretic! Clara! Help!"

I knew there was no way that I was going to be able to hold her for very long, and I certainly wasn't strong enough to pull her back up over the edge. Help was our only hope.

"Heretic! Clara!"

I realized that Sammy was staring up at me, tears falling freely from her eyes.

"Please don't let me fall." Her words were barely a whisper. "Don't let go."

"I won't." It was all I could manage.

I didn't know if it was moments or minutes that we hung there. The only progression I paid any attention to was the growing ache in my shoulders and the increasing screaming pain of cramping in my fingers, palms, and forearms as I clenched Sammy's wrists. Sammy fell silent after a while, and her breathing grew shallow and quick, punctuated by hisses and stifled groans every time she shifted.

Just when I was sure I couldn't sustain my grip on

her wrists for a moment longer, I felt a hand on my back, then a dark sleeve rushed past my face.

"You're going to have to pull her up just a few inches. I can't reach her." The sound of Heretic's flat, electronic voice had never been so welcome. I felt tears squeeze from the corners of my eyes and felt them run down and off my nose. I watched as they fell onto Sammy's upturned cheeks, and then made eye contact with her. Her own eyes watered anew.

I nodded, then heaved. Every muscle in my upper body tensed as I tried to raise Sammy up the face. My chest lifted off the ground, my shoulders flexed outward, and my elbows bent to give me enough inches of lift to allow Heretic to grab a hold of Sammy. It was just enough. He clamped down on her good wrist and lifted slowly and steadily. As she rose, I released the arm that had dislocated, but it stayed above her head. Sammy wailed as Heretic lifted her higher.

Finally, I was able to hook my elbow behind one of her knees and helped to pull her up. We dragged her up and over the lip of the edge, then rolled her onto her back.

Sammy's right arm still contorted oddly at the shoulder and pointed up above her head.

"Please try to hold still." Heretic said softly. Sammy nodded, eyes squeezed shut. Heretic moved this way and that around Sammy, emitting a few soft clicks from his head. *X-rays.*

"This is going to hurt." Heretic said briefly. He took off Sammy's belt and doubled it over, then put it in her mouth. "Bite down on this." To me, he said, "Give me your shirt."

I took off my tee and handed it to him. He wrapped it around the top of Sammy's shoulder, then handed me the two ends. "Pull downward on this when I tell you."

Heretic positioned himself at Sammy's head, over the injured shoulder. He lifted Sammy's arm gently in his hands. She whimpered.

"Pull," he said. At the same that I pulled, he lifted her arm up, palm toward her feet, and rotated it upward. Sammy screamed around the belt in her mouth, and I felt a subtle pop through the taut fibers of my shirt.

"Release," Heretic said to me. He held Sammy's arm a moment more, moving it in gentle circles. "Does that hurt?"

Sammy's chest was heaving, but she shook her head, tears forming a glistening trail that disappeared into the hair above her ears.

I leaned over and put my hands on my knees, my entire upper body tremoring.

Heretic looked over the two of us, silent. "Might I suggest staying away from edges in the future?" he asked.

Sammy and I looked at each other and started laughing, which devolved into something involving nervous chuckles and tears.

Chapter 15

By the time we got back down to the lodge, there were three vehicles parked in front of it that we didn't recognize. When we walked inside, Clara was talking quietly with three different couples varying from her own age to that of my parents, and three young people, a girl who looked to be about ten, a teenage boy, and a young adult woman. The first of the Mythic refugees had arrived.

Sammy disappeared toward her room, still nursing her right shoulder. Heretic followed her, a wordless shadow. Not knowing how else to make myself of use, I wandered back to the conference room and cleared away and cleaned up breakfast. I was halfway through the dishes before my hands stopped shaking and I could breathe normally again. I was drying and putting away the last of them when Clara walked in, a rifle case in one hand, and another tucked under the other, casted arm.

"You busy?" she asked, looking around at the cleaned countertops and the bowl in my hands.

"Nope. Just finishing up."

She indicated the cases. "Help me out with these?"

I nodded, put away the bowl, and wiped my hands on the towel, then followed her out the door. As we walked through the lobby, she nodded toward the pile of cases. "Grab a few."

I scooped up a few of the other cases and followed Clara into Conference Room A.

In a moment she had her cases down and one of them opened, a rifle in her hands.

"We cleaning them?" I asked.

She nodded, proceeding to break down the rifle to its smallest parts, collecting them on the mat she pulled from her case.

I opened one of the cases I held and followed suit, reaching for the AR rifle to start. As my hands went about the familiar task of removing pins, bolts, and the rest, my mind traveled back a year to my brief stint serving with Safeguard. While in training at the now-nonexistent facility in Kansas, I had become good friends with Pat and Clara. I mentally contrasted the crusty, yet kind Clara—"Like a Tootsie Pop: hard on the outside, gooey in the center!", Pat had often described her—with the sunken-eyed, emotionless Clara who sat a table away from me. I wondered if I'd looked after losing my parents the way Clara looked now. I remembered well the nights of medication-induced sleep that were the only form of relief from the days when I chased away every thought, every reminder of my loss.

I paused in my brushing and glanced at Clara. She

was examining a minute piece of metal, studying it for signs of corrosion or cracking, and paid no attention to me.

I brushed a few more times, then stopped again. I cleared my throat. "Clara—" I began.

"No." She didn't even look up.

I set the parts I was cleaning down and pulled up a chair at her table. "I just wanted to say, I get it. After my parents died, I—"

She slammed both hands down on the table—the cast banged loudly against the tabletop— and jumped up, sending the pieces she had so carefully set aside and placed jumping and skittering over the plastic tabletop. The only sound was the soft hollow scratching as one of the small pieces moved in a small circle on the table, finally coming to a stop with a gentle wiggle.

When Clara finally spoke, it was with her head still down, palms on the table. It was in the faintest of quivering whispers. "I can't sleep. I haven't slept more than a few minutes at a time since that night." She wiped the back of a hand across her nose and sniffed, raising her head to look at her hands. "The last thing every night and the first thing every morning, he'd take my hand and he'd put it under his cheek like a pillow. It was stupid, but I—" A coughing sob cut her off, and her head dropped back down. She sat slowly down, and clasped her head in her hands, her elbows propped up on the table.

I sighed. When I lost my parents, the smallest

things set me off. A scent in my mom's kitchen, the smell of oil in my dad's shop. I understood a bit of what she was going through.

"What do you need from me?" I asked in a whisper.

She sniffed. "I have no idea." She mashed her palms against her eyes. "I have several thousand Mythics arriving in the next two days who are going to look to me for leadership, for direction. There's an unkillable psychopath who'd very much like us all dead, and who's directly responsible for... Who..."

"For Pat."

She nodded, wiping tears from her eyes. "So, you tell me, James, what can you do for me?" She laughed, but there was no humor in it, only pain. "I can't even help myself out of this pit I find myself in."

"I know what you mean," I said. "That's exactly how I felt when I showed up on Safeguard's doorstep and asked Pat to Sweep me. Do you remember? I felt like anything, like even feeling nothing at that point would have been better."

Clara nodded. She must have been remembering, too, because her eyes lost their focus and just stared out ahead of her. I continued.

"Training with Safeguard for those first months after he Swept me felt amazing in the moment. It felt fantastic! But it wasn't real. The second Heretic found me and did a Reversal, the phoniness, the farce of it, was so clear. All that time, training with Jose and the rest of the team, I—" I stopped. I'd had a sudden thought.

Clara looked up at me, confusion on her face. "What?"

"We run the op again," I muttered.

"What?"

I said it again, louder. "We run the op again." I reached into my pants pocket and took out my wristband. "We connect a team and go after him that way. If it would have worked for Danton, it will work for Caine. Why haven't we thought of this before?"

Clara squinted, her already puffy, swollen eyes getting even smaller. "Because it feels a lot like suicide."

I shook my head. "It's exactly the same thing. Danton's manipulation of sickness, Caine's manipulation of antimatter, it's all the same at its root: Mythic ability."

"But where do Mythic abilities end and natural laws of theoretical physics begin?" Clara asked. She seemed to have more focus now. It may have been a distraction, but at least she was somewhat her old self.

"That, I'm not sure about," I admitted.

"You may be immune to atomic reactions, but the rest of us definitely aren't," Clara said. It had some of her old edge. I inwardly cheered.

"Still, it's a better chance than we thought we had a few hours ago. What do you think?" I pressed.

Clara frowned and turned back to the rifle strewn across her table. She stood up and walked to the other side of the table, looking at all the pieces carefully. She bent down to the floor and started patting around her. A moment later, she came up with a tiny bar of metal, no longer than her pinky nail, in the palm of her hand. In a flash, she had the rifle put back together. She pulled the charging handle and pulled the trigger. At the click of the firing pin, she looked up at me.

"It's a better chance than we thought we had a few hours ago."

I smiled, and we both returned to our cleaning. For now, I had a shadow of the old Clara back. I just didn't know for how long.

***

By the time Henry arrived back the following day, well over three hundred Mythics had arrived, along with a fleet of caterers and trucks with food shipments. Considering the fact that we'd only arrived at the camp ourselves a couple of days before, I felt like we did a pretty good job assigning everyone to different cabins and groupings.

Each cabin slept a total of eight individuals and was grouped into clumps of ten around a larger central pavilion with a rudimentary kitchen setup. Basically, all the food could be prepped at the main kitchen in the lodge, then dispersed around the camp to be cooked, served, and eaten in the multiple mini-camps.

Henry was impressed. Had he known Clara even a little better, he wouldn't have been surprised in the slightest.

"Seems like everything is going pretty well," he commented. We had just finished a tour of the filled camps so far, Henry filling his role as a gracious host to the utmost, offering additional bedding and blankets, and soliciting recommendations from his guests. You'd have thought he was hosting a retreat, not a refugee camp.

"They're used to following orders," Clara offered.

"So, what's our next move?" Henry asked, maneuvering the small side-by-side Utility Task Vehicle we were all riding in around a parked car and waving at the people in the camp. "Anyone come up with a solution to the bigger problem at hand?"

Clara turned slightly from where she sat in the front seat to look at me. "Your plan, your move."

Henry sought my eyes in the rearview mirror. "You got something, James?"

I nodded. "We think so. It's a start, at least." I pulled the wristband from my pocket and held it out. "I know this doesn't look like much without your Tinkervision, or whatever, but we used it last year—well, would have used it last year—against a Mythic named Julian Danton."

Henry took the bracelet and held it up where he could alternate between looking at it and the road ahead. He reached up to raise his sunglasses off his eyes and onto his forehead. "Huh! What is that? Some kind of alloy?" He dropped it flat on his palm and hefted it a couple of times. "Heavy." He handed it back to me. "What's it do?"

"Well, when I wear it, it nullifies Mythic abilities." I slipped the wristband back into my pocket.

He stared at me in the mirror. "Are you serious? Not to sound rude, but why didn't you list that among our assets in the first place?"

I squinted. "I know that line..."

He smiled in the mirror. "Great movie, isn't it?"

"Focus." Clara brought us back. I saw her brush her eye and remembered Pat's penchant for quoting movies. I regretted the diversion.

"So, it's like a bubble? An unpoppable bubble?" Henry asked.

"I've never thought of it in exactly those terms, but yeah, I suppose so," I nodded. "It's more than that, though. It can extend to other people if you're connected with metal cables. We tested it pretty rigorously."

"Well, that gives us a fighting chance, I suppose." Henry pulled the UTV into the garage space beneath the main lodge. "Heretic still out riding fence?"

"What?" I asked.

"Riding fence. Walking the perimeter and getting to know the area?" Henry climbed out of the vehicle and returned the keys to the bank of boxes that housed all the keys to the veritable fleet of vehicles beneath the lodge.

"Oh, yeah, for the last couple of days." I unfolded myself from the back seat and dropped to the ground.

"Was he able to make contact with Raven like we mentioned before I left?"

Clara shook her head as she walked around the side-by-side. "We were waiting for you to get back, and more of the refugees to show up. Somehow, Caine can travel crazy fast. Once we let them know where we are, we don't think it'll be very long before he shows up."

"I've been thinking more about that," I offered. "I'm pretty sure Caine can teleport."

Henry dropped the socket wrench he'd picked up from a workbench nearby and turned to me, his mouth open and his eyes wide.

"Seriously? What makes you say that?"

I shrugged. "The first time I saw him, back after he destroyed the Safeguard training facility, he and the Danton kids just disappeared into thin air."

Henry cupped his chin and started pacing slowly, his other hand scratching absently at the hair behind his ear. "What would that even require? I haven't looked into teleportation yet..." He muttered to himself for a moment.

Clara snapped her fingers several times. "Focus. No shiny objects, Henry. One thing at a time."

"Sorry, you're right." He inhaled sharply through gritted teeth and scratched furiously at his hair with both hands, then smoothed it down again. "Okay, so for now, we wait for more of the refugees to arrive before we prank call Caine. In the meantime, what do you need for this Mythic-proof bubble of yours, James?"

Chapter 16

The camp filled quickly to capacity over the next several days. In true billionaire fashion, Henry had arranged for several refrigerated coolers to be delivered, along with food to fill them and enough fuel and generators to keep them running for months. I was genuinely impressed with his forethought, but it blew my mind that someone could just do that, without thinking about it or even pausing. The money he threw around was evidenced throughout the camp. Not frivolously, but to incredible effect.

I watched from the lobby window one dark afternoon as the mealtime line of UTVs filed out from the lodge and down toward the camps. As it turned out, the first couple of days we'd been here had been anomalies. Most days here in the Uintas, the onset of the afternoon brought thunderstorms that Henry kept referring to as "flashies". The first time he called them that, I stared at him. He just shrugged and laughed it off.

I looked down the valley that I now knew housed the camp, knowing that the line of UTVs would be making their way across it, making stops at the now 30 encampments that housed Mythics. At last count, we'd welcomed over 2,300 Mythics. The majority were Safeguard Host families and members, but we'd been surprised by groups here and there of Mythics whom Heretic had liberated from Safeguard over the years. There had been a few small scuffles and disagreements over the last few days, but certainly not as many as there could have been.

"It's kind of neat when you think about who's out there," Clara said from a chair a few feet away. "There's never been a gathering like this before. It makes you think, you know? I wish..." she paused, and I heard her take a deep shuddering breath. "I wish Pat were here to see this."

I nodded and turned back to watch the last of the vehicles disappear down the road into the trees. "If only it were under different circumstances." I stared out over the valley. At the far end, I could see the rain already starting to come down. It would reach the lodge in the next few minutes. I bit my lip. "Hey, do you remember a time before you were with Safeguard?"

Clara turned to look at me. "No, my parents were Mythics with Safeguard, too. I guess I always knew about it."

I winced inwardly, clenching my jaw. I knew the truth, that most members of Safeguard had started out as abducted children, placed with Host parents who even themselves were Swept to think they'd always been a family. Everyone thought that their family was the exception to the Hosting protocol. That was part of what had driven the final wedge for me in striking out against Safeguard as an organization before Caine had surfaced and driven the issue to the back burner.

I sidestepped that particular secret and pushed on to my originating question. "Do you ever wonder what it would be like to just live out in the open?"

Clara snorted. "What, as a Mythic, you mean?"

"Yeah."

"There's no way. Think about how people react to other people who even just have different beliefs than they do. We're not talking about beliefs here, James, we're talking about radical fundamental differences."

"Why is it any different from skin color? Nationality? Anything else you're just born with?" I pushed harder.

"Well, for one thing, *your* specific 'nationality' gives you the destructive capability of a world superpower. That's not necessarily something that the world is likely to welcome sharing a fence line with if you know what I mean."

"What are we talking about?" Sammy walked into the lobby, followed closely by Heretic. Her right arm was in a sling, but I noticed that she kept adjusting the arm by itself. I had a feeling that the sling was something being forced on her by Heretic. I smiled in spite of myself.

"What are you smiling at?" Sammy fired at me.

"I—Sorry, something else. We were just talking

about living out in the open as Mythics. Clara doesn't think it's possible."

"I've thought that we should head in that direction for a long time," Sammy said, off-hand.

I looked at Clara and held my hands out toward Sammy. "Thank you!"

Clara glanced at Sammy, then back at me. "Congratulations; you'll make a wonderful couple."

I backpedaled furiously. "No! It's not like that. She just agreed with me. It's not—We aren't—"

"Who broke you?" Sammy asked, throwing herself down across a couch.

"Broke me? Really?" I looked from woman to woman. Clara smiled out the window, Sammy leaned her head on her arm and grinned at me.

Henry walked through the door down to the garage, drying his hands with a paper towel. "Oh, good, you're all here. What are we talking about?"

"Nothing!" I said loudly before either Clara or Sammy could speak.

Henry stopped, looking around at each of us and blinking furiously. "Okay. I think we're ready."

Clara turned around to face him, and Sammy sat up straighter on the couch.

Heretic turned toward Henry from where he stood near the hall to the guest rooms. "Shall I send the signal to Raven?"

Henry looked around at each of our faces. "What do you think? Are we ready for this? How confident are we about how this will go down?"

"According to Raven's memory files, Caine keeps his following of Faithful intentionally small. The Brick affords us protection from their Mythic abilities, which gives us the distinct tactical advantage if they come ready for a firefight." Heretic spoke rapidly as if he were anxious to get it all out there.

Clara lifted up out of the chair she was in and went and stood a few feet from Henry, her arms folded. "I say go. No time like the present."

Henry looked at me. I stood, my hands in my back pockets, and looked up at the ceiling. I sighed. We had hopes for how this would go, but the short of it was that we truly had no idea what would happen when Caine showed up. Finally, I nodded. "Do it."

Henry returned my nod, then looked at Heretic. Heretic stayed silent, then nodded himself. "Done. I've left an email with enough detail about what we've done in one of your inboxes, Henry, and used Raven's unique tag in the underlying code to get her attention. Now, it's only a question of how fast they'll get here."

Clara held up her left hand, still in a cast. "I'm gonna need this taken off. You got a saw?" she asked Henry.

He laughed and beckoned behind him at the door to the garage. "We'll find something."

Clara went through the door Henry held for her, and Heretic went along, spewing protests.

"Clara, you should really consider leaving it on for another week. It's not been the full recommended six to eight..."

I laughed, then made accidental eye contact with Sammy. We hadn't seen much of one another since her almost fall. Part of it was my doing; I'd been actively avoiding her. Being alone with her, at least.

She brushed a strand of hair back behind her ear. Before, when everyone else had been in the room, she'd been relaxed, sprawled the length of one of the several couches. Now, she huddled back against the far arm, knees pulled up in front of her and a pillow gripped securely in front of her, hiding the lower half of her face.

What do you say to someone whose life you probably saved, but you weren't sure how you felt about them, still?

"How's your shoulder?" I asked, trying not to come across as openly hostile.

She laughed quietly. "It's fine. A little sore, but not that bad. The robot insists I wear the sling."

"Yeah, he can be pretty insistent," I replied, offering a courtesy smile. I couldn't deny that it had been my very first instinct to save her on the clifftop. It wasn't anything I'd needed to think about or consider. I couldn't feel *that* negatively toward her.

She picked at the seam on the pillow. "I never had a chance to say..." She looked up at me. "Thanks."

"It's fine." I scratched at some stubble on my face. I hadn't bothered shaving for a day or two.

She stopped picking at the seam and dropped the pillow away from her face, toward her knees.

"It's fine?" she asked. "What does that mean? I just

thanked you for saving my life, and that's all you have to say, is 'it's fine?'"

I shrugged. "You're welcome, I guess?"

Sammy shook her head, lips parted in a smile. "You're really terrible at this."

I shrugged, holding up my hands. "At what, exactly?" I knew exactly what I was terrible at, but I wasn't about to admit it.

"This. Flirting. Me. Girls in general? I don't know yet." She pushed the pillow away and put one leg on the ground. The other she curled under her. "I need to level with you, James. I like you. Like, a lot."

We were definitely into uncomfortable territory now. I never knew how to act around a girl who might like me. I didn't want to do anything that would make them feel like I disliked them, but I didn't want to do anything that would lead them on, either. The result was a limbo, where I felt like there was no option left but to avoid them. That was no longer an option with Sammy.

"How can you say that?" I protested weakly. "You don't even know me."

She laughed, harder this time. "James, there are certain advantages to being a Tech. I've been watching you ever since we met at that first op at the Dantons. I thought you were cute, then. When you did what you did, ran off with the kids, I became *really* curious. I'm the reason Safeguard was able to find you in North Dakota and track you to California." She pulled the sleeves of the hoodie she was wearing over her hands and rubbed them together. "I hacked your dad's helmet."

"You did what?" Mostly, I was just surprised. I hadn't even considered that someone could hack into the helmet. I must have come across angrier than I'd intended, though. Sammy pulled up the knee that had been folded under her again, hugging it to her chest.

"I hacked the helmet. Early on. I listened to what you did—what you did for those kids." She reached for the pillow again. "I heard everything. Then, once you came back to Safeguard, I watched you. I used the cameras at the training facility to watch you— not in like, an invasive way. There were only cameras in the public areas of the facility." Her head shot up. "Not that I would have used cameras in private areas if they'd been there. It wasn't like that. I didn't—I'm not..." She swore. "I just wanted to get to know you. It wasn't anything weird."

"You don't find that at all weird?" I asked, crossing my arms and raising my eyebrows. I was equally parts embarrassed, flattered, and upset. I didn't know which emotion to give priority to.

"No! For a Tech, it's basically just like stalking someone's social media. I just wanted to get to know you. And I did!" She leaned forward, and for a moment, I thought she was about to get up and come at me off the couch. "I do know you, James. You're kind. I saw it everywhere. You're respectful to everyone; you don't put people down or try to make yourself appear better than everyone else. You lift people up. You work hard.

You always try to do the right thing. Your roommate, Dougan? He was a tool. They're everywhere; even in Safeguard."

She smiled, and her voice lowered. "But not you."

"You like me because I'm not a tool?" I asked. "That seems like a pretty low bar."

She laughed again. "I don't *not* like you because you're not a tool."

"Isn't that like a triple-negative?" I asked. I couldn't think. Nothing was clicking, I couldn't get past the superficial. Sammy liked me. Sure, I'd been attracted to her from the very first time I'd met her, but that was before she'd betrayed all of Safeguard and *literally* shot people down in front of me.

"That's what you're taking away from all this?" she asked, her face falling.

"What am I supposed to say, Sammy? What do you want me to say?" I could feel my cheeks and forehead heating up. "You killed four people in front of me, then helped the man who tortured me for weeks. How am I supposed to just move past that? Forget about it? Pretend it didn't happen? It *did* happen! Jose, Olivia, Brian, and Candace are all dead because of you." I said louder, "Not just dead because of you, but *by* you!"

Sammy's hand covered her mouth, the other wrapped across her stomach. I watched her eyes fill with tears. Real, hot tears. "I know. If there were any way I could, I would go back to the moment that Julian Danton approached me and made me the offer he did, and I would spit in his face. You know why?

Because it's what *you* would have done." Her voice dropped even lower.

"He found me pretty soon after the first op. I said yes then. If he had asked me later? After I'd gotten to know you, saw what you were willing to do and go through for those kids, for the sake of doing the right thing? I'd have told him where he could stick it after that."

She stood up and adjusted the sling. "I just wanted you to know. Now you do. Do whatever you want." She walked quickly out of the room, leaving me standing in the same place, my thoughts still refusing to move beyond the dichotomy of "she likes you" and "she's a murderer." I closed my eyes and took several deep breaths.

Why, even when the girl is straightforward, is this process so complicated? I cursed romance and its problems, then walked to my room to get ready to face Caine. *Sammy is just going to have to wait.*

Chapter 17

"We're establishing a perimeter around the camp! I want sentries staged within visual distance of one another all the way around the Brick! Everyone keep your comms on, monitoring the main frequency, as well as a secondary frequency for dedicated sentry communication." Clara stood at the top of the stairs, speaking into the audio system we'd moved outside. Across the clearing in front of us, the full contingent of Mythics, with the exception of the children, stood shoulder to shoulder, dressed and armed for a confrontation.

Clara scratched at the pale skin of her wrist where the cast impressions could still be seen.

"I want rotating 3-hour shifts, through the night, if need be. If you encounter anyone, do not engage! Stay within the boundaries of the Brick, notify us on the main frequency, and maintain the perimeter."

She looked out over the crowd of helmeted heads and green shoulders. Apparently, the liquid armor suits also had color-shifting pigments that allowed them to camouflage. I had no idea. The group gathered below the lodge was covered in dark green camo patterns. The matte covering of the visors of their helmets made it seem like a crowd of giant, attentive bugs, all armed with at least two different firearms.

"We're going to make it through this. Without abilities, we hold every advantage. We know they're coming, we have the element of surprise, and we have the home field. Today, we make this man pay for our friends, our brothers, our sisters, who he took from us!"

"I believe it's 'whom,'" Heretic said quietly behind me. I stamped on his foot. It hurt my heel.

Clara raised her rifle above her head. "For Safeguard!"

"For Safeguard!!" The words were roared back at her, and nearly two thousand rifle barrels shook at the sky.

Clara switched off the microphone and handed it back to Henry.

"Beautiful," he said. "How many times did you have to repeat that to yourself in the mirror this morning?" He grinned.

Clara ignored him. She turned back to the crowd and put on her helmet. Opening the visor, she said, "Signal check. High sign if you can hear my voice." She raised her hand in a thumbs-up sign. The crowd reciprocated, every thumb pointing to the sky.

"Affirmative. Dismissed."

The crowd dissipated rapidly back to the camps.

Henry raised his eyebrows. "That's all you need to

tell them? No organizing schedule, no roster, anything like that?"

Clara shook her head. "We train for this. Each camp has a captain who will have already divided everyone up into fireteams of 6, and they'll rotate through the six for sentry duty over the next 18 hours. We're good."

Heretic nodded his approval. "For all our differences of opinion over the past several years, I can't deny that your efficiency is impressive. Well done."

Clara nodded without smiling. I wasn't sure how she felt about Heretic at this point.

Sammy and I stood at opposite ends of the deck, not looking at each other. Everyone was wearing their liquid armor, as well as the plates to protect against Tamers. Henry was the only one not so outfitted, and he provided a stark contrast, wearing yet another beautiful three-piece suit, this one a light blue with subtle pinstriping that only stood out in direct sunlight.

Despite his suit, I watched as he reached back on his belt inside his jacket and brought out a large pistol, which he charged and checked, then put back under the suit coat. As he buttoned the jacket, he caught me looking and winked broadly.

"It's Utah," he said.

A lightning strike several miles away set the sky above us rumbling a few moments later.

"So what now," I asked. "We just wait for Caine to show up?"

"That's about the long and short of it," Clara said, pulling the charging handle on her rifle to prepare it for firing. She thumbed on the safety, then slung the weapon on her shoulder as she checked first her extra magazines at her waist, then her Con-gun sidearm on her hip. I saw her jaw muscles clench, then slowly release as she looked out over the trees of the valley.

I looked around at everyone on the porch. "Anyone figured out yet how he's getting around so fast? Is he actually teleporting or something?" I looked at Heretic as I checked over my own weapons. "Raven, have you already weighed in on this?"

Heretic pulled up the goggles and down the face covering so that Raven's face could look out at us. "No idea. In all my time with him, I've only been witness to the absorbing part of his abilities. But, I don't really know; he plays things very close to his chest, even where I'm concerned. A lot goes on behind closed doors."

I nodded, disappointed. The way I'd seen him disappear with the Danton children didn't leave much room for any other explanation than teleportation. But how did it work? It had to have something to do with the Space. I stole a glance around the deck. Everyone was involved in their own thoughts and tasks.

"Henry." I shouldered my rifle as I walked over to him. I dropped my voice low enough that no one else would hear me. "I need to borrow one of the side-by-sides."

"Oh?" He asked, looking up. "Where are you going?"

"I have a theory that I want to test. I can't do it under the Brick."

"That's all you're giving me?" he asked. "No details?"

"The less you know, for now, the better." I had no idea why I said this. I think I just wanted to intimidate him a bit. I hated myself for it immediately. It was something a tool would say.

"Okay, I like it. I'm in. I'll go with you." He snapped his fingers, and Clara looked at him. "Hey, we're going off-Brick. Super hush-hush, so tone it down. We'll be back."

Clara frowned at him but didn't say anything. She frowned at me, I offered a shrug in return. I had no choice but to follow Henry through the lobby down to the garage and climb into the UTV he picked out.

"You want to drive?" he asked.

I swallowed. I had to quell the impulse to take the keys and jump in. It didn't matter. "You go ahead." *Don't be a tool.*

He started up the engine, which thrummed sharply as he backed out of the garage.

We didn't speak as he drove us down the road toward the main entrance to the ranch. Several minutes after driving through the gate, he stopped. "The boundary is just beyond that tree ahead."

I nodded my thanks and climbed out of the UTV, leaving my rifle on the seat.

The instant I felt the effect of the Brick drop, I sat down on the trunk of a downed tree just beyond the tire-churned mud of the dirt road.

I closed my eyes and slowed my breathing, suddenly conscious of the beating of my heart and the sound of air going in and out of my lungs. When the now-familiar sensation of weightlessness and complete silence came over me, I opened my eyes. I looked around at the blue-grey dimness that was this Space and I racked my brain for possibilities.

I was still in the process of looking around for inspiration when I heard a noise. I almost dismissed it, because it sounded like a strong wind blowing through trees outside a window. Then I remembered that there were none of those things in my Space. I looked around in a sudden panic. *What's happening?*

I broke out in a cold sweat when I heard a low, male voice echo though faintly muffled, as if we were underground, "No one moves without my say so. We will not set foot within the infected area."

I closed my eyes and tried to still my breath, but it was too erratic. Caine was here! I forced my lungs to comply, taking in a long, shaking breath and squeezing it out slowly. With a rush, I felt the air move across my face and heard the last of a peal of thunder rumble in the distance.

"He's here!" I yelled, standing up and running back to the UTV.

"Whoa, what?!" Henry shouted, only now just getting around to shutting the engine off. "James, what are you talking about? You sat down on that log, then jumped up again like something bit you. What do you mean, he's here?"

"I went into my Space, and I heard him. I don't know how, I don't know why, but I heard him speak. He was telling the Faithful that they weren't to move except on his command, then something about not going into the infected area. I think he means the Brick." I pounded my palm on the dash of the side-by-side. "Let's go!"

I flicked the switch on my helmet that turned on my comms and dialed in a private frequency with Clara, then tried my best not to yell into it. "Clara, this is James. Caine is here. Repeat, Caine is here."

Clara's voice came through my helmet speakers. "Where? What's your location? Are you still at the front gate with Henry? I need visual confirmation before I send people in."

I hesitated. "I—I haven't seen him exactly, so I'm not sure where he is, but I heard him." I glanced at Henry, wincing beneath my helmet. "In my Space."

There was silence for a moment, then Clara spoke up, tentatively. "Say again?"

"I'm not exactly sure, myself. Just tell everyone to be on the close lookout, because I'm pretty sure he's here."

I had only barely finished speaking when a woman's voice spoke over the main frequency. "Sighting on East perimeter. We have a confirmed count of forty-six individuals, none visibly armed. Waiting on your direction."

"Hold your positions. We're on our way to you." Clara's voice clicked off on the main channel, then clicked on what I assumed was our direct channel. "James, get your ass back to the lodge, now."

Henry whipped the UTV around, spinning the rear tires until we'd done an about-face, then letting off enough to allow the tires to catch before leaning heavily on the gas. We whipped around the corners and left the ground on the larger bumps. My eyes watered from the wind. In significantly less time than it took to get away, we were back at the lodge.

Clara, Heretic, and Sammy were waiting on the bottom step. Clara threw a large spool of cable in, then jumped up into the back, standing up and leaning on the roll cage frame.

"C'mon, c'mon, c'mon!" Clara yelled. Sammy and Heretic scrambled into the back seat as well, barely seated before Henry gunned the accelerator, driving us forward again.

"Head for the East ridge!" I yelled over the sound of the engine.

"I know!" Henry shouted back. "I rigged up an earpiece last night! I heard!" He gave me a thumbs-up, grinning.

It was a good thing Henry drove. It would have taken me or Clara several tries to navigate the maze of crisscrossing paths and roads that turned the valley into a veritable maze. Instead, Henry drifted around corners and took invisible off-shoot trails that had us up to the ridge in no time. A crowd of Mythics had gathered, though I was convinced I was only seeing a few of them, due to their camouflage. It was insanely effective.

We skidded to a stop just below the crest of the ridge, able to see back into the valley. Several yards ahead of us, we'd be able to see over the ridge and down across the next valley. A Mythic walked up to the side of the UTV and I heard her voice come over the comms.

"Forty-six hostiles: twenty-two men, twenty-four women, mostly adults, but several teens. Waiting for your orders, Director."

No children? I wonder why he didn't bring the Dantons?

Clara jumped out of the side-by-side and reached back in for the spool she'd tossed earlier. She un-rolled a length of cable, and gestured to me, her face obscured by the helmet she wore.

"James, let's get this thing rigged up. You've got the wristband?"

I dug in my pocket and brought out the innocuous piece of metal. I slipped it onto my wrist, then ac-cepted the bit of cable she'd offered me. She tossed me a small metal clamp and a screwdriver. "Around your waist."

I nodded and pulled up the liquid armor top I wore, wrapping the cold cable around my middle. Once I had it secured with the clamp, Clara played out another several feet from the spool and wrapped it around her own middle, then handed the spool to Henry. She pulled several more clamps from a pocket and caught the screwdriver I tossed to her.

"James."

Heretic had walked up behind me without my noticing. I jumped, and a jolt ran down my arms, prickling the hairs up on their backs. I swore under my breath beneath my helmet.

"If Raven is here, it is imperative that you all not betray that you recognize or know her. Caine would almost certainly eliminate her if he suspected that she has been plotting against him all this time."

I nodded.

"Tell the others." Heretic walked backward, going to stand next to the side-by-side.

Henry held the last of the spooled cable and cut the line with a pair of cutters from the side-by-side. I heard him sigh, then he untucked his shirt and wrapped the line around his belly beneath the undershirt he wore. Once he had it secured with a clamp, he undid several buttons from the bottom of the shirt, pulled the cable up to the gap, then redid the buttons below it, so that the cable protruded from the gap between buttons. He then proceeded to tuck back in his shirt.

"Really?" I asked, smiling incredulously.

"Order and a clean appearance are kind of my thing," he said, unapologetic.

I noted that Clara very visibly removed the safety from her rifle, keeping her finger clear of the trigger guard.

"I want everyone currently within sight of the hostiles in position to have as clean a shot as possible. If they make a wrong step and I call for it, I want a hundred rounds into them before they finish a second one." Clara's voice was low, flat. I wished that I could see her face. She sounded back to the way I'd felt two years ago. That concerned me.

"Just remember that my sister's out there, too, and that she's on our side," I whispered to her on our direct channel. Clara didn't answer.

"Are we ready, Miriam?" she asked instead, looking at the Mythic woman who'd first reported to us.

"Fireteams, check in. Are we in position?" A cascade of confirmations answered her question. She nodded at Clara. "We're good to go, Director."

Clara returned the nod. "Let's go."

The three of us walked up the road that crested the ridge. A few steps before we got high enough to see the road on the other side, I paused, took a deep breath, and forced myself to let it out slowly. It shook. I shook. I glanced down the line from me at Clara and Henry. They'd both stopped, and I could see their chests rising and falling faster than normal, too.

"Ready?" I whispered.

They both nodded, then we took the last several steps to the top of the ridge.

He was the first thing I saw when I looked down the road.

Caine stood in the middle of the dirt path, his hands held behind his back, feet wide apart, like a soldier at ease. His long, dark, curly hair was just like mine, only longer. Though his skin was a darker tone than mine, we shared the same angular nose and oval face.

The dark coat he wore, an oddity in the summer heat, hung open around him and moved sporadically around his calves in the wind of the approaching storm.

I didn't even have time to notice anything or anyone else before I heard Clara hiss in a breath and then shout over the comms in my helmet.

"Fire! Fire now!"

She raised her own rifle to her shoulder, and I heard the rifle crack several times as my helmet's ear-protection filters took effect.

"Wait!" I screamed, throwing my hand out to push her muzzle down to the ground.

I was too late. The air around me hummed with energy as an avalanche of cracks rolled over me. The fireteams had followed their order without hesitation.

My heart stopped, returned to normal, then plummeted into my belly as I turned my eyes back to Caine.

I barely registered the group of people standing behind him on the road. As the reports from the rifles firing all around us echoed in my head, there was a ripple in the air about Caine, and a web of what looked like black spider webs of smoke appeared and grew dense in the air around him and the others.

Clara held up a single closed fist, and the cracks halted.

The spider webs began flowing, looking for all the world like a series of tiny rivers flowing together through the air, toward Caine. They collected into a single large stream that flowed around him to disappear where his hands must be behind his back.

Caine took several more steps toward us but stopped again quickly, hands still held behind his back. He spoke, and the same low, rumbly voice I'd heard in my Space crossed the distance between us.

"That was a mistake."

Chapter 18

Caine didn't say anything more for several moments. He just stood there, his eyes traveling up and down the line of the ridge as if searching for where each and every bullet had come from. *The bullets. How did he do that?* I had known that I could absorb things, and Heretic had told me a long time ago that I could potentially absorb even gunfire, but I'd never been successful at it. I'd nearly given up and resigned myself to the softball-sized bruises that came with the stopping of the bullet by my liquid armor. But that! What Caine had done was beyond comprehension. There had to have been several hundred rounds fired in those few moments. Not one of them had made its target.

Clara, her rifle still shouldered but pointed at the ground, took several confident steps forward. I couldn't help but admire her courage. As the cable tugged at my waist, I had no choice but to follow after her, walking toward Caine and his Faithful. To his credit, Henry, whose face was one of the few on our side not hidden under a Safeguard helmet, looked as calm as if he were enjoying a morning walk down the dirt path, instead of walking forward with neither physical protection nor guarantee other than our word and hope that our makeshift tether would be an effective deterrent against Caine's abilities. I watched him out of the corner of my eye as he casually reached up to remove his sunglasses and slip them into the outside breast pocket of his jacket.

I looked back to Caine, whose eyebrows had raised somewhat, and a smile bent the corners of his mouth. I had the distinct impression that he found our aggressive advance more than mildly amusing. There was movement from several of the Mythics behind him, but he raised his hand, forestalling any retaliation.

To my relief, Clara stopped her advance probably twenty yards away from the group on the road. She spoke quietly over the comms. "Are we far enough to be out from under the Brick? I want him off balance."

Henry nodded subtly.

Caine took several steps of his own forward, raising his hands out to the sides, palms upward. "It's not every day that my quarry meets me so willingly. I promise it will be quick." He extended one hand toward the three of us and slowly closed his fist.

I instinctively closed my eyes, wincing.

When nothing happened, I opened them again, in time to see Caine's smile fall from his face, and his brows clench together.

"It's not possible..." I heard him say. He put both hands out and squeezed them sharply into fists. Nothing happened that time, either.

Caine's breathing became erratic, and his shoulders heaved. His eyes bore into Clara's and my helmeted faces. "Which one of you is an Interstitial?" He was rubbing a spot on his right forearm with his left hand as if he had an insistent itch. He was staring at our forearms, as well. I had no idea what that was about.

There was a murmur from behind Caine as his followers looked at one another, confusion on every face.

"I don't know what an Interstitial is, or what business it is of yours, but I *do* know that you're trespassing," Henry spoke up, his hands in his pockets. *How did the man always seem so in control?* "I'd appreciate it if you took your little entourage and left my land the same way you came." He looked around, as if for a vehicle. "Whatever that is."

Caine still rubbed his right arm absently, but he seemed to have recovered somewhat.

"Your confidence is amusing, worm, but ultimately misattributed."

Caine spoke with just the hint of an accent, but I couldn't for the life of me place it.

He continued, reverting to his wide-legged stance with his hands behind his back. He still stared at Clara and me. "I wish to know which of you is an Interstitial, and why you would voluntarily defile yourself with the shackles of the Oppressors." He paused to look between us, then continued. "Make yourself known to me, and I will spare you." His eyes lost their focus, and his voice quieted to just above a whisper. "It's been lifetimes since I've encountered any of my own kind."

"Father Caine," someone behind him spoke. One of the Faithful, a young man, not more than a teenager, stepped forward. "We should just destroy everyone and be done with it. I could do it. Let me rain fire down on them."

Rain fire? "Steven?" I asked before I could stop myself. Looking closer, it *was* Steven. He had the same prominent forehead, the unruly cowlick on the back of his head. But how could that possibly be? Steven wasn't even ten years old. This young man looked like he could be nearly sixteen or seventeen. *It's not possible.*

When I'd said his name, the young man had looked up at me, a mix of fear and confusion contorting his face. He took several steps backward, back into the ranks of the Faithful. For the first time, I truly considered the individual faces of the Mythics behind Caine, seeing them as individuals for the first time.

There, to Caine's left, putting a hand out toward Steven, Elizabeth Danton stared at me. To her right, both Jessica and Mary reached out to put hands on Steven's arms or shoulder, pulling him back in line with them and holding arms protectively out in front of him. How could it possibly be them? They all appeared roughly the same age, instead of the nearly eight years difference that should have divided Jessica and Mary. Standing immediately behind Caine, over his left shoulder, I also picked out Raven's face with a jolt.

"You know these exceptional children?" Caine asked, a sudden edge to his voice. "Then you are aligned with the creed of the Oppressors. Most likely you participated in their subjugation, the blasphemous mind-sculpt that left them with no memory of who they truly are, or where the others were." He turned, gesturing the four to step forward. They did so, standing with shoulders thrown back, chins held high, and eyes cold as they considered us across from them.

"As you can see, I liberated them. I saw to it that they were raised together, aware of their nature and their purpose." He clapped Steven on the shoulder and touched Mary's elbow. They both turned to smile at him. My stomach lurched. *What has he done to them?*

"I'm here to continue my work, the work of liberation and protection from all who uphold the Oppressors' creed."

At my side, Clara pushed the release and her helmet slid open. She hung her rifle on its sling from her shoulder. "You know what? You are one big pile of—" the rest of what she said was lost as, in one smooth motion, she drew her Con-gun from her hip and fired it several times at Caine.

Pandemonium ensued. Because the Con-gun didn't fire projectiles, there was no matter for Caine to absorb. Instead, a wave of pure concussive energy blew over him and the rest of the Faithful, knocking everyone to the ground. Three of them, two men and a woman, were the first back on their feet and ran at the three of us, wordless screams issuing from each of their throats.

Clara let off several more shots at the man bearing down on her, and Henry drew his own pistol from concealment. I heard him get several shots off as I raised my own con gun at the third man, who was now a matter of feet away from me.

I fired one shot, but it wasn't enough to knock him down again. Not with his forward momentum. *Tanks.* I pulled the trigger several more times, but my shots went wide. I was distracted by the yells and grunts to my left, where I knew Clara and Henry were dealing with their own problems.

The Tank facing me knocked my con gun aside, then drove his fist into my middle with a feral snarl. Even with both liquid and metal armor, I was convinced that, had his blow had the effect he intended and assumed it would, my chest would have caved in. Or, maybe he simply intended on punching right *through* me. As it was, it knocked me backward, but there was also a sickening series of crunches from his hand, accompanied by a howl of agony. Because of my wristband, his Mythic ability had been negated, and he'd shattered what sounded like every bone in his hand against my armor.

The man collapsed to the ground, his hand limp

in front of him, his other hand clutching his wrist. I stepped away but was tugged back by the cable around my waist. Clara had a knife and was struggling against the Tank who'd come after her. Having grappled against her many times in the past in training, I knew she could typically hold her own in hand-to-hand combat against a wide variety of opponents, but the man was just so much bigger than she was. I raised my con gun, but they were too close. I couldn't hit him without also hitting Clara. Suddenly, there was another crack, and the man wrestling Clara stiffened, then hunched over, his hand on his stomach. There were several more cracks, and he jerked with each one, then fell to the ground. Beyond Clara, Henry slowly lowered his pistol, his face sweaty, his eyes wide, and his shoulders heaving. The Mythic woman he'd squared off against lay on the ground, either dead or unconscious, I couldn't tell.

All three of us stepped back, suddenly aware of the quiet around us. Looking back toward Caine, I took another involuntary step backward.

The man's face was unrecognizable in the snarl that pulled his lips back over his teeth and shadowed his eyes in slits. He took several steps forward, tentatively, as if he were walking on glass.

Clara, Henry, and I retreated further, Clara and I holding our Con-guns trained firmly on Caine.

When he reached the three Tanks on the ground, he knelt to speak with the man whimpering with the broken hand first. After a few quiet exchanges that

I couldn't make out, Caine waved his hand, and the man dissipated into a cloud of white dust that swirled and collected in the palm of his right hand, then disappeared. *Did he just...?*

He stood and went to the side of the woman. I saw him put a few fingers to her neck, checking for a pulse. I wasn't sure what he found, but a moment later, she, too, dissolved into a white cloud that disappeared over his right hand.

Finally, he crouched over the man who'd been grappling with Clara. The man was perfectly still, and his eyes were open, staring blankly at nothing. Caine put out one hand and gently closed the man's eyes.

I realized we were all watching, everyone on both sides of this conflict, with breath held.

Caine rearranged the man's limbs, straightening his body and folding the arms over the man's chest. After a moment, he closed his eyes and spoke quietly to himself. Finally, he placed his left hand on top of the man's crossed arms, and the body dissolved into dark swirling matter that disappeared into his hand.

Caine stood up, and I heard and felt a hundred guns rise with him.

His voice was a quiet hiss that made the hair on the back of my neck stand up. "These people have been at my side for generations. We've toppled regimes, orchestrated revolutions, and assassinated Oppressors throughout this world's history who gained too much power for their own good. The man whose life you just took has done more for the good of this world than you will ever know. His name was Mehmed Hamid; mark it well. His death is your sentence." Caine glared out from beneath his eyebrows at Henry.

Caine swept back toward his line of followers, his long black coat rippling behind him.

I had a very bad feeling about this. "We need to get back," I said, turning and walking quickly back to the edge of the Brick, behind which all of the Safeguard Mythics huddled in small groups, not bothering to hide anymore. I had to tug on the cable to get Clara and Henry to follow me.

We turned back around in time to watch Caine wave his hand in an angry swat, and the rest of the Mythics, including Jessica, Steven, Elizabeth, Mary, and Raven, disappeared in a cloud of white dust.

I involuntarily took a step forward. "No!"

He whirled around at my shout, his face again an angry mask. He advanced in quick, forceful steps. "And suddenly you're concerned for my people's safety? Do you think that I would ever hurt them? They have been nothing but loyal, my Faithful." He stopped after a few more steps, then paced back and forth side-to-side on the road, his eyes never leaving our group. He reminded me of a caged predator, searching for a weakness, an opportunity to exploit in escaping and tearing apart his captor. *Only we're the ones in the cage.*

"They turned their backs on the corrupt and self-serving predilections of their heritage and swore an oath to keep this world from becoming an echo of what has happened to others before it." He stared right at me. "You, on the other hand, you betray your own kind." He nodded to himself as I took a step backward. "Yes; I know it's you; you are the Interstitial." He stopped pacing and faced us head-on. "Why do you allow them to bind you, to deprive you of your potential, while they only strengthen their own positions of power?" He held out a hand to me. "Join me. I can see that you recognize Translation. Yet you know nothing of Deliverance. I don't know who you are, but surely you can see that you're on the wrong side. I'm not a madman: I'm a liberator!" He held his hand up higher, beckoning with his fingers.

It was Clara's turn to take several angry steps forward. Luckily, Henry and I were still connected to her via the cable. We both reeled her carefully in as she exploded.

She swore. "Not a murderer?! Tell that to my husband!" She let loose with a string of expletives and oaths that left my ears ringing.

Caine only looked at her, his face quizzical. "I don't recall your face."

Clara folded her arms. "We've never had the pleasure before now. Your mutt took my husband a week ago."

Caine's face broke its angry set as surprise softened his forehead. "Vasily? You haven't killed him, then?"

I looked at Clara. Her face had gone slack. Her hands slowly dropped until she was holding her hands at the level of her belly, clasped lightly together. She whispered, "He's alive?" I knew she wasn't talking about Vasily.

I turned back to Caine. "Look, I don't know why you're doing this, but no one here is an Oppressor like you keep talking about. We're just people, trying to exist."

He scoffed, his long black hair falling back from his face. "They're all Oppressors. The fact that you align yourself with them is appalling. Nevertheless, you're free to choose your fate. My conscience will be clear."

With that, he suddenly flew up into the air above us, a black waving figure against the dark gray of the storm.

"Everyone get under cover, quick!" I shouted, yanking Clara and Henry back further under the Brick." Mythics behind us were screaming, breaking formation, and running who knew where. I heard more screams behind us from the direction of the camp.

I watched in horrified fascination as a gleaming sphere of brilliant gold light began emanating from Caine's middle, where I assumed his hands were.

The light grew and expanded until I couldn't see Caine any longer. I barely had time to flinch before the sphere of light left his hands and plummeted to earth.

Chapter 19

I don't think any of us knew what would happen at that point. We'd hypothesized and hoped that the power of the Brick would negate Caine's abilities, but we weren't one hundred percent certain.

The screams continued, then slowly dropped off as people, like me, realized they weren't dead or dying. I heard more than one voice sobbing uncontrollably. My own heart felt like it had leaped into my throat, and an uncontrollable shiver rolled across my body.

The ball of light, which had seemed to fill the entire sky, had shone with a light that must have been blinding for most of the others around me. When the light began to fade, I looked around and saw that many people were stumbling or carefully walking with hands out in front of them, eyes either closed or blinking furiously. Clara had dropped to one knee, holding her eyes tightly closed while holding her Congun pointed at the ground in front of her, turning her head this way and that, as if she were listening.

Henry wasn't in any better shape than Clara or the

rest. He stood bent over, hands on his knees, wincing as he tried to get his eyes to adjust.

"Where is he?" Clara called. "I can't see! James, Henry? Does anyone have eyes on Caine?"

I put a hand out on Clara's shoulder. "I can see. I don't see Caine anywhere, though," I said, looking up to where he'd hung in the sky a few moments before, and sweeping down to the road. The light had finally dimmed enough for me to see outside the Brick. What I saw stopped my breath dead in my throat.

For several hundred yards out from the edge of the Brick, the trees and brush had been incinerated, leaving nothing but white ash and blackened stones and dirt. There were fires burning at the far edge of the incinerated swath, in the trees that were far enough away to have survived the blast. Suddenly, though, as if they'd been put out with a candle snuffer, the fires went out, the flames simply dancing into nothingness. *Steven.*

"What's the damage?" Clara asked, standing up.

"Not bad, on the whole," I said. "The Brick seems to have deflected Caine's blast. There's a pretty wide area just outside that took the brunt of it, though. Anything there aside from rocks and dirt was just obliterated. It's covered in white ash."

"It worked," Henry said, his voice low and shaky.

I nodded, then remembered that they couldn't see. "Seems to have, yeah," I said.

"Pat's alive!" Clara practically yelled, putting a hand

out blindly until it found my chest, then went to my shoulder.

"We don't know that," I said, not wanting her to be hurt more than she already had been. "Vasily just hasn't connected back up with Caine like we thought he would."

Clara was already shaking her head. "No. If Vasily never made it back to Caine, it's because Pat managed to take him down. I need to go back. I need to find him."

It was my turn to shake my head with every ounce of my conviction. "Clara, there's no way we're getting out of here. If you could see what he did, what he's capable of... We're trapped here. You were right. This just turned into a siege."

***

"What do we know now?" Clara spoke up from where she leaned against the side-by-side, her con gun still in hand, her helmet opened so that we could see her face.

Henry sat in the passenger side seat, hands clasped with fingers intertwined, thumbs pressed to his lips. Sammy sat in the back, feet propped up on the side of the vehicle, tossing a water bottle back and forth between her hands.

Heretic spoke up from where he leaned against a tree on the side of the road. "Let's reflect on what we learned from our brief encounter with Caine."

I continued my pacing. "He's insane! All of his

'Deliverance,' 'Translation,' and 'Oppressor' garbage? What even is that?"

"If Vasily isn't back with Caine, he's got to be with Pat. This is what we talked about, remember? Keep Vasily away from Caine, so that he can't keep leading him to Mythics. Pat did it! He's alive!" There was more life in Clara's eyes than I'd seen since the day Pat had been taken. I couldn't bring myself to be the one to stamp it out.

"Okay, but even if he is, we can't do anything about it. I don't know if it's what he was intending, but Caine very effectively cut us off from any escape. There's no sneaking people out without any cover. You heard the lookouts: the explosion wrapped around the entire perimeter of the Brick. We're on an island, and Caine's the shark in the water outside." I kicked at a rock in the dirt.

"Why was some of the smoke white, and some black?" Henry asked.

I turned. "You noticed that, too?"

He nodded. "Black smoke to his left hand, white smoke to his right. What's the difference, James?"

I shrugged, but inside I was panicking. Sammy didn't know that I had abilities, let alone that they were like Caine's. "I—I don't know." I glanced at Sammy. She was staring at me, her mouth open, her forehead creased.

"I'm sorry," she snapped, sitting up in the rear seat. "You're like him?"

I couldn't look at her. I didn't know how to answer her.

She didn't let it go. She stood up in the back of the side-by-side, but Clara stepped away, gun at the ready, to remind Sammy that she still wasn't trusted.

"That's where Danton went. He didn't 'disappear'." She air-quoted her fingers. "You—you what, disintegrated him?" She dropped out of the far side of the side-by-side, then turned back to glare at me. "You're just like him. You're just like both of them!"

No one said anything as she stomped away up the road back toward the lodge. Heretic turned to look at Henry, Clara, and me, then said, "I'll accompany her and keep an eye on her." He jogged off in pursuit of Sammy.

Henry turned back to me. "Did he say other worlds?"

I grabbed my head. "What does that even mean? What, like space?"

Henry's eyes glazed over, and he leaned his head back onto the headrest of the passenger seat, lost in thought.

I paced rapidly back and forth in front of the side-by-side, digging my fingernails into my scalp.

I stopped. "I think I need to talk to him."

Clara and Henry both looked up. "What?" Clara blurted.

"That's insane," Henry agreed.

"I think he'll talk to me. You heard him; he wants me to join him, and he doesn't seem to be particularly guarded where I'm concerned for some reason. What did he call us?"

"Interstitial," Henry offered.

"Right," I murmured. "What does that mean? Isn't that like the space between objects or something? Is that what my Space is?"

Clara nodded. "Right. Didn't you say that before Caine was ever spotted, you heard him when you were inside of your space?"

"Yeah, I did." I tried to remember what that had been like. "I could hear his voice, but it was like he was in another room behind thick walls, or something. It was weird."

Clara frowned as she thought. Henry was lost in thought as well.

"You guys, I think I could go talk to him. I honestly think I could collect more information about him in a few minutes of conversation than Raven has over the last several years." I grimaced when I heard how that sounded out loud.

"I didn't mean that in a competitive or a critical way. Just that, for some reason, he seems willing to tell me things. You heard him out there."

Clara nodded. "What have we got to lose, at this point? He can't hurt you, one way or the other, can he?"

"I honestly don't know if he can straight-up absorb me, or not," I hesitated. "I'm blast-proof, but I don't know whether or not I'm disintegrate-proof."

"That changes how good I feel about it," Clara groaned.

"I say we let him try it," Henry interjected.

Both Clara and I looked over at him.

"Think about what we have to gain. We're talking about a chance to interview a man who has not only potentially visited other worlds but has also lived through most of this world's history, as well as apparently kept a small, committed band of followers alive throughout that time, too." He looked from face to face. "Is no one else even fractionally interested in how he's accomplished any of that? I mean, the secret is obviously in your whatever space, but as of right now, we don't get that at all."

"You're completely right," I admitted. I thought of something else. "You know, all of the living people turned into white smoke. Only the dead guy, Mermed—"

"Mehmed," Henry corrected me.

"Right," I glossed over it. "Only he turned into black smoke. Maybe the color of the smoke has to do with whether they're alive or dead."

"Could be," Henry conceded. "Have you ever absorbed anything living to observe?"

"No," I said forcefully until I remembered. "Not consciously, at least."

"Consciously?" Henry asked.

I squirmed, suddenly uncomfortable. "Twice in my life, now, I've absorbed people who caused me pain, both at different ages, and both without meaning to."

"All right, you can try it," Clara interrupted. I'm sure she was just trying to get me out of dwelling on what was quickly becoming my least favorite part about myself. "But you wear the wristband, and you don't take any risks beyond what you already are simply by talking with him, you understand?" She looked right into my eyes, and I saw the care there, etched deep. *She's lost a lot of people, too.*

I nodded.

Henry nearly fell out of the vehicle in his haste to get out the door before he had it opened.

"Do you have a phone? Maybe you should record the conversation." He reached into his pocket, removed his phone— the latest model— and tapped a few buttons on the screen before he put it in my hands. "Here, use mine. Keep the conversation going for as long as you possibly can. We want to learn everything we can about this man, and even more importantly, we want to learn about where he comes from and how."

I laughed, putting my hand out on Henry's shoulder. All of his confidence, his calm and assured demeanor, was gone with the fervor of his curiosity. He was like a child. "I'll do my best."

Leaving the two of them there, I sealed up my helmet and walked out toward the newly formed and easily visible border of the Brick. Making certain that the wristband was solidly in place behind the wrist of my glove and beneath my armor, I took a deep breath and stepped beyond the line. I almost expected something to happen, I just didn't know what, exactly. But, nothing did.

I started toward the far tree line, following the compacted dirt, free of large stones, that was now the only difference between the road and the rest of the land in the blast zone. *No man's land.* The term seemed appropriate. I turned around to look behind me at the line of trees under the Brick. I could see Clara's white armor and Henry's blue suit standing among the trees, and the movement in several different spots that indicated other Safeguard members. I raised my hand in what I hoped was a brave, confident wave, then turned around and stepped into the trees, forcing myself to breathe out, slowly.

I wasn't sure how to go about finding Caine, but I figured, more likely than not, he'd find me. I wasn't wrong. I hadn't been walking but a few minutes in the quiet of the woods when I heard a high, guttural scream from somewhere behind me, and I wheeled about, Con-gun in hand and raised. A mountain lion, long, lithe tawny body tense, crouched openly behind me on the road I'd been following.

"Hold!" a sharp female voice called out from the trees, and a woman stepped out of concealment from behind one of the large trunks. Putting a hand out, she made several signals to the big cat, and it padded to her side, rubbed its head against her thigh, then turned its face back toward me. Its eyes narrowed.

The woman examined me, one eyebrow raised, just

as I studied her from behind the anonymity of my helmet. She had long black hair that was brought back in a single thick braid that fell over the front of one of her shoulders. Her facial features told me that she probably had ancestry somewhere in eastern Asia, but I couldn't say where. She was dressed very similarly to the rest of the Faithful with Caine, simple brown pants with high brown boots and a loose white shirt with no collar. They looked like they could have stepped right out of something like the 1800s.

"You are the Interstitial?" she asked.

"How did you know that?" I pushed back. I looked like most of the other Safeguard members in my armor and helmet. How could she tell a difference?

"Drops-from-tree-death," here she patted the cougar's thick hide, "wouldn't touch you when you entered the tree line. If you weren't the Interstitial, she would be feasting on your corpse, per my instructions."

I guess that answered the question of whether we could escape from the Brick undetected. I shivered.

"Follow," she said, then turned and walked away into the trees, away from the road. I holstered my gun at my thigh and followed.

We walked for a few minutes deep into the forest, with no roads or paths visible. After another several, I heard a branch snap behind me and looked back to find that there were several Faithful behind me, along with two mountain lions, a large elk, and three coyotes. I continued walking after the woman and the mountain lion with whom I'd first made contact, suddenly sweating heavily beneath my armor.

A moment later, we walked through a large, jagged opening in an abrupt high bluff in the trees. The dirt at the base of the bluff looked dark and wet, as if freshly disturbed. Walking through the opening, I realized that this bluff wasn't natural, and had probably only just been created.

The bluff was really a wall of solid, rough stone that formed a perfect circle, perhaps a hundred feet across inside. *Mary.*

I looked around eagerly and spotted the four Danton teens, all sitting comfortably on large hunks of earth that resembled armchairs covered in lichen. Several other Faithful stood up and eyed me as I walked in, flanked by my escort.

Caine, sitting in another seat provided by Mary, stood when I came closer, and held up a single hand, his face contorted in anger.

"Stop where you are!" he said, looking directly at me. "The Oppressor's mark is not welcome here! Remove it, or we remove your head!"

The cold sweat began running down my side from my armpits again. "How do I know you won't just kill me when I take it off?"

Caine spread his arms wide, looking around at the Faithful. "If I wanted you dead, do you think you would have been allowed to reach the very heart of our camp?"

He made a good point. Abilities or not, they could

have killed me a long time ago. I certainly would have taken more than a few with me, if they'd tried, but I would certainly be dead by now if they'd had any orders otherwise.

I nodded, trying to keep my head and hands from shaking visibly, and removed the wristband, putting it in my pocket. There was one promise broken to Clara, already.

A tall, thin Black man with long, thick dreadlocks stepped forward. "He has a phone in his pocket recording everything we're saying," he said. "Shall I destroy it?"

Caine looked at me in surprise. He laughed. "A recording? What possible advantage does a recording give you?"

"We're curious about you," I said honestly. "I was hoping to record everything I could learn about you."

"Ah," Caine said quietly, smiling slightly. He nodded at the man with the dreadlocks. A moment later, there was a loud pop from my pocket with the phone in it. I panicked when I realized that the pocket was on fire. I guessed he'd blown the battery. Before I even had time to swat at it, the flame disappeared. I looked up and made eye contact with Steven, who raised his head as if to coolly acknowledge responsibility.

"I'm afraid I'm normally a very private man," Caine said simply. "Is that the only reason you've come?"

There goes my hope of getting him to talk freely. Unless...

I reached up and pushed the release on my helmet and tugged it off, putting it under my arm.

"I came because I'm your son."

Chapter 20

Caine blinked slowly, and his eyes narrowed, but not angrily. "I would speak with this man alone."

A muttered whispering spread throughout the group of Faithful, men and women buzzing quietly.

Caine seemed to ignore them. He gestured back the way I'd come, to the gap in the high bluff wall. Glancing one last time back toward the Danton children, I saw them, heads gathered together, whispering fiercely and eyes darting repeatedly to me. I hadn't seen Raven anywhere. Caine followed me out of the gap, and we walked away from the encampment, back into the trees.

He didn't say anything for several full minutes as we climbed steadily upward through the growth. I had no idea what he was thinking. He moved up to walk next to me, rather than behind me, but I never saw him look at me at all.

Several minutes later, he stopped. We were standing on a tall ridge, a different one than we had been below several hours earlier. From here, I looked around and could pick out both the ranch, Henry's lodge, the camp, and the ring of bluff that was Caine's camp in opposite directions. I didn't say anything. I was hoping that he would fill the silence. I didn't have to wait much longer.

"You do have my hair, and my height, but everything else you got from your mother." I turned to face him and found him carefully considering me, one arm across his stomach, the other resting atop it, fingers on his lips. "Your mother's name?" he asked. His face was inscrutable.

"Rachel Kline." I decided that was okay to offer up. I just couldn't give away that I knew who Raven was, or that she was helping us through Heretic.

He nodded slowly. "It was Safeguard, wasn't it? That day in the hospital?" His voice was a low hiss, and I nodded. I saw no point in lying. He already wanted all Mythics dead. How could I make it any worse?

He said something sharp under his breath, but it sounded like another language. I couldn't make it out.

"And your name?" he asked.

"James. Strader."

"Strader. Your kidnappers?"

"My adoptive parents."

He snorted and turned away for a moment, and I could see his fists clench and his whole body went rigid beneath his dark coat. He turned back to face me.

"You lived. And you became an Interstitial like me. How long have you known? It can't have been long; we've seen nothing from you, not a whiff of rumor or happenstance." He was tapping the heel of a boot on the ground now, eyes boring into me.

"It's only been recent that I even found out," I said. "Did you kill Rachel?" I had to know.

He shook his head. A weight lifted from my gut, and a thrill sprouted through my chest to my fingertips.

"She's alive?" I breathed.

"Of course," he said as if offended. "She isn't even a Mythic. I hold no ill will toward Rachel."

"No ill will? That seems like a strange way to talk about someone you were married to."

He looked away from me, out across the valley that held the Faithful's camp. "That was a very long time ago." His eyes regained their focus, and he took a long, audible breath through his nose. I heard him slowly release it. "I've lost so much since that day." The last he said quietly, almost as if to himself, but I was able to make it out. I didn't interrupt his musing.

He snapped his fingers and turned on me. I had to resist the urge to put my hand on my con gun.

"What do you know of Translation? Of Deliverance?"

I blinked. "I—I still don't know what that is."

He smiled. "I think you do." He bent and picked up a piece of granite, about the size of his fist. He held it up in his right hand. The stone burst into white smoke that rapidly swirled into nonexistence above his palm.

"Deliverance."

He flicked his hand down and the stone reappeared in his hand. My eyes went wide. He hadn't changed position, hadn't gone anywhere. Was this what it was like being on the other side of my ability? Time didn't pass inside my Space. Is this what it looked like to an outside viewer?

"Did you go into—"

"No. Be still." His voice wasn't angry, but it was lined with hardness, a teacher who was used to being heeded. He switched the rock to his other hand and this time it dissipated in black smoke.

"Translation."

With an identical flick, the rock reappeared, but it was glowing white-hot.

"Look out!" I threw my arms up to shield myself.

From the other side of my arms, he laughed.

"You see? You're more familiar with them than you might believe."

I peeked out. The stone sat inert in his left hand, still glowing, but most definitely not exploding.

"How... Why isn't it exploding?" I stared at the stone, the light warm against my face.

"When you've lived as long as I have, you don't leave things to chance. I can teach you to control every aspect of the process of Translation."

He laid his right hand over the top of the stone and pressed down. The stone melted in front of my eyes, and he shaped it like a lump of bread dough, smoothing corners and erasing folds with nothing but his hands. Soon, the stone was a nearly perfect sphere of light that pulsed and throbbed with energy and light. He held it out toward me.

In spite of every instinct that told me otherwise, I held out a hand to receive it, entranced.

The moment the sphere dropped into my hand, it exploded, throwing me backward through the air and onto the ground. Surprised that there was still enough of me to sit up, I did so. My eyes were immediately drawn back over the dozen feet I'd been thrown to where Caine stood, hands in the air like a magician, bathed in fire and light, the sphere that had been no larger than a softball expanded to a circle of golden light ten feet in any direction, crackling and shimmering in its captured state.

Slowly, as I watched with my mouth hanging open, the sphere contracted, compressing and collapsing in on itself until it once again sat with blistering intensity on Caine's palm.

"You have a long way to go." His eyes smiled. The ball disappeared once more in a puff of black smoke. He walked to me and held out a hand.

I allowed him to help me up, and I automatically started brushing my hand over my armor to remove the dust and twigs I assumed would be there. My hands brushed over a few melted pieces of liquid armor and twisted remnants of the metal armor plates on my thighs.

I swore loudly and tried to cover myself, realizing

I was practically naked. Everything on me had been destroyed by the blast.

Caine laughed. I looked up to see him holding out several articles of clothing and a tall pair of boots to me.

"You'll want these," was all he said.

I retreated awkwardly with the clothing behind a large tree and a few bushes to change. There was a shirt, much like the one Caine and the rest of the Faithful wore; a pair of dark pants that looked to be some sort of leather; a buttoned vest made of what looked to be a similar material; and a tall pair of boots, heavier leather than either the pants or the vest, that were a tad on the small side, but not too bad, all things considered. I looked for the con gun in the remains of the liquid armor and found a lump of metal and circuits. I cursed in my head and slipped the wristband from the ruined pocket and into the pocket of the new vest.

I walked back around to where Caine stood. His arms were crossed, and he was considering the valley where Henry's ranch and the Mythic camp were nested. He turned around when he heard me approach and nodded approvingly.

"They suit you."

I pulled both sides of the vest open, looking down at myself. "What is it made of?" I looked at Caine's clothes, which showed no worse for the blast that had completely decimated my armor, both liquid and metal.

The smile was back in his eyes. "You wouldn't believe me if I told you."

The whole situation seemed impossible. I liked this man. My father. He was very likable. Was it all a misunderstanding? He seemed so rational, so concerned. *What the heck?*

"So, you can't really be serious with all this. What are you really doing with all of the missing Mythics?"

His face went impassive and stony again. He muttered another word in that other language.

"Mythics? Is that truly what they call themselves in these circles? You don't see the arrogance in that?"

"I hadn't really considered it." I hadn't. "What's the problem you have with them, anyway?"

"The problem?" he repeated. He pulled up the sleeve of both his coat and his long sleeve shirt, exposing the forearm I'd seen him rubbing during the incident earlier that morning. In the middle of his forearm, just a few inches above his wrist, there was a large, dark dimple in the skin. He pushed a finger, and the dimple expanded, showing itself to be a large hole, about the size of a pencil. "This," he held out the dimple for me to examine myself. "Is the mark of the Oppressors."

"What is it from?" I asked, not quite able to reach out a finger and touch his arm.

He lowered the sleeves again, adjusting the cuffs. "Where I come from, the Oppressors, the Mythics, as you call them, pierce all Interstitials with a ring, made from a metal that dampens our ability." He held out a hand. "May I see yours?"

I reached into my pocket and held out the wrist-band, uncertain. If he were to destroy it...

He took it and brought it close to his eyes. Examining the rigid, c-shaped piece of solid metal, a groan of disgust rolled off his tongue. "It's been reworked slightly, but it's the very same ring I removed from my own arm millennia ago, I'm sure of it." He handed it back. "I had hoped never to see it again. Why do you keep it?"

I accepted it and returned it to my pocket. "It's saved my life on multiple occasions."

He raised an eyebrow. "Indeed? Then it's brought you far more luck than it ever did me. To me, it was only ever the mark of a slave, a possession, a symbol of status."

"Where exactly *do* you come from?" I pressed. This was what I'd come for. This was why I was here.

"On the planet where I was born, these 'Mythics,' as you call them, are the ruling class. Interstitials like us are nothing but symbols and sources of wealth to them. With our enslavement, they hold everything all dictators desire: wealth, energy, control of resources, and immortality."

"Come again?" I choked.

He ignored my outburst and continued. "When I orchestrated my escape, I had hoped to eliminate all of them that were with me at the time. I underesti-mated their resilience. I've been trying to keep them from getting a toehold on this planet throughout its existence. They now have no memory of their origin, but the instinct to dominate, to rule, to enslave, is strong. In recent years, with the humans' Industrial Revolution, it has become more difficult to weed them out. My fight has gone to the shadows."

My head was reeling. Here, standing in front of me, my own father, was a self-professed real-life alien. I was an alien. My origins weren't on earth. Half of them, at least.

I had to sit down. The world around me was spinning.

As if noticing my struggle for the first time, Caine put a hand out, helping me down to the ground.

"You didn't know any of this. I apologize. I can't imagine how difficult and shocking it must be."

I took long, deep breaths, closing my eyes to keep from being sick due to how much my vision was swimming.

"You don't have to do this," I gasped, rising to my feet. "The Mythics of Safeguard don't want to rule, they don't want to enslave. They only want to live without being bothered."

Caine laughed, but it was not a cheerful one.

"What do you call Julian Danton's instinct? Was he alone in his ideals? Was he a lunatic without a platform or following?"

I looked over at him. "It *was* you, then, who came to Danton, after his transformation?" I remembered that the Danton children had talked about a man, Caine, who had shown up to speak with their father, but that their father had returned several weeks later, angry and driven.

Caine nodded. "It was. I had intended to recruit him, to invite him to become one of my Faithful, but he refused. I had intended to go after him, but I was in the middle of a lengthy campaign against the British King's Men and couldn't get away until after word reached me of his demise and his children's disappearance."

I kicked a stone near my feet and stared out across the valley. Evening fires had been lit in both camps, and the flickering, quavering orange light provided a cheery contrast against the bleak grey of the remains of the afternoon's rainstorm.

"How did you find the children?" I asked.

He waved a hand, dismissing my question, and moved on. "James, I tire of this exchange. I've afforded you the courtesy of conversation and life because you are my son, and that is to be acknowledged. But you must know: you now have a decision to make." He folded his arms across his chest. "You may join me. Your mother is alive and in my care, as is your sister. Though, you probably have no memory or knowledge of her."

I tried to make my face a believable mask of disbelief. "I have a sister?" I winced inwardly. I only hoped that he was too focused on the impossible choice I felt he was about to offer me to notice my middle-school-trained acting.

He nodded. "We can be together, standing against the spawn of the Oppressors." His voice dropped significantly. "If not, if you choose these 'Mythics', I will not spare you. I will not allow them to bring another planet under their subjugation, be they connected to the Dynasty or not."

He turned his back to me, walking away through the trees. "You have the night and tomorrow to decide. The following morning, we come after them, infection notwithstanding." His black coat disappeared into the shadows of the pines.

***

Thirty hot, sweaty minutes later, I walked out of the tree line on my way into camp. A large tuft of ground exploded near my feet, and a fraction of a moment later, the crack of the rifle that had fired reached my ears.

"Take one step closer, I dare you!" came a faint yell from somewhere within the opposing tree line.

"It's James! James Strader!" I raised my hands over my head and tried to locate the shooter within the trees, without luck.

"I don't care if you're Elvis Freaking Presley! Put one foot closer and the next round goes through your skull!"

I thoroughly regretted not spending more time in the camps and getting to know more of the people in them. I sat down and crossed my legs. "Look, I'm not going anywhere! Just call Clara Walker and tell her James is back!" I decided courtesy was a good idea. "Please!"

Silence. I'd have just called Clara myself, but my helmet hadn't made it through Caine's blast, either.

Several uncomfortable minutes later, I heard Clara's voice shout across the distance.

"James? Is that you?"

I stood up and dusted myself off. "It's me."

"What the hell are you wearing?"

I jogged across the distance and Clara stepped out from cover.

"My clothes are the least interesting thing about what I just learned. Where are Henry and Heretic? They're gonna want to hear this!"

Chapter 21

I ran my hands through my hair and scrubbed at my eyes with my palms, then simply held my face in my hands, shaking my head. The fluorescent lights of the garage made my eyes water and my head hurt. Clara, Henry, Heretic, and Sammy all stared at me. *Like I'm an alien. Well, technically, we all are.*

"Are you kidding me?" Clara stood with her hands on her hips, facing me from the doorway of the garage. "So he's—what, he's on some mission of revenge for something that was done to him *thousands of years ago?!*" Clara was as mad as I'd seen her since the night Pat had been taken. Then, she'd been cool, detached. Tonight, she was red-hot and clearly engaged.

"No, it's not like revenge, it sounds more like he thinks he's the good guy like he's saving the world or something."

"Psssh!" Clara shook her head, pacing back and forth.

Henry's eyes were gleaming as he rubbed his chin, staring into space. "What do you think he meant when he said that you and he—Interstitials, did he call you?—were the source of wealth and immortality? Energy seems obvious enough, but immortality? How does that even..." He trailed off, muttering to himself and scratching at some shadow on his chin. It was the first time I'd seen him less than perfectly groomed.

I glanced at Sammy, then immediately wished I hadn't. She sat on a high stool at the workbench, her arms folded across her chest, and her eyes were boring holes into my face. She didn't say anything.

"It makes sense that the origin of Mythics should be extraterrestrial," Heretic said from a place near the workbench. "Life on this planet is fairly pedestrian in comparison with what it could be. I must say that I'm surprised that he kept that from Raven so effectively for so many years. There's absolutely no mention of anything like that in her memories."

The face screen lit up with Raven's image. "That's because I didn't know. I had no idea! Why wouldn't he tell even the Faithful about that?"

I shook my head. "I don't know. How do you sit on that? How do you keep something like that quiet? For a thousand years? You heard what he said this morning about the Faithful being with him throughout history, right? I didn't misunderstand that?"

Henry was nodding again, now wiping down his workbench frantically. "Exactly! See? That's the question. How is he doing that? It's one thing for him to be able to live off the lives he absorbs. How have they? Is he somehow transferring it to them? If we could just—" he turned to me, rag still in his hand.

Clara was shaking her head. "No! James is better than that. He and Caine aren't the same."

"You don't think so?" Sammy spat. "They seem pretty similar from where I'm sitting."

Clara turned on her. "James was unconscious, the last time he absorbed someone. What's your excuse? You were wide awake when you pulled the trigger. Four times, I believe it was?"

Sammy took in a sharp, shaky breath and slid off the stool. She didn't say anything more. She looked at me one more time with something I couldn't identify in her eyes. It wasn't the eyebrow-knitting anger she'd been treating me to all night since I'd returned to camp. It was something softer. Something sadder. She stomped up the stairs into the lodge.

"Once again, we're left pondering on our next course of action," Heretic observed.

"No pondering," Clara said. "You said that he said that he works in the shadows, right?"

I nodded in confirmation.

"Perfect. So, we shine the light on him, like the cockroach that he is!"

Henry paused in his frenetic cleaning and organizing. He stared into space, then began nodding and poking a finger at the air. "Yes! We take the whole thing public! I have a contact in the news, and even a few people in the Governor's office I can talk to. He wants to work in the shadows, he's going to have to do it from somewhere else!" With that, he flung the rag into a basket in a corner and practically sprinted upstairs.

Clara blinked. "I forgot how well-connected he is. This might work a little too well!"

My face must have shown what I was thinking, because Clara took one look at me and said, "This is the right thing to do, James. It's what you were talking about the other day! What if we can live out in the open, unafraid to use our abilities, not scared of discovery? Can you even imagine?"

I leaned onto the workbench, sighing heavily as I thought.

"What if it backfires?" I thought aloud. "What if even more people die, because of what we do? I mean, we don't know how Caine will react to this. What if he just *literally* blows up? Bigger than ever? Are we prepared to be responsible for whatever he does after?"

Clara shifted on her feet, hands still on her hips, but her elbows tucked in, then she slowly brought her arms across her chest, clasping herself.

"James, the sooner this ends, the sooner I can get out there and find Pat. You have no idea what it's like, to know he's out there, to not know where he is, to not be able to go find him."

I shook my head. "You're right. I don't. I just hope that this doesn't come back to bite us."

Clara nodded, but I could see she wasn't as confident in her decision as she'd been before.

I walked upstairs, leaving Heretic and Clara in the

basement garage. Back on the main floor, I saw Henry through the glass of the front windows, cell phone up to his ear, talking and laughing animatedly. I sat down in an overstuffed armchair and let my head drop onto the back, suddenly realizing how exhausted I was. Out of habit, I closed my eyes and counted slowly to ten, counting every inhale and exhale of my lungs.

I didn't look up or even open my eyes until several minutes later when I heard the front doors swing open and shush closed, and the sound of Henry dropping onto the couch a few feet away from me.

"It's done," he said simply. "I told my best contact in the governor's office everything. In a few minutes, the governor will be made aware that there's a terrorist group holding a group of refugees hostage out here, and he'll do something about it. My contact assured me."

I nodded faintly several times.

I heard Henry shift on the couch, the leather squeaking slightly beneath him, then he cleared his throat softly. "Hey, James, how are you? I mean, how are you doing with everything?"

I opened my eyes and dragged my head upright, surprised.

He looked immediately uncomfortable, hands rubbing each other, looking down at the ground, and his shoulders tightly hunched.

"It's a lot," I tested, curious at how far he would see this experiment through.

"I bet," he replied, shoulders widening just a bit. "What—What feels the heaviest right now?"

I forced my eyebrows to stay neutral as I choked on my surprise. Working as I had around women in early childhood for so long, I'd had conversations like this before, but never with another man. I reached over the discomfort to mentally sort through everything I felt like I was carrying at the moment. There was a lot.

"I think right now, it's just the weight of the consequences of what we're doing. I mean, we left the realm of decisions that impact just us a long, long time ago. That call you just made to the governor's office? That's going to change the world. I'm not sure yet how that feels to me, other than heavy."

Henry was nodding. "Yeah, it's big. I didn't really think of it like that, you know? Sometimes, I just get so focused on the parts of the whole, I forget about the emotional fallout for people." He chuckled. "At least, that's what both my therapist and my marriage counselor tell me."

I blinked. "Wait, you're married?"

He chuckled again. "Yeah, I never mentioned that did I?" He looked down at his hands, flexing them wide open. "No, I'm not a very good husband. Or father. I'm a pretty terrible one, actually." His smile was sad, and it didn't reach his eyes.

"Well, you thought to ask me about my problems. You must do all right at home." I could see he felt terrible. I felt bad for him.

He shook his head. "The marriage counselor suggested that type of question. I'm not that good with it." He stood up and started pacing in front of the couch, visibly agitated. "It's just that if I can see a situation, a problem, and just watch it for a while, I can usually figure out how to fix it. How to address the problem, solve it, and make it one hundred percent better. I've done that with my software," he was counting on his fingers now. "With my business, and most systems and other companies. I've even started doing a good bit of consulting, because I can just see the problem and know how to fix it, you know?" His hands closed into fists, and he sagged back into the couch. "That doesn't work for my wife. Doesn't work for my daughter. At work, everything's just so easy! You see the problem, you figure out whose responsibility it should be, you assign it to them, you reward them and recognize them for it, and you move on." He propped his elbow up on the arm of the couch and leaned his head on his fist. "It's not that easy at home."

I was blown away. I couldn't believe how much this man had just dumped on me. Or what he was dumping. Here he was, Henry Hoover, tech billionaire, confessing to me that he didn't know how to run his marriage or his family. He was just a man, too, it turned out.

Suddenly he laughed. "My wife will be relieved to find out that I'm part alien. That much, at least, will make sense to her."

I laughed too. "You know, I was super intimidated by you."

He looked up, his eyes wide. "Really? Why?"

I snorted. "Why? Because you've literally got that whole, 'billionaire playboy philanthropist' thing going on."

He squinted. "Wait, isn't that from…"

I continued. "The point is that we're both just men, trying to figure things out. I mean, now that I know you're married, you're not so much the playboy, but we don't have the answers."

"No, we don't." Henry looked up at the ceiling and blew out a deep breath. "It's going to be an interesting night."

***

That evening, I went down among the Mythics in the camp. My experience that afternoon had driven home that I needed to spend more time with them and gain their trust.

I changed out of the clothes that Caine had given me. I'd been shot at once based on that resemblance. I didn't need to add getting shot to my list of recent new experiences, especially since I didn't have any protection, neither ability nor armor, to save me. So, I went out in a tee shirt and jeans, determined to mingle with the locals.

At the first camp, I felt decidedly out of place. By this point, it was a well-oiled machine, people young and old darting here and there, accomplishing every-thing that living in a camp required. At this point in the day, dinner was over, and folks were finishing with cleanup and preparing for bed in a few hours. I passed one woman carrying a tub full of disinfected plates to be dried and put away in the small central pavilion outfitted with a stove, an oven, a large sink that could be filled from the camp water spigot, and a shed that served as a pantry. She stared at me openly as I passed, not even attempting to hide that she didn't recognize me.

I tried to defuse the tension by smiling broadly. "Can I carry that for you?"

She turned slightly away and shook her head at me. "I'm fine. Who are you? Can I help you?" Her words were polite, but her face was tight, her mouth pursed. People were on edge, especially with people they didn't recognize.

"No, I'm just out walking this evening, meeting people. I'm James Strader." I offered a hand after she set the bin down on the counter, but she didn't take it. I lowered it slightly, my face flushing with heat. "Were you with Safeguard? I'm Jared and Deby Strader's son."

She blinked, and her eyes widened with recog-nition. "Oh! The former directors? Oh, I didn't know they had a son!" She took the hand I'd lowered en-thusiastically and pumped it a few times. "I'm Ashley Turner. Tucson unit." She looked around at the several people passing by us, some of them looking on with open curiosity, most glancing or looking out of the corners of their eyes. "What brings you down here? Are you staying up in the lodge with Director Walker and the Hoover guy? Oh, I've seen you riding around with them. I remember now!"

I nodded. "Yeah, that's me. I just thought I'd go around and see how people are hanging in there. How are things going?"

Ashley shrugged. "All right, I guess. I mean, we're refugees. What can we expect?" She leaned in, looking around. "Hey, were you around this morning when those people showed up? People are saying some people were killed. Is that true?"

I hadn't considered the fact that the camp was almost assuredly a rumor mill. I couldn't imagine the different versions of today's events that were swirling around over the meals and chores.

"One of Caine's people, yeah. It's a shame. It didn't have to happen that way."

"Is it true he ate the body? I heard someone say he ate the body, and he killed some of them that were wounded. It gives me the creeps! It's like something out of a horror movie!" She shuddered.

I frowned. "He didn't—"

"I don't know why we didn't just mow the whole line of them down. Nothing the business end of a rifle couldn't solve! I've heard the cowards ran off after that, and now they're hiding in the trees." Ashley talked without taking a breath. "Hey, what was the flash of light earlier? That was bizarre! Did they really burn down the forest in a ring around the Brick? What's their game there, do you think?"

"I... They..." I didn't know which to address first.

"You don't know either? That's okay. I just figured I'd ask. Nobody seems to really know for sure." She shrugged. "Anyway, it was nice to meet you. I gotta go get my girl ready for bed. G'night!"

I stood under the pavilion, bewildered. So much wrong information. How was that even possible?

I exchanged nods with another man who walked past, his eyes only barely meeting mine. I noticed his hand hovering over the pistol on his belt as he walked past. A few steps beyond me, he twisted his head around to glance back at me.

It was the same in each camp I visited. I was met with suspicious eyes for several minutes, before finally being able to introduce myself and set a few people at ease, at which point more of the others seemed to relax. Each camp was the same in that speculation and misinformation ran rampant. One other thing I noticed was that the further I went away from the lodge, the more extreme the views I heard expressed. Considering the fact that Ashley, way back in the first camp, had actively advocated simply mowing down the whole lot of them, that shocked me.

I sat down at the fire of what I'd decided would be my last camp visit of the night. In the dark and given the late hour, people were getting too jumpy for my liking.

"Cam Mezner," the young man next to me introduced himself. "Who are your parents?"

"Oh, I'm not from this camp," I offered, shaking his hand. "I'm staying up in the lodge. But my parents were Jared and Deby Strader."

The young man blinked, and his eyes narrowed. "Really? How was that?"

"Fine, I guess. They were good people."

He snorted. "Really? That's not what my parents say."

I leaned away from him slightly, turning to face him. "What do you mean?"

"Oh, my parents thought they were control freaks. They were always so rigid with the protocols and everything. My parents were always talking about how we should just take over, fix the country, and stuff. They always said that they thought the Straders were cowards." He poked a stick at the fire, seemingly unbothered in the slightest by what he was saying.

My mouth hung open, and I stared at him. I couldn't decide which bothered me more: his lack of filters, or the subject matter of his opinion.

"I'm sorry, 'we'?" I stammered.

"Yeah." He glanced at me, unperturbed. "Mythics."

My head was reeling. I stood up, shaking my head. Caine's words and his warning echoed around my skull.

The young man looked up from the fire. "Where ya goin'?"

"To bed," I lied, then headed for the lodge, racing through the dark.

Chapter 22

I checked the time when I entered the lodge: a few minutes after eleven. I didn't see anyone in the lobby, and the kitchen and conference room hallways were dark.

I rushed down the hall toward the guest rooms and stopped in front of Clara's room. I tapped at the door, trying to find a balance between waking up the others and not waking up Clara. She opened the door a moment later, still fully dressed, and wide awake.

"James? What's up?"

"I need to talk to you."

I think she could tell from my tone that something was up. She stepped aside and invited me in.

I stepped inside, and, as soon as she closed the door, blurted, "Are people talking about taking over?"

"What?" Her hands were in her back pockets, and she drew in her chin in confusion.

"Mythics within Safeguard. Are they talking about rising up and taking over?"

"James, what are you talking about? Taking what over?"

"The country! The government, the world, whatever! Have you heard people talking about it?"

She nodded her head from side to side, her face screwed into a grimace. "Yeah, there's always a few. I mean, you know how it is; there are fringes in every movement, kooks in every party."

I paced back and forth in front of the window, cursing.

"Why? James, what's wrong?"

"I was just outside, down in the camps, trying to meet people. I talked to a kid who was talking about it and acting like it wasn't even a big deal."

Clara nodded again, closing her eyes as if she found it distasteful. "I'm not surprised." She pointed at me, palm up. "It shouldn't be news to you, either, James. I mean, where do you think the people who took up with Danton came from? Just out of the woodwork? We're always trying to deradicalize our members. It's what makes rogue Mythics like Danton so dangerous. I mean, Safeguard has always tried to hide our existence from the outside world, from its inception. Don't you think that ruling the world runs just a little bit contrary to our mission statement?"

I ran my hands through my hair, still pacing. I folded my arms, tapping one clenched fist on my lips.

"James, what's wrong?"

"He called it. He freaking called it!" I barked through clenched teeth.

"Who?"

"Caine! That's his whole thing, his whole argument

for why he does what he does. He says that Mythics have always been and will always be 'the Oppressors' that he refers to them as." I spun to face Clara.

"What if he's right?"

Clara jumped back as if I'd struck her with a branding iron. "What does that mean?"

"I mean, what if he's right about Mythics? What if they can't *not* rule or enslave others? Exploit others? You said it yourself: Danton had followers, and he didn't even have to try very hard."

"James, think about what you're saying." Clara stepped back in, her face somber. "You know me. You know Pat. Does that sound like something we would ever do? Like something we would ever allow to happen?"

I shook my head. "No, see, that's just it. You and I, we sit up here, in the lodge, and we make plans, and we pretend like we have control of this situation, but we don't! I mean, those people out there, they're not robots. They're not gonna' just blindly do what they're told. And if they decide they want to take over a country, who's to stop them, huh? Not the people of that country. What would they do against a Tank, who suddenly decided he was going to force people to do what he said? Or a Thinker who decided to take control? Any one of them could bring society to its knees, given the right opportunity."

"That's exactly why Safeguard was formed, James. It wasn't just for our protection. It was for the world's." Clara crossed her arms. "Have you still never read your great-grandpa's journals? Adopted great-grandpa. Whatever."

I blinked. "No. Those are a thing?"

She laughed. "Hell yes, they're a thing. Some of the founding documents came straight from his notes. You really should take a look at 'em, first chance you get, when all this is over." She shifted on her feet, visibly relaxing somewhat. "Yeah, that's exactly what he was trying to prevent. He wanted to prevent another Hitler."

I started. "Hitler? Are you saying Hitler was a Mythic?" I couldn't believe what I was hearing.

"Yeah! Of course he was a Mythic. A Thinker, for sure. You honestly think a guy as ugly as that got by purely on charisma?" She shook her head. "No way. No, Safeguard was formed as a means of protection, for sure, but it was also about accountability and security. A way of preventing something like that from happening ever again."

"So, this line of thinking isn't anything new to you?" I asked, my heart still racing and my head still reeling from the Hitler revelation.

"Shoot, no. I think about it all the time. It's actually one of the primary directives and objectives in the by-laws. You really should read them sometime soon."

"So, what do you do about it?" I pressed, sitting down on the edge of the bed.

Clara pulled out the chair from the desk near the door. "Well, as soon as possible, we put it down, as calmly as we can. We have informants in every one of the Mythic cells across the country. In fact, I bet I already know about them. Who was it you talked to?" She pulled out her phone and opened a file on it.

"Cam…" I had to think. "Mezner."

"Mezner?" she repeated, squinting as she scrolled through the phone. "Oh, yeah, Mike and Judy Mezner. Based in Idaho." She turned the phone around so I could look. "See? we're on top of it. No homicidal psychopaths necessary." She put the phone back in her pocket.

I blew out. I felt a lot better, but it didn't answer all the questions or solve all the problems. "So, how does what's happening tomorrow figure into the bylaws?" I scooted back on the bed and leaned back on my palms. "What'd my great-grandpa have to say about going public with Mythics, putting us in front of the world?"

Clara laughed. "Yeah, I'll admit, we're going seriously off-book with this. But, what choice do we have? Your great-grandpa definitely didn't know about Caine. Something tells me he wouldn't have liked him very much."

I laughed, in spite of the weight of the moment. "You're probably right. A family reunion for me would be very, very complicated."

We both chuckled. *Maybe things would be all right, after all.*

***

I woke up early the next morning, despite having gone to bed so late. It was still dark, and I felt simultaneously incredibly groggy, yet impossibly awake. I knew that trying to go back to sleep was pointless. I knew I wouldn't be getting anything more than what I already had. I dressed quickly and stepped out into the dark hallway, a few dim lights every several dozen feet along the wall the only illumination. After tip-toeing through the hall and across the lifeless lobby, I stepped outside and took in several breaths of the still-cool morning air. I was glad for the jacket I'd pulled on over the shirt and vest from Caine.

On a whim, I started up the hillside behind the lodge, retracing my steps from my ill-fated hike with Sammy. As terribly as that hike had ended, it really had been a fantastic viewpoint. The flashlight I'd taken to keeping in my pocket paid off, as well. I was able to make it up the slope in one piece, knowing I'd gone the right way when I hit the cliff face.

A few minutes later, I was sitting a dozen feet from the edge, watching the eastern piece of the sky slowly fade in from black, then blue, then purple and finally to pink. By the time I could see the color of the vegetation, the light hitting the mountain behind me was fantastic. The landscape out West was very different from home. Some of it I liked, bits of it I didn't hate, and others straight up freaked me out. But this, the "alpine glow" of the rising sun hitting the face of the mountains? This I loved. This, I would miss when I returned home.

Home. Where even was that, anymore? I thought about how the last several times I'd returned to my adoptive parents' house, it hadn't actually felt like *home*. Where was that, now? Where was I going to get that, "all is well" feeling of coming home?

I was startled out of my reflections by the sounds of footsteps on stone and sliding scree. I whipped my head around, hand reflexively dropping to the con gun I normally carried there. It found only empty air.

Sammy gasped and stopped when she saw me. Our eyes met for just a moment, then she turned away and started back the way she came without saying anything, her backside bouncing as she jogged away.

I stood up. "Sammy," I called.

"I didn't know anyone was up here." She said without stopping.

"Sammy, wait!" I took several steps after her. "Sammy, stop! Please!"

She stopped but didn't turn around.

"I—When you..." I had no idea what to say, so instead, I punted. "I want to know what you're thinking."

She whirled around on me. "You want to know what I'm thinking?"

I was very suddenly regretting the request. "Yes?" I tried not to whimper.

She took a few steps toward me, and I took pride in the fact that I didn't take any steps backward.

"I'll tell you what I'm thinking. I'm thinking that I'm an idiot for ever believing that you were anything different." She stopped only a few feet away and continued her rant. "I thought it was special, that you did everything you did for the Danton kids, and you weren't even a Mythic. For someone so different than you, you risked your life." Her voice started to crack and she cleared her throat. "Then I find out, not only did you keep the fact that you're a Mythic from most everyone, but you're also the same kind of Mythic as Caine is, and, the best part of all, you've killed people, too!" She took a breath and wiped her eyes.

"You want to know what I'm thinking? I'm thinking I'm a fool for building you up into something you're not. I had you on a pedestal. I thought I had you figured out, and you were this great, selfless guy who I could look up to, aspire to be like, and really like. You were going to be my template, who I could say to myself, 'what would James do in this situation?'" She folded her arms. "But you're not any better than me. And I hate you for that." There were tears in her eyes.

Everything in me wanted to scream back at her, throw her own failings and massive mistakes in her face, yet again. What she said hurt. It hurt because it was true. Lord knew I'd had every one of the thoughts she'd just expressed about me, about myself. Nothing was new. No one was as aware of my shortcomings as I was.

Instead, I took a deep breath, and let it out. It was cool enough that I could see the vapor, a million tiny reflections in the air as my breath froze.

"I understand."

She scoffed. "What do you understand?" She said, wiping her cheeks.

"You built me up in your head into something. For you, it was something big. Something important to you. When the truth came out about me, it didn't fit with that perfect image of me you'd created, because that's not me. I'm not this perfect guy. I'm not *that* guy. That time with the Danton kids? I had no idea what was right. I spent those weeks completely broken. I was just trying not to self-destruct, let alone do the right thing." I dug my hands into the pockets of my jacket. "I'm sorry that it meant so much to you, and I'm sorry that you found out the truth about me the way you did."

It was my turn to clear my throat. "If I'm being entirely honest, I was actually terrified for you to find out that I was a Mythic. When Henry spilled it yesterday, that was my first thought, was what you would think."

I shrugged. "I know it's not a secret that I'm attracted to you. It was obvious that very first time we met, and you turned on Pat's seat warmer because he wouldn't leave it alone."

She smiled and actually laughed through her tears.

"I think I have an idea of how betrayed you felt when you found that out because that was exactly how I felt when you were standing over me that night on Danton's property, holding a gun in my face."

She lowered her face again.

"I say that not to rub your face in your mistakes, because that's not what I want to do. I tell you that because I know what it feels like to think the world of someone and have that world come crashing down in a single instant."

"You thought the world of me?" she whispered.

I smiled. "That's what you're taking away from all this?"

We both laughed nervously.

"I— I like you, too." She met my eyes fully for the first time. "It's just really confusing, because I really hate what you did, and I'm incredibly mad at you for that. Still." She looked back down again.

I nodded. "I get that, too," I whispered. "But—I don't know. It's very confusing. All around. I mean, we both have blood on our hands. That's not exactly a simple situation." I was out of things to say.

"Shall we just finish watching the sunrise together?" I asked.

Her eyes met mine again. She smiled and nodded.

Chapter 23

Soon after lunch, a call came in over the comms that Caine had been spotted, alone, on the main road outside the camp, on the far side of the newly established no-man's-land.

"He's asking for a James?" the man's voice on the other end asked as a question.

Clara looked up at me. Henry had rigged up another headset for me to use since I no longer had a helmet of my own. I nodded and headed for the garage. Henry and Clara followed me. We all climbed into the side-by-side nearest the exit and Henry sent us roaring down the road, the engine whining and the dust billowing up behind us.

We skidded to a stop at the edge of the tree line, the gathered Safeguard commandos giving me a strange sensation of déjà vu.

We all climbed out of the vehicle, and one of the commandos pointed across the empty space, where we could all see Caine standing coolly, his hands again behind his back, his black coat shaking lazily in the breeze.

"I've got this," I said to Henry and Clara. "You give the order that nobody fires. I don't want to get shot. He might be able to stop bullets, but that's not something I can do yet." I looked intently at Clara, waiting on her nod.

"Hold your fire!" She ordered through her comms. A small army's worth of rifles and weaponry was either lowered or put on safety with an audible series of clatters and clicks. She nodded at me.

I nodded back and walked toward Caine. I shivered when I thought about how many rifle barrels would have been pointed more or less at my back just a moment before. The hairs on my arm shocked up, and a tingle went up my spine. I quelled the urge to shake myself off like an animal.

"James, I'm disappointed."

His voice held none of the casual ease with which he'd addressed me yesterday. Something had changed.

"My scouts down the mountain have reported that there's a large motorcade of SWAT vehicles headed in our direction. I can only assume that you and those with you have notified the authorities about what's happening here. It's clear, however, that you haven't fully considered how this is going to unfold."

Caine pointed generally behind him, in the direction the road ran. "They can't even get along with themselves. The moment they cross a line of 'different-enough', the veneer of their civility and kindness wears out, and they turn on even each other."

He shook his head. "I've watched the same thing happen across millennia, James. They can't change. They *won't* change. Humans are just as consistent in their natures as the Oppressors."

His hands disappeared behind his back again. In that moment, I hated how calm, how confident he looked. Every muscle in my body was screaming from trying not to shake. Every joint ached with the effort of not shivering.

"They're here because of you," I said stiffly. "We told them what you're here trying to do. You're in the wrong, Caine. And you're wrong about them. They're just like us. We're just like them. When people are in trouble, there will always be others who want to help them."

Caine was shaking his head. "You didn't tell them the full truth, though, did you? You told them just enough to get them involved in our story in the way that you want them to be." He again pointed down the mountain. "Do you think they'd be here to rescue you if they knew you had the power in your hands to wipe their entire civilization from history itself?" He shook his head once more. "There's a reason I work from the shadows, James. It's because I've learned, time after time, at great cost, that those who stand up in the spotlight hoping for adoration and validation realize too late that it's the illumination of a searchlight, instead, receiving only violence as their reward."

I shivered, despite my best efforts. I could see the

cloud rising from the road further down the valley now, where I knew the approaching vehicles would be. "You're wrong."

"I wish that I were." He turned away, putting his back to me, but he turned to look over his shoulder. "As an Interstitial, I will always have your back, James. Our kind shares an unbreakable kinship, thicker even than blood. When the bullets begin to fly and the bombs begin to drop, I will come for you. Please realize where your true allegiance lies."

With that final promise, he simply disappeared.

He can enter his Space so easily!

I turned back across the no-man's-land to the line of Safeguard troops, Clara and Henry at the forefront near the side-by-side. With new eyes, I looked at the Safeguard line of defense. Weapons bristled everywhere. Futuristic armor and tech glistened in the harsh early afternoon sun.

"We need to stand down!" I said, broadcasting into my headset. "The police are on their way, and we need to not be the threat they're prepared to find."

Clara nodded but didn't say anything over the comms. "I hadn't thought about it like that. What about Caine?"

I shrugged, the shakes that I'd suppressed now wreaking havoc on my nervous system. "He made it sound like they were pulling back, at least for now. He's pretty sure the police are going to turn on us when they find out what we are."

Henry spoke up. "We'll just have to do our best not to let that happen. I'm well-connected to most of these guys. I like our chances."

"Still," Clara said, "It doesn't hurt to not look like the military is already here. If the police don't take men reporting domestic violence against them seriously, they aren't going to believe that a well-armed paramilitary force is under any threat." She spoke into her comm mike. "All Safeguards stand down and dress down. I don't want anything more threatening than a popgun visible when the police arrive."

There was silence on the comms for a few moments. I watched as the commandos visible nearest us exchanged looks and heard whispers of what I assumed was dissent. Finally, a single male voice crackled over the comms.

"Say again, Director? Did you say dress down?"

Clara's reply would have blistered fresh paint. "Stand down and dress down. That's a direct order! Anyone in violation of this command will be expelled from Safeguard without any hearing or recourse. If you want to keep your place among us, you will stand down and dress down, immediately!" She whirled on the commandos nearest her to emphasize her point. The unfortunate Safeguard woman at her elbow hastily dropped the magazine out of her rifle and cleared the round from the chamber, then set off at a rapid jog toward the camp. Commandos in pairs and small groups began following her example.

Clara turned to look back down the road, squinting at the approaching dust cloud. "How long do you think we have?"

"Maybe ten minutes?" Henry said, scratching at the stubble on his chin.

"That will have to be enough," I said, looking down at my watch.

"Let's head back to the lodge," Clara said, shouldering her own rifle. She spoke into the comms again. "All Safeguard need to pull back into their respective camps. I don't want any stray encounters with SWAT forces before we have a chance to explain to them what's going on."

"Seeking confirmation, Director, you said to pull back? What about sentries monitoring the border of the Brick?"

"Callahan, you heard me perfectly well!" Clara growled into her mike. "I said *all* Safeguard pull back." She waited, but there was no reply. The last visible commandos accelerated into a full-out run back toward the camps.

"You're a little scary at times," Henry observed to Clara.

"You have no idea," she replied, smiling.

***

Turned out, we had more than ten minutes. Fifteen minutes or so later, a helicopter roared overhead several times, then hovered directly over the lodge for a minute, and finally disappeared back down the valley. A few minutes later, the first SWAT truck squeaked to a stop in front of the lodge.

Clara, Henry, and I stood from where we'd been sitting on the steps of the lodge, waiting for them to arrive. I shot a glance up through the glass front of the building and saw Sammy standing with arms crossed across her chest, her face drawn tight with what I assumed was worry. I only saw a shadow that I assumed was Heretic darting out of sight.

Henry held his hands out and slightly up, making obvious the fact that he was unarmed. Clara and I followed suit. He stepped down to the bottom of the steps and knelt, facing away.

"What—" I started to ask.

Clara silently imitated his pose. She whispered out the side of her mouth to me, "They're nervous."

"How can you tell?" I asked, kneeling in the dust.

"Because they haven't come out of the truck yet," Clara whispered. She looked up at the front of the lodge and jerked her head at Sammy. Sammy obligingly left the window, retreating further into the lodge.

I heard a squeak behind us as the doors of the truck opened up.

"Kneeling in the dust, Henry? That doesn't really seem like you."

Henry turned around to look and smiled. "Ben Foster? I had no idea you would be the one to come all the way out here."

I turned my head just enough to glance behind me to see who was speaking.

A hulking man in body armor and a helmet came pounding through the dirt to Henry's side, reaching out a hand to help lift him from his knees. Clapping the shorter man's arm with his other hand, Ben Foster grinned at him.

"I had to pull some interesting political strings to manage it, but you know I had to when I heard the governor ordered an investigation into what was going on out here." He looked down at me, then Clara, in the dust, then all around him. "What exactly is going on out here? I read the initial report, but all of our scouts and even our aerial surveillance of the place couldn't see anything that looked like what was described. He glanced down the road toward the camps. "What sort of conference are you holding this weekend, Henry?" He laughed.

Henry offered first Clara, then me a hand up, then turned to face Foster.

The rest of the SWAT officers had clamored out of the back of the vehicle, milling around nervously, heads swiveling, eyes devouring everything, and fingers just outside trigger guards.

Henry turned back to Foster. "I'm glad you're here, Ben. Your initial report was accurate. I'm assuming, anyway. I'm hoping it captured what I reported about a refugee situation with a hostile and armed force?"

Foster nodded his head at Henry's words as he

turned his head this way and that. "That's about the sum of it. So where is this hostile force?"

It was Henry's turn to nod. "It's complicated."

Foster laughed. "Well, not to seem rude, but you'd better start simplifying it for me, otherwise you'll be finding yourself with a hefty public services bill. Respectfully, of course."

I made eye contact with Clara. They didn't believe us. Without Caine around to validate the claim, they might very well simply dismiss us and return to the city, friendship with Henry Hoover or not.

"Sir?" I spoke up.

Henry and Foster turned to me. Foster looked me over one more time, and I saw him stand up a little straighter as he took in my height.

"What is it, son?"

I groaned inwardly. Ben Foster was one of *those* men.

"The report was accurate. I don't know what you think is going on here instead, but there really is a group of people who wants everyone in this camp dead. They're led by a man named Caine." I glanced at Henry and Clara for support. Foster put his hands on his hips and glanced between them himself, following my cue. Both Clara and Henry nodded their heads, backing me up.

"He's extremely dangerous," I continued.

Seeing both Clara and Henry's support, Foster's right hand dropped to his side and the large black revolver holstered there.

"Dangerous how?" he asked, suddenly all business. "The report said they were armed. What are we talking about? Is this some fringe extremist group?"

"I mean, you could call it that," Henry broke in.

"Well, what would you rather I call it?" Foster asked, his tone deepening.

I watched Henry swallow. "They... that is, he..." He trailed off, unsure how to finish.

Clara rescued him. "They're a super-powered international terrorist group."

Foster stared at Clara, looked at Henry and me, then chuckled. "Look, little lady—"

He didn't actually just say that, did he?

I glanced at Clara. Terrifyingly, she was smiling.

"Officer Foster, I think we'd like to show you something." She looked at me. "Wouldn't we, James? Isn't there something we'd like to show the man?"

I nodded against my will, held hostage by the tone in Clara's voice.

"What is it?" Foster asked, looking around. "It should probably wait until after we've addressed this threat, don't you think?"

Clara shook her head. "Oh, no. I think, if you're going to adequately understand what you're up against, you need to see this."

Foster was apparently smart enough to hear the edge in Clara's voice because his eyes narrowed somewhat, and his considerable eyebrows knit into a single fantastic unit across his forehead. "I'm going to need more information than that to go on, young lady. I've got my men's safety to think of. I don't want to be leading them into anything. As a matter of fact, I'm going to need to see some ID, please. Henry, I know, but I'm afraid I don't know either of you two."

He looked menacingly from Clara and back to me as if we were the threat he'd been called out to deal with.

"Of course," Clara said, reaching into a cargo pocket for a slim wallet. She handed Foster her driver's license and stood calmly, hands clasped behind her back.

I dug into my own pocket, fishing for my wallet, and handed it to the large SWAT officer.

He looked them both over, making an exaggerated show of comparing the pictures on the cards to our faces. He looked over the top of Clara's, his eyes barely visible behind the slits of his eyelids.

"You military?" he asked Clara.

"Former," she said. "Army Rangers, ten years."

I turned to look at Clara, my mouth open and my eyes bugging from my skull.

She shrugged in dismissal. "Never came up," she murmured.

Foster grunted in approval, but if he was surprised, he did a good job of not showing it. He handed back our licenses.

"What was it you wanted to show us?"

Clara must have taken his change in tone as a form of apology because her own attitude changed drastically.

"We'll need to go back up the road a short way, to the dead zone I'm sure you noticed on your way in."

Foster nodded. "Yeah, we wondered about that. What's the deal there, Henry?"

Henry shrugged. "It'll make more sense when you see what I think Clara's wanting to show you." Henry looked at me pointedly. I took his expression to mean more or less, "Are you ready?" I nodded slowly, taking a deep breath in through my nose and letting it out through my mouth.

With a few short hand signals and barked commands, Foster and his men disappeared back into the rear of the SWAT truck. Henry again got behind the wheel of the side-by-side, and I climbed in shotgun while Clara clambered into the back, spewing orders and updates into her comms.

The SWAT vehicle lumbered after us along the road, and I had to suppress an insane urge to laugh when I realized that the huge black bumper across the front reminded me impressively of Ben Foster's scowling unibrow.

Henry pulled us off the side of the road just outside the border of the remaining trees on our side of the dead zone. I stepped out of the UTV and felt the familiar slight tingle behind my belly button and between my ears as I crossed out of the Brick.

The SWAT vehicle behind us pulled off also, and another three vehicles left the forest on the other side of the new clearing.

Foster and several of his men joined us a moment

later, and he hollered like a wounded walrus for the others from the other vehicles to join us.

"Now, what are we looking at, Henry?" His words were addressed at Henry, but I saw that Foster was looking at Clara as he spoke. Apparently, Clara had risen more than a few rungs on the ladder of his esteem.

In reply, Clara uncrossed one of her arms and pointed to me, palm up, with just the hint of a smile about her mouth. I made a mental reminder to glue her helmet shut at some point in retaliation.

"You're going to want to have your men stand back," I said, stepping off the road and facing the empty field in front of us. I heard the clatter of body armor and more than a few mutters as the men behind me shifted back nervously.

I closed my eyes, took one more long breath, then opened them, focusing on a large rock several dozen yards away from us. "Watch that big rock ahead of us," I said without turning. I raised both hands and pointed my palms in the direction of the rock. *Just a small blast. I don't want to panic them, just show them what we're up against.*

I felt the familiar slight impression of warmth in each palm, then sent the atoms racing toward each other in the direction of my target.

The blast made a fantastic explosion on the under-side of the rock, blowing the entire chunk and an impressive spray of dark red dirt several feet into the air away from us.

I smiled despite my nervousness. *I'm getting better at this.*

I turned around, putting on my most somber face to meet the looks of astonishment and awe I expected.

Foster stood, thoroughly unimpressed, the frown on his mouth accented by the frown in his brows.

"So, this guy's got what, a flair for the dramatic and some land mines?"

There were a few chuckles from his men.

Clara took a step forward. "That's not what you just witnessed, Officer."

"Ben, it's more than that. They aren't land mines, James just did that," Henry spoke up, as well.

"I don't get it. If you triggered it, why are we in any danger from this Caine? Just go ahead and detonate the rest of them. What'd you do, patch into his trigger frequency or something?"

I shook my head. "No, that's not—" I sighed. Foster was going to need something he couldn't explain away. I thought back to Caine's demonstration the day before when he'd handed me the ball of pure atomic reaction. I hadn't had good luck with it before, but it certainly wouldn't be something Foster could dismiss out of hand.

Without saying anything more, I took several more steps out into the field.

I tried not to feel too hardcore when I heard several of Foster's men panic and start swearing, yelling for me to come back. They thought I was walking into a field riddled with active landmines. Let them think that, at least for another few seconds.

I stopped when I got to the freshly tumbled and charred rock. I stepped a few feet away from it and stopped. I didn't want to hit my head on it when this crazy idea went south.

Many of the officers were scanning the ground at the edge of the road, undoubtedly trying to figure out how to rescue me from my self-imposed predicament. Foster stood with his hands on his waist, his face a hilarious shade of red.

I tuned them all out, focusing on the space just above both of my palms. I gently pressed both hands together, palms flat. I felt warmth, and bright light started emanating from the cracks between my fingers and palms. I rotated my hands slowly, forming a ball with them. Light continued to pour from my hands, and the warmth increased as the reaction strengthened. My heart was hammering in my chest and my hands shook as I eased them apart.

Pure energy started arcing out from my palms. I used my fingers to nudge it back, and *it responded*, pulling back and recoiling into a more concentrated lump. Trying to quell the excitement building up in my gut, I corralled the energy, shaping it more and more into something that resembled a rough sphere. I stared between my hands, grinning. The golden light was only the size of a marble, but I thought it was the most beautiful thing I'd ever seen in my life. Staring into the depths of it, there was power, freedom, and pure potential. The swirls and fluctuations of energy filled my entire range of vision, mesmerizing in their unpredictability and sporadic movement.

I gradually became aware of someone yelling my name. When I looked up, it was down the barrels of well over a dozen rifles. Foster was shouting something, yelling at Clara, who was yelling right back at him, gesturing at me. Henry Hoover was simply standing in the field, holding his sunglasses in his hand, staring at me, and shielding his eyes with a hand from the glow in my hands.

There was a loud blast from a rifle, the earth at my feet exploded, and I instinctively raised my hands to shield my face. When I did, the world around me erupted in brilliant gold.

Chapter 24

As I picked myself up from the ground, my ears were ringing and my eyes were having trouble focusing. I blinked and rubbed at them, digging dirt and mud from the corners. I lowered my hands and looked around, still blinking fiercely. I immediately wished I hadn't.

Several officers who must have been running toward me when I'd lost control of the energy ball lay strewn about like rag dolls, their armor and clothing scorched and in tatters. The skin that I could see was blistered and burnt. The stench of burning hair and searing meat roiled my stomach. I turned my head and threw up.

None of the officers closest to me moved as I stumbled past them. I retched again, but my stomach was already empty. Further from me, the blast must have dissipated quickly. By the time I got to the road, the bodies were intact and largely unscathed; I prayed that they were merely unconscious. I ran to Clara and Henry where they, too, were lying unconscious from the blast. As I walked past Foster, his hand suddenly shot out and grabbed my ankle.

"What the hell are you?" he slurred. His eyes were slightly crossed, and his grip on my ankle was weak.

"I—I'm so sorry," I stammered. I couldn't look back out at the field, at the consequences of my actions. "This wasn't supposed to happen."

"My men—are they..." Foster's eyes began to roll back in his head.

Hot tears burned my eyes. I couldn't breathe. *Some of them are dead. I'm a murderer.*

Foster lapsed into unconsciousness, and I kicked my ankle out of his grip.

What now? Nothing had gone according to plan. I had just attacked and killed several highly-trained officers of the law. There was no way anyone was going to protect us from Caine. Caine had been right. Somehow, this had always been the outcome, and he'd known it. I didn't know how, but he'd known it.

My mind was spinning. *What do I do?* The only thing I could think to do was to load Clara and Henry into the side-by-side and retreat to the camp. I didn't know what else to do.

As I watched the SWAT vehicles and the various bodies of the officers shrink in the rearview mirror, then disappear entirely behind the trees, I knew that things had changed. Nothing would be the same after this. Unintentionally, I had just declared war on humanity.

***

As I pulled up to the lodge, Heretic and Sammy both ran down the steps from the balcony. They'd been waiting.

"What happened?" It was Raven's voice from Heretic.

"I—the police... I—" I couldn't finish any of my thoughts as I clambered out of the side-by-side.

"Are they okay?" Sammy asked, pointing at Henry and Clara.

I shook my head and shrugged. "I don't know. I hope so?"

"Jamie?" My adoptive mother, Deby, spoke from Heretic. "You don't look good. What happened? Where are the police?"

In my mind, I saw again the melted armor, the blisters, and the burns. My knees buckled beneath me and I had to grab onto the side-by-side to keep from falling, lowering myself to the ground. "They're dead." It came out as barely a whisper.

"What?" Mom leaned down to get closer to my mouth.

"They're dead!" My voice cracked, and the tears returned as I said the words out loud. I looked up at Sammy, and our eyes connected. *What must she think of me now?* I tried to read what I saw in her eyes, but all I could see was my own reflected revulsion and horror. It didn't help me feel any better. "It was an accident," I stammered. But the words felt hollow, even as I said them.

"What happens now?" Sammy asked.

It was Raven's voice that spoke up from Heretic again. "We're screwed."

Heretic's own formal voice chimed in. "It's true. Given this unfortunate turn of events, there is only a very slight chance, .0003, precisely, that the authorities will not retaliate negatively. Our ability to maintain control of the situation has drastically declined. We now face extinction from Caine and his Faithful if we leave the House of Bricks, and every likelihood of death by law enforcement or criminal prosecution if we stay. I do not like our options."

I looked at Clara and Henry, still unconscious in the side-by-side. *What would they do?*

I pulled myself to my feet and tried to square my shoulders. "That won't happen."

Sammy snorted, then looked embarrassed. "I'm sorry, I just—What are you going to do about it, James? No offense, but it was you who got us into this mess."

I flinched inwardly. Her words hurt. Not just because they just so happened to be true, but because I thought she and I had patched up some of the distance between us. *I guess some things are harder to forgive than others.* After all, hadn't I just done what she'd done, killed people? We'd had a hard time forgiving her, and we'd had weeks.

"I don't know yet. But I refuse to sit here and die, either way. There's got to be a way out of this."

Heretic stepped forward and began lifting Henry out of the side-by-side. "I find that unlikely. Without the introduction of some previously unaccounted-for variable, my models suggest that we are, as Raven so eloquently put, 'screwed.'"

At that very moment, beyond all reason and belief, a small grey pickup truck droned out of the trees down the road. When it pulled to a stop, Pat Walker climbed out of the driver's seat, threw an empty energy drink can into the back of the truck, and said, "Do you guys have any idea how hard it was to find you here? Not one of these roads is marked."

"Pat?!" I rushed over and swept him up in a crushing hug. "We thought for sure you were dead!" I pushed him back slightly to look at him. "How did you find us?"

"CPS," he said, pointing with his thumb at the truck. "Canine Positioning System."

Vasily Novakov unfolded himself from the small pickup, stretching his huge tattooed limbs, and finished adjusting the shirt he'd just put on with his de-transition within the Brick.

When he saw me looking, he waved slightly and smiled nervously. "Hey."

Pat patted my shoulder when I tensed and said, "It's all right. He's more or less with us now. We had a lot of opportunities to talk, driving across the country."

Pat caught sight of Clara still slumped in the side-by-side, threw my arms off him, and rushed to her side. "What happened? Clara?" He patted her cheek gently, but she didn't respond. He turned back to me. "What happened? We drove past all the SWAT vans.

Some of those guys didn't look good. What the heck's been going on here? Did Caine do that? Why are the police involved?"

I winced. "You've missed a lot, Pat. Let's get Clara inside, and we'll explain everything as quickly as we can. I don't know how long we have." I looked at Heretic. "Heretic, we've got to see if we can help the police. Maybe we can still patch this up."

"You killed officers of the law, James. I'm afraid that diplomacy at this point is a moot effort. I will, however, see what I can put together as far as first aid is concerned for those who survived."

Sometimes, the android had absolutely no tact or sensitivity.

***

By the time Heretic and a team of field-medic-trained Safeguard commandos went back for the police, they'd already loaded up and disappeared. Wary of Caine, the group returned within the Brick quickly and Heretic initiated a reinstatement of the sentries and watch around the perimeter.

Inside the lodge, Pat sat on the couch, gently holding the icepack to Clara's head and brushing her hair from her face lightly. Her left hand on his thigh looked more like a vice grip than a gentle caress. I didn't think she'd ever let him go again.

Vasily clutched a mixing bowl of mashed potatoes, a large spoon making the trip from bowl to mouth in a constant unwavering rhythm, occasionally punctuated by grunts or smacks of satisfaction.

Sammy was helping Henry, also applying ice to his head.

Heretic stood at my elbow, silent and unreadable.

I stood, my arms crossed, foot tapping impatiently as my mind raced.

"What are our options?" I hardly waited for an answer before I spoke again. "I could turn myself in."

Pat swore. "Are you serious? Do you not watch movies? Name one single movie where turning yourself in ever worked out!"

"Life isn't the movies, Pat," I said, gritting my teeth.

"No, but what would that solve?" Henry asked. "They know people like us exist, and we've made it clear that we're dangerous, however unintentionally," he said, in what felt almost like an apology to me. "They aren't going to stop at just you, James. As soon as they realize that there are others with abilities, we'll all be rounded up and 'controlled.' Think back to the Japanese during World War II." He winced as he shifted, putting a hand to his head. "They'll be back; as soon as Ben gets off the mountain and has service, he'll have backup swarming the ranch. Maybe even the National Guard." He shook his head minutely. "Long story short, the ranch is no longer safe."

"But where else do we go?" Sammy asked quietly.

Clara nodded. "And how do we get out of here? Let's not forget that Caine is still somewhere outside, waiting for his window."

Vasily burped loudly, and put down the mixing bowl, sucking on the end of the spoon still in his mouth. He took it out and pointed at me with it. "Is simple. You are destroyer like Caine, yes?"

I hated both his comparison and the term he used, but I couldn't refute either, so I simply nodded.

"Yes. Is simple. Use portal to escape."

Every eye turned to look at him.

"Excuse me?" I blinked rapidly. I remembered my previous conversation with Henry, speculating about how Caine was able to travel so quickly. "Are you actually saying that Caine can teleport?"

Vasily nodded, turning to the chair next to him, where he had several more containers and packages of food stacked.

I snapped my fingers and whistled impatiently at him. "Hey, dog-boy, focus!"

Vasily looked hurt and looked at Pat. Pat made some calming motions with his hand, then turned to me. "James, that was unnecessary and hurtful." He looked back at Vasily and nodded comfortingly.

Vasily returned the nod, then looked back at me. "Yes. Is how we come to America; Caine pull everyone into his portal, and we step out in Washington DC, near..." He stopped to think. "Po-toe-mack River." He picked up a container that held some sort of casserole and lifted the lid to smell its contents. He smiled, going in with his spoon.

I turned to look at Heretic. Raven's face lit the

screen. Her eyes were wide. "Don't look at me; that's new. At least, he never showed me before!"

I turned back to Vasily. "How does it work?" I asked, resisting the urge to snap and whistle again. Apparently, I hadn't forgiven him for his previous role in Caine's operation.

"Don't know," Vasily managed to spray around a mouthful of mixed vegetables and chicken. "Caine have us hold hands, then touch one of us." He waved the spoon around in circles above his head. "Then suddenly we in some between-place, gray, blue all around. Then—" He flourished his hands like a magician finishing a trick and blew a poof of melodramatic air. "America."

I looked at Henry and Clara. "Is it possible?"

Clara winced, closing her eyes, then said, "It seems to me that we're constantly rewriting the book on what's possible these days."

Henry simply nodded. "I see no reason to doubt what our new ally Mr. Novakov has told us."

"There's only one problem with that," I said, putting my hands on my waist. "Everyone and everything that I've ever put into my Space has converted to anti-matter and ceased to be who or what it was before." I turned to look at Vasily. "So, how is it that you aren't a glittering, floating puddle of anti-atoms?"

Vasily paused, his mouth full of food, and stared at me as if I'd sprouted three heads. He shook his head minutely, then shrugged largely, returning to his chewing.

"Any ideas?" I threw it out to the group at large. Everyone stared at the floor, the ceiling, and anywhere but at me. I clapped loudly, impatience eating at the base of my brain and making every second feel like a wasted hour. "C'mon! We need ideas! You all heard Henry. We have as long as it takes Foster and his men to get off the mountain and reinforcements to get to us! There's no time for brain farts!"

"James, calm down." Henry peered up at me through his squinted eyes. "And for heaven's sake, please stop yelling. We're not being unreasonable. None of us knows anything about your pocket dimension. Tell us about it."

"I don't know what to say." I began pacing, nervous energy burning in every cell. It felt as if I could feel every revolution of Foster's tires taking him further down the mountain, closer to making the call that would bring imprisonment or death raining down on each and every one of us, and it was all because of me.

"I don't know how to describe it. There's just a place that I go, right through here—" I held up my left hand. I looked up at it. "Wait..." I looked at both hands. Black smoke. White smoke. Translation. Deliverance. My eyes went wide. *Could it be that simple?*

"I need to get off the Brick. Now."

Everyone's eyes went wide.

"Why? What's wrong?" Clara winced around her icepack.

"Nothing's wrong. I just think that Caine may have

given me the secret to teleportation already. But I'm not sure, and I need to test it. So, who's coming?"

Sammy, Heretic, Pat, and Vasily all raised their hands. Clara and Henry closed their eyes to avoid making eye contact with anyone.

I nodded. "Let's hurry. We're running out of time."

The five of us filed downstairs into the garage and piled into a side-by-side, Vasily carrying an armful of food containers, then sped down the road, stopping at the border and waving off the Safeguard sentries at the roadside.

I was the first to climb out and crossed the border, feeling the tingle as my abilities returned.

"Vasily, toss me one of those containers."

The insatiable Russian turned to the pile on the seat next to him, looking over the menu. "What you want? Noodles? Soup? Chicken or beef?"

"I don't care, just toss me one of the containers! I'm not after food."

He shrugged and tossed me the recently emptied mixing bowl. I caught it in both hands. Then, holding it in my left hand, I focused on specifically absorbing it with that hand. It disintegrated in a puff of black smoke.

"Okay, another one."

I had all eyes in the side-by-side on me, now. Vasily grumbled and looked over the containers one more time.

"Just hand me one of the containers!" I practically screamed at him.

"All right!" He picked up one, lifted the lid to smell it, grimaced, returned the lid, then tossed it to me.

Again, I caught it in both hands, then held it up specifically in my right hand. Concentrating, I absorbed it with that hand, a puff of white smoke marking its departure.

"What are you—" Pat started to ask. I cut him off with a wave of my other hand, then sat down in the dirt of the road, cross-legged, and started taking some deep breaths. I tuned out everything happening around me, focusing only on my body, on the beat of my heart, on the feel of the breath coming in and out of my nostrils, and the rise and fall of my torso as my lungs filled and emptied. After a moment, I opened my eyes and found myself in the familiar expanse of my Space. Except this time, there, directly in front of me, floated the plastic container of leftovers. It was unchanged, intact, and when I picked it up, solid.

I held it in my hands for a moment, disbelieving, then crowed in victory, chucking the container as hard as I could, sending it spinning and tumbling unendingly in a straight line.

"Yes! Deliverance!" I closed my eyes and tried to calm my breathing in order to leave. It took me several moments and a handful of tries to calm myself enough to do so.

When I did, I was standing up, and everyone yelled at once.

"Whoa!"

"The heck?"

"What just happened?"

I was grinning. "What?"

"You just blipped!"

I balked, pulling my chin inward, still smiling. "I what?"

Sammy pointed down at the ground. "You were sitting on the ground, there was a puff of white smoke, then it's like you glitched, like a video game, and suddenly you were standing there."

I nodded, grinning. "I went to my Space."

Pat snorted, tittering behind his teeth. "You've *got* to stop calling it that. You're gonna get hit with a copyright infringement or something."

I ignored him. I held up my left hand. "Translation." I held up my right hand. "Deliverance. He told me. He freaking told me then, the difference between the two. I just didn't see it."

I turned to Heretic. "Let me take you there."

The android looked at me, face-screen dark and blank for several seconds, then nodded. I reached out and took one of his gloved hands, pulling him across the border outside the Brick.

"Whoa, whoa, whoa!" Pat leaped out of the side-by-side. "Look, James, I know Harry has been a real pain in the rear in the past, but you know he deserves better than being turned into atom soup!"

"I appreciate your candor and concern, Pat. However, I trust James. I have observed him for several years now; if he has asked me to take this risk, it is because he himself is confident in his ability to manage that risk. I'll let him do what he wants."

My own eyes went wide, aware of the compliment Heretic had just paid me, even if he didn't intend it that way, and nodded.

Pat looked between the two of us, threw up both of his hands, and turned his back on us, muttering.

I looked at Heretic, suddenly very aware that the uploads of both my parents, as well as my biological sister, were housed in his frame. I squeezed the hand in mine gently, and it disappeared in a cloud of white smoke.

"I sure hope you know what you're doing," Sammy spoke up. "You just disappeared the most advanced example of artificial intelligence and robotics achievement I've ever seen." She looked around. "Also, if any of you tells him I said that I'll kill you."

"I'm sure." I once again closed my eyes, attention turning inward. In a moment's time, I was standing in my Space, facing Heretic, who was holding the container of food.

"I am relieved that I was not destroyed."

"So am I," I laughed.

"What now?" Heretic pressed. "Do you know how to change location?"

My smile faded. "Caine didn't really mention that, I don't think."

Heretic stood blankly, then said, "This is still a win. It is easier to hide a single individual than several thousand. You can flee, while everyone else takes shelter in... your Space."

I nodded slowly. "I think you're right. I think that's going to be our best way out of this mess. Even if I get caught, at least everyone else will be safe, no matter what happens."

"Perhaps," Heretic mused. "We don't know what happens to your pocket dimension if you die."

The air went out of my lungs. However blunt, he made an excellent point.

"Well," I said slowly. "I'm just going to have to make sure that I don't die."

The android nodded his head curtly. "Agreed."

Chapter 25

"Look, we're running out of time! The authorities will be back soon, and they're going to be playing hardball!" I practically had to yell into the comms to hear myself over the shouts of the throng of Mythics in front of me, all clamoring to be heard over the person next to them. Every so often, I could make out individual objections. They spanned the entire continuum, from hot to cold.

"We should turn you over! We haven't done anything! This is still America!"

"Let 'em come! It's past time we took control, anyway!"

"Save us, James! Please! Take my daughter!"

"Enough!" Pat's shout over the comms had me clamping a hand to my ear and doubling over in pain. Most of the crowd did the same.

"Director Pat Walker speaking, for those of you who don't know me!" Pat stalked back and forth on the stairs of the lodge where the small group of us faced the writhing mob. "The reports of my death have been greatly exaggerated!"

I saw Clara roll her eyes and look toward the sky.

"I think some of you have forgotten what Safeguard is. This is not a democracy! We're not asking for your permission; we're not begging you for your support!" He stopped, his hands behind his back, and looked out over the crowd dramatically. "What we have here is a simple matter of life and death! As I see it, you all have three options."

He held up one finger. "One, you can choose to stay on the Brick, and risk whatever retribution the government is preparing to mete out, now that they know we exist, and we've demonstrated ourselves a threat."

There was a loud snarling rumble that spread over a considerable segment of the crowd at that point, and I saw quite a few obscene gestures flash in my direction.

Pat put up a second finger. "Two, you can flee on your own and pray that Caine and his goonies don't find you, because we know exactly what he intends for each of us."

Another more fearful rumble overtook the crowd.

Pat raised his third and final finger. "Or three, you can choose to trust James, as you've trusted his parents before him." Here he looked at me. "As I trust him." I lowered my eyes. "And maybe, just maybe, we can escape and live to fight another day!"

"Enough with the movie quotes!" Clara hissed at Pat. He waved her off, but his eyes had smile lines around them.

"We're through debating. Those are your choices, and we're deciding now! Anyone choosing option James, follow us to the edge of the Brick. All others—" he saluted. "Good freaking luck."

At that moment, Henry came out of the lodge with a large hiking backpack draped over one shoulder. He handed it to me. "This is for you. We don't know how long you'll be out there on your own, so I went ahead and packed you a pack with supplies for maybe a few days. You already transported the MRE meals I showed you in the dry storage?"

I nodded. Henry had had the forethought to have a large stockpile of Meals Ready to Eat, MREs, brought in before everything had gotten hairy, in the event that the catering didn't work out. It was lucky that he had. I'd emptied the shelves in a matter of a few seconds.

The crowd milled about, no one moving in any specific direction just yet.

"Well, that's it," Pat said. "We've dropped the gauntlet, we've laid out their options, now it's everyone's decision what they'll do to help themselves."

"All right, let's head out, then." Sammy headed for the road, going down the steps and pushing past several people in her way without even looking at them.

"For once, I'm with her!" Clara spoke up. She moved down the steps and Pat darted to her side, taking her hand in his and pressing it to his lips briefly as they followed Sammy down the road.

Heretic and Vasily were quick to follow after. I

turned to look at Henry. "I guess we better keep up, huh?" I took a few steps down the staircase but stopped. Henry hadn't moved. I turned to look at him. "Did you forget something?"

Henry shook his head, smiling in a way that made my heart drop.

"I can't go with you, James."

"What?!" I turned to look toward the road, where several small factions of Mythics had broken out from the main crowd and were following after Sammy, Pat, Clara, and the rest. I turned back and went up several steps to stand next to Henry. "What do you mean, you're not coming?"

"James, I can't become a fugitive from the law. If I flee the scene of a crime, I make myself guilty. I can't do that; I have a wife and a daughter out there who need me." He clapped me on the arm gently. "You go —you're everyone else's best chance. They need you. My family needs me."

I searched his eyes, wide but calm, behind his designer sunglasses. "Are you sure?"

He nodded, then pointed with his chin toward the growing line of Mythics headed down the road. "I'm sure. But tell them to hurry. Ben Foster has a temper, and I'm afraid a bit of a reputation. He's not real big on community relations."

I nodded, shouldering the cumbersome backpack, and clipping up the waist belt. "Thank you. For every-thing you've done for all of us. It—" My voice cracked slightly, and I cleared it, my face burning. "You gave everyone a place to gather and treated every one of us like members of your family. Your wife and daughter are lucky to have you."

He laughed. "Go, James!"

I turned and started jogging down the road, unable to look back. First, I couldn't see behind me because of the huge pack, and second, it was stupid, and I knew it was stupid, but I didn't want Henry to see the tears in my eyes. *Stop trying to be macho!*

I was in the process of turning and waving to Henry one last time when a loud rhythmic roar exploded overhead as an Apache helicopter whipped the trees into waves and the road into a rising flood of dust. *We're too late. They're already here.*

My heartbeat matched the slap of my feet against the road as I sprinted, the weight of the pack flailing back and forth wildly and nearly taking me off my feet. I didn't slow down. I raced past screaming people, Mythics clasping their children and fleeing into the shelter and cover of the trees. I stuck to the road. If I couldn't get to the front of the line, to the edge of the Brick, no one had any chance. I kept sprinting.

I tried to shout, to encourage people to keep heading for the border, but no one would have heard me. The roar of the Apache's engines was too loud. Instead, I looked side to side, trying to catch anyone's eyes who would look. To those who did, I gestured wildly, pointing in the direction of the border down the road. Some of them took my advice, breaking into a run, others simply fled, running into the forest, and disappearing.

My lungs burned. The backs of my quads felt like they were on fire. My feet and ankles were screaming from the added weight of the pack. But I couldn't leave it. Assuming I could get to the edge of the Brick, transport anyone within reach into my Space, and get away, I was going to need what was in that pack. Without it, I didn't like my chances in this unfamiliar terrain and climate.

I heard something amid the receding roar of the engines. It could have been a voice over speakers of some kind. The helicopter must have gone for the clearing around the lodge; it wasn't as loud as it had been.

I ran for several minutes without encountering any resistance. There was nothing but the silent huff and puff of the thinning crowd of fleeing Mythics around me as we ran for the border of the Brick. Up ahead of me, I could see the border. The road led out of the pines into the clearing. I could see shapes of people standing at the edge, still beneath the shelter of the forest. I forced my legs to move faster, my arms trying to support some of the weight of the pack and mini-mize its wild pitching side to side.

I was getting close enough that I thought I could make out Sammy, Pat, and Clara among those at the mouth where the road left the forest. I couldn't see Heretic's or Vasily's distinctive forms anywhere.

Suddenly I heard a distinctly Russian accent scream, "Run!"

It was too late. I could only watch as a squad of soldiers left the shelter of the trees opposite and fired several launchers in the direction of the group on this side of the break. I couldn't see the canisters but billowing clouds of smoke began spewing up like geysers from the ground all around the huddled group. I wasn't close enough to hear their coughing, but I could see them doubling over, grasping knees, trying in vain to escape.

I couldn't breathe myself. The air caught in my throat, and I couldn't breathe in, couldn't breathe out, couldn't swallow, couldn't look away.

A heavy hand clapped me on the shoulder, and I jumped, swinging a fist wildly at whoever had me. Vasily blocked the punch easily, then pulled me down to the ground, army-crawling in the dust and the pine needles to the nearest tree. He looked behind me at something and flattened his hand, indicating to get down. I tried to look behind me, but the pack was too big and heavy, forcing me to fight just to keep my face from grinding into the dirt. I scrambled to undo the large stiff waist belt, then the smaller sternum strap, and finally shrugged out from beneath the bulging pack.

Peering behind me now, I saw Heretic, peeking out from behind a tree. Turning back to the road, I tried to see what was happening. A few straggler Mythics fled from the road in terror, choking on the gas from the canisters. There was no movement from the several bodies I could see strewn across the road at the forest's edge. I had to fight to keep from screaming. Pat. Clara. Sammy. Some of those shapes were my friends. The rest were innocents. This was happening because of me.

The helplessness crushed me as I watched the soldiers file down the road, rifles pivoting and sweeping over the landscape constantly until they reached the crumpled shapes of the fallen Mythics. I pressed my hands into the dirt and was about to push myself to my feet, when a hand pushed me down with the strength of a hydraulic press, halting any upward movement I would have made.

"Don't." Raven's voice was barely audible, it was so quiet. "There's nothing you can do for them right now. You can't stop bullets. Not yet, and don't forget we're still under the Brick."

"What about you? You're bulletproof, aren't you? And you don't breathe, so the gas wouldn't hurt you!" I hissed. "Go after them!"

"As soon as they realized the gas had no effect on me, they would use their rifles. This casing's good against lower calibers, but those rifles are designed to hurt."

"Then what do we do?"

"We get ourselves to safety, then we go from there," Raven whispered. She waved a hand gently to get Vasily's attention, then pointed in a direction away from the road and the clearing. He nodded and began sliding on his belly through the debris of the forest floor, leaving a huge swept track like some giant snake.

Raven started after him, dragging the heavy pack with ease at her side. I swallowed stiffly several times and took several breaths, closing my eyes and trying not to look in the direction of the road and my friends.

"Hey!"

I opened my eyes to see Raven's face peering dimly back at me from Heretic's face screen. "We have better chances of being able to help them outside the Brick with access to our powers."

I nodded and crawled after the two of them, making my own track on the woodland floor.

Several hundred yards later, Vasily tentatively raised his head, bobbing and ducking as he looked for troops. He sniffed deeply several times and looked at Raven, shaking his head. She, in turn, looked around, then too shook her head. They both stood up and began running further in the direction we'd been crawling. I jumped to my feet and followed suit. Within several dozen yards, the trees opened up, and we were at the edge of the clearing made by Caine's initial blast, which now felt like it had happened weeks ago.

Vasily pressed his back to one of the pines at the edge and eased his head around the side of the tree. I watched Raven do the same from her own tree. After another moment, they looked at each other and shook their heads. At that, Vasily reached down and pulled up his shirt, shucking the entire thing off over his head. He took several steps out of the trees, and suddenly I knew why he'd peeled the shirt off. Everything first stretched, then ballooned as he made the transition. The dark, thick, coarse fur sprouted all over his body, and he had barely pulled his pants down before a large, bushy tail sprouted over the waistline. When he turned to face the two of us, the lips pulled back over the long, pointed teeth and I stifled the urge to scream.

"Do not scream." The thick Russian accent was an octave lower than normal, yet unmistakable as Vasily. "American troops five hundred meters to right." The huge gray beast stuck its snout in the air and took several deep inhales. "One of them prediabetic. Two taking ketamine..." He sniffed again. "Not sure if bodybuilders or depressed."

My mouth sagged, and I had nothing but questions flooding my brain.

The gaping mouth somehow revealed more teeth, and I realized with some horror that Vasily was smiling. "One of them is Mythic. We may have ally."

Raven shook her head and whispered, "I'm not sure we can count on that. American troops are known for their loyalty to each other. I'm not sure that we would have enough time to exploit that before we were captured."

I took an involuntary step backward as a loud gurgle emanated from Vasily's midsection. He took one more sniff, then licked his lips. I panicked, looking around for a weapon and realizing I had none. I mourned yet again the loss of my con gun.

"I very hungry. Be back in moment." Without another word of explanation, the monstrous werewolf dropped to all fours and loped quickly off into the woods, weaving through the trees like a ghost.

I exhaled, trying to jumpstart my heart and lungs into remembering their jobs.

"I, for one, am curious about exactly what sort of conversation Pat was able to have with that thing that convinced it to switch sides," Raven mused in a whisper.

"I'm not sure, but I'm really glad he did," I stammered back. "Can you imagine meeting him in a dark alley some night?" I involuntarily shivered.

"Strangely enough, he seems all right." Raven seemed distracted, her head on a swivel as she searched the woods.

I nodded in agreement.

After ten minutes or so of watchful silence, Raven's head jerked to one side, and she said, "He's back."

As if on cue, the large grey figure materialized from the shadows of the woods, licking blood from his muzzle and clawed hands.

I grimaced. "Do we want to know?"

More teeth: another smile. "Moose. Less fatty than brown bear or boar. I like."

I tried to return the smile, failing miserably. "Good." I turned to face Raven. "What now, do you think?"

She looked at me. "This just changed from an

evacuation to a rescue operation. The parameters have changed, but the objective is the same: the military has arrived, and we need to find and rescue as many Mythics as we can without getting caught, ourselves."

I nodded. "That makes sense. I think in order to do that, we definitely stay outside the Brick. If people have any sense, they'll be fleeing the Brick in order to regain their powers. I think we need to patrol the perimeter of the Brick for as long as we can, collecting people until we can't evade capture anymore."

The other two nodded. "Is good plan. I can help." Vasily's deep rumbling reply was suddenly very comforting. I looked him over one more time, taking him all in. The towering height; the thick, maned ruff around the neck; the pointed, triangular ears that swiveled constantly, hearing who-knew-what; heavy, thickly-muscled arms and chest, more human-like than I expected, that ended in strong, large hands with long, sharp claws. He slimmed in the waist, but only slightly. The legs, which were jointed and pawed like a wolf's, were muscled to match the rest of him. The bushy, wiry tail swished happily behind him, like an eager dog's. *He's genuinely happy to be with us.*

"Let's find some Mythics," I said, rubbing my hands together.

Chapter 26

We cached the pack somewhere we could come back to it later. We decided to temporarily split up: Heretic had volunteered to go back to the lodge as a scout to take stock of how many Mythics had been captured, and their status. After watching the android sprint lightly off into the distance and disappear into the forest, Vasily and I turned to the task at hand: gathering Mythics. It didn't take very long for Vasily to begin sniffing out small groups, pairs, and stragglers who were all making their way out from beneath the Brick. One by one, we convinced them to allow me to hide them, sheltering them in my Space.

Most of them, the Thinkers, Tinkers, Tamers, and Techs, simply froze in fear when they turned to see the gigantic werewolf bounding toward them, mouth open and tongue lolling. How were they supposed to know that the bared teeth and slavering tongue were actually betraying just how ecstatic the werewolf was to be doing something helpful?

The Tanks turned out to be far more problematic. With the return of their powers must have come a certain feeling of superiority and invulnerability. The first male Tank we encountered, a man wearing a black "Guns N' Roses" T-shirt, managed to get a few swings at Vasily, to his credit. The werewolf managed to dodge them easily, circling and whining in pleasure. Luckily, he was so occupied by Vasily that I was able to slip on my wristband and get behind him, grabbing a wrist as it wound up for another punch. The sudden loss of his powers startled the man enough that Vasily was able to dart in, catching him up in a bear hug—wolf hug?—that allowed me to speak to the man and convince him that we were friends, not enemies.

We worked that way for what felt like hours, Vasily constantly on the lookout for troops, but also Caine or his Faithful. I hadn't been into my Space to check on things inside since we started finding Mythics, but I estimated that we'd met up with easily hundreds. Compared to the several thousand I knew had been on the ranch, I couldn't escape the nagging guilt that there were thousands of them who were unaccounted for.

In front of me, Vasily paused in his zigzagging, tail still and straight out behind him, looking into the trees back toward the Brick.

"Harry," he rumbled.

Sure enough, Heretic dropped from the trees and walked toward us, straightening his jacket and his gloves.

"What's it look like back at the ranch?" I asked, nervous to hear the answer.

"As we suspected, they've set up their base of operations at the lodge. I would assume that Henry is their prisoner, though I didn't see him. They may be keeping him inside the lodge. The other Mythics, they've rounded up and are holding in several of the closer campsites under armed guard."

I groaned. "How many? Could you tell?"

The android shrugged, shaking his head. "I estimate a few hundred."

"That's all?" I grimaced. "That means there are still several thousand unaccounted for!"

The android nodded. "I fear that the more time that passes, the less likely it becomes that *we* will be the ones to find them. The military is instituting grid searches, aided by their helicopter, and Caine and his Faithful are still on the outskirts of the Brick, waiting for stragglers. It seems that things played out more or less just as he anticipated they would. No doubt he sees his role as merely cleanup at this point."

I hated just how true his statement felt.

"Is there any signal or a warning that we could send? How are the comms?"

Heretic shook his head. "Too risky. There's every likelihood that the military would intercept any message we sent. Anything accessible to Mythics will also be visible to the military or Caine."

"Then what's our play?" I asked, feeling entirely without options.

A deep rumble cut off any further discussion.

Vasily crouched low to the ground, his tail straight and stiff out behind him, his eyes and ears both fixed on the tree line at the far side of the no-man's-land.

He gave a single-word explanation: "Caine."

My stomach fell and my legs felt cold. I didn't think Caine could or would hurt me, but what about Vasily? What about Heretic?

Caine stepped from the trees, hands clasped behind his back, standing boldly and seemingly without concern outside the shelter of the trees. He raised one hand, beckoning with two fingers to the three of us.

Beside me, Vasily growled again, and Heretic stood loosely, hands slightly raised. He reminded me of a cornered cat, bunched up and ready to spring.

There was movement beneath the trees beyond Caine and I saw him wave back, shaking his head and saying something to those behind him. I saw more movement, then the shadows went still. He must have sent off whoever had approached. He looked back toward us, his shoulders squared and chin raised, the picture of brazen confidence.

"Do we run?" I asked quietly.

"No." Vasily let out a snarl and exploded into motion, launching himself forward, his feet throwing up chunks of charred dirt.

Caine didn't move. Vasily gave one last huge bound and flew through the air toward Caine, his claws reaching. Caine raised a single hand, and Vasily disappeared in a puff of white smoke. A tingle of equal parts panic and relief flooded through me as the were-wolf disintegrated; the white smoke meant he at least was alive, but Caine hadn't even flinched.

"Run." Heretic's voice beside me held something I'd never heard from the android. I felt certain that it was the edge of fear. I kicked my legs into motion, trying to build into a sprint across the bare dirt and rock.

"Head for the Brick!" Heretic said, turning sharply to the left. I turned just in time to be blasted off my feet by a blossoming gold explosion. I hit the earth heavily, landing on my back and pounding the air from my lungs. I threw myself over onto my front, trying to remember how to pull oxygen down my throat and failing. I managed to pull my knees beneath me and push up onto my hands and knees. I watched in horror as a pair of boots landed lightly in the dirt at the edge of my vision and walked slowly toward something to my left. Still scrambling for breath, I turned my head and saw Heretic launch onto his feet from his back, but only in time to disappear in a puff of white smoke.

My lungs remembered their role and filled with air. I gasped, gulping in oxygen as I struggled to stand. I turned to face him, but Caine had already started moving away, jogging quickly across the bare dirt. He turned to yell behind him, "Come, James. No doubt the humans heard that. It will not be long before they arrive to investigate. Follow me."

I couldn't yell. I couldn't scream. I wanted to, but I was afraid that if I did, I wouldn't stop. This man, my father, had destroyed everything. He'd left us with no alternative but to reveal ourselves to the rest of the world. He'd taken the Danton children from Safeguard custody and destroyed the Safeguard training facility, along with a significant number of its members. If it all came down to it, I was fairly certain that it was his influence that had put Julian Danton over the edge in driving him into madness and delusions of grandeur. Everything negative that had happened in my life for the last several years could be tied to this man and his insane mission of annihilation. I ran after him, pushing my legs into the earth and driving myself forward. With every pounding step, my anger built. He disappeared into the trees in front of me. I pumped my arms harder, leaning forward on the balls of my feet, everything I could think of to make myself move faster.

Entering into the perpetual twilight of the shadows beneath the trees, I slowed down for a moment as my eyes adjusted. It didn't take but a few seconds, then I pushed off again, my eyes boring holes in the back of his ridiculous trench coat.

He probably heard me coming; I wasn't trying to be quiet. He turned to face me. A few steps ahead of him, I slowed and raised my fist, fully intending on putting it straight through his skull. Just before I reached him, he sidestepped, pushing my arm further in the direction it was swinging and stealing my balance. I stumbled, trying to keep my feet beneath me. I felt a hard shove against my ribs and my balance failed completely, my shoulder driving down toward the ground again. I tried to recover into a roll, but the hard ground was punctuated with roots here, and the pain as several punched into my shoulder and sides as I crashed to the ground was awful.

Again lying on my back, I craned my head backward to try and keep Caine in view. It was difficult. He'd hardly moved from where he had stopped. I scrambled to my feet and started reaching out with my hand for a few atoms from my Space. He must have recognized what I was doing, because he darted forward and seized my left hand, clapping his own to mine, as if in a handshake. I had the strange impression that I'd just stuck my hand against the hose of a large vacuum, because our palms sucked together, my dirty and dusty one against his clean one.

Caine gripped my hand harder and clasped my elbow with his other hand. "James, I need you to calm down. It occurred to me that you still have an incomplete view of me. You surely noticed that I didn't Translate your strange mechanical companion, nor even the traitorous Vasily." He paused for a moment as if giving me time to think about what he'd said.

I relaxed the hand in his, and his own grip slackened in response.

"That's it," he encouraged.

I hated him for his patronizing tone.

He released my hand and stepped slowly backward, holding both his hands up in an attempt at a peaceful gesture.

I glared and squeezed my hands into fists. "What

makes you think you deserve a chance at further explanation?"

"The fact that you have neither allies nor options left."

His words bit into me, and I took several shuddering breaths.

"I am an open book to you, James. Ask me anything you will. I will not lie, nor will I shy from the truth. As an Interstitial, you deserve to have your questions answered and to make your choice from a position of knowledge and confidence, rather than the fear and half-truths of the Oppressors." He spread his arms. "Ask me anything."

I was torn. The last thing I wanted to do right now was to talk to this person, yet the opportunity to learn more about my abilities and my apparent heritage was too tempting to remain truly silent.

I folded my arms and channeled all of my anger and resentment into a glare, but still managed to ask, "How do you travel?"

He blinked and I saw his eyes smile, though he kept it off his lips. I pretended not to notice, holding onto my bitterness.

"I'll show you. Come with me."

"Where are we going?"

"Into the Fold. The space of Deliverance." He held his right hand out to me.

I hesitated, keeping both hands in my armpits for a moment longer. Finally, I managed to reach my right hand out without it shaking.

As soon as our hands touched, the world around me disappeared in white smoke, and the familiar blue dawn light of my Space—*his* space, rather—settled into existence. I looked around, expecting to see Heretic and Vasily.

"The Fold is infinite," Caine said quietly, releasing my hand. "Your friends are here, but they are also elsewhere for the time being. I assure you, they remain safe."

I shrugged, not sure what else to say.

He slipped out of his coat, letting it go, where it hung in midair.

"Travel within the Fold is one of the most critical abilities an Interstitial can master. It allows you to transport across lightyears or mere feet in the blink of an eye. Distance becomes no obstacle for you."

"Spare me the lecture. Can we just get to the point?" I found myself using the same tone of voice I'd used when I was a young teenager. My face went red, but I coughed and rubbed at my nose to cover it up.

Caine laughed. It wasn't a cackle or a cruel laugh; it was warm and full. It bothered me that it sounded so normal. It made me want to smile, which in turn made me want to vomit.

"Spoken with the impatience of true youth. Very well; less talk."

He closed his eyes and pushed his palms together. Light began filtering out between his fingers, and he suddenly spread his hands apart. As he did, the golden light between expanded, filling the expanse of the Fold, as he called it.

I blinked reflexively. As I did, the light collected and coalesced throughout the Fold, in groups and pockets that seemed random at first. After another moment and a slight refocus of my eyes, I gasped. I was looking at galaxies and star systems. I wasn't an expert, but I'd seen enough pictures of space formations to recognize the tell-tale swirl of galaxies.

"What is this?" I asked breathlessly.

"This is everything. All of existence, extrapolated from a single atom." He raised an arm and waved it from left to right, and everything around me slid to the right. My stomach lurched, and I had to put my head between my knees to resist throwing up.

"If we left the Fold now, you would find yourself in the immensity of empty space, beyond the pull of gravity from even the closest star." He put a finger out to a point just in front of his eyes. "Here."

"It's that easy?"

He laughed again. "Every task performed by the master appears easy to the novice. Also, if you were to attempt such a jump, the energy required to do so would consume every cell in your body. There wouldn't even be dust left. And even if you had the energy, the gravity fluctuations would rip you apart."

I stared at him, trying to gauge whether he was joking or not. "I can't tell if you're being serious right now."

He nodded, smiling with only his eyes. "Quite serious. The mechanics are simple; the cost is not."

"But you could make that jump?" I asked sarcastically.

Again, he nodded. The smile faded from his eyes. "With the right tools, yes. I could."

"What's the difference between the two of us?"

For the first time, Caine looked tired and I saw wrinkles form around his eyes. "The weight of a thousand lifetimes," he said quietly.

"What does that mean?" I pressed. If I was being honest, seeing that it caused him pain gave me a perverse satisfaction that left me ashamed.

He gave no immediate answer. Instead, he let out a breath as if he were relaxing and the lights of the entire universe simply dropped out of formation and winked out, like billions of embers disappearing in the night above a blaze.

Reaching for his coat, he pulled it on. After adjusting the lapels, he reached out with two fingers from his right hand and stabbed them into the air at his eyeline. The tips of both fingers disappeared. He lowered them through the air as if working an immense zipper.

I watched in growing disbelief as he created a large tear in the air in front of him, just slightly shorter than he was tall. He brought his hands together and pushed them into the tear at chest height, then separated them, creating an opening. Gold light, like the reflection of light on water, spilled out. Stepping aside, he held one hand up, as if holding a door for a stranger.

"After you," he said.

I took a step forward, my curiosity and amazement outweighing my fear and anger for the moment. I could fight him after I learned everything I could from him.

I squeezed through the opening he'd created, ducking my head and turning sideways to fit through. When I straightened, looking out ahead of me, I couldn't keep in the gasp that passed my lips.

Swirling, floating masses of bluish matter alight with gold flashes stretched as far as I could see in every direction. Ahead of me, behind me, to either side, even above and below, rows and rows and rows of swirling bubbles. From my own traumatic experience, I knew what these were. Each one of these orbs used to be a person.

Behind me, Caine stepped through.

"Behold," he said, heaviness and just a touch of bitterness in his voice. "The birthright and legacy of the Interstitial; the weight of a thousand lifetimes." He turned to look at me. "Behold your destiny."

Chapter 27

"I'm sorry, what?" I asked, my mouth beginning to fill with the taste of bile. My heart was hammering against my ribs; I could feel its chaotic flailing in my neck and face. I was dangerously close to throwing up. My arms were shaking as I supported myself on my knees. *People. These are all people.*

"I've been keeping this world free from Oppression for well over a thousand lifetimes now. This—" he turned slowly with his arms outstretched, taking in all directions. "Is both the spoils and the cost."

"The spoils? What the hell does that even mean?" My head was still reeling, and I struggled to catch my breath. *How many are there?*

"I know what you must think of me. I know what anyone who sees only part of what I do must think of me. It's monstrous." He turned again, his eyes reflecting the gold flashes as he took them all in. "But it's the price of true freedom." His eyes found mine again. There was an intensity and an openness in his face that I couldn't ignore. I knew, without a doubt, that what he was about to tell me would be his earnest, honest, raw truth.

"If you had any idea, James, what I've saved this world from. How many times I, and those who fight with me, have brought down a rising Oppressor? This world would be a very different place." He shifted uncomfortably, rubbing the cuff of one sleeve of his coat between the fingers of the opposite hand. "It's awful, I know—I'll be the first to agree—but what the humans have done with it is what they've chosen themselves. I pray—well..." He chuckled. "I *hope* every day that they make better choices, but it's undeniable that their choices remain their own. It's the most precious gift I can give."

I swallowed, but it was rough, and it took effort. "You think you're God," I spat. It was an accusation.

He straightened. "I didn't bring you here to debate the morality of my decisions. You asked about the energy required to travel. It lies here." He stepped to the nearest floating puddle and thrust his hand into the center of it. As he stood there, the shape dripped and flowed into a new form: a person. Like a three-dimensional swirling shadow, the gold light-infused puddle of blue became a woman, with bushy hair, and an athletic silhouette.

As I watched, the golden light swirling across the surface intensified, quickening and spiraling around Caine's hand. The light swirled faster and faster until it formed a solid ring that contracted and condensed until Caine withdrew his hand from the puddle, holding a shining sphere of golden light the size of a golf ball. Holding it in front of him, the gold light lit up his features, shadows exaggerating the furrow of his brow and the downturn of his mouth. *He genuinely takes no pleasure in what he's doing.*

Caine clenched his fist, and the light diffused into his hand, then traveled up his arm and throughout the rest of his body, gradually fading as it dispersed across his person.

"Why?" I asked quietly.

"I'm sorry?" he asked, his breathing rapid. He looked somehow younger.

"Why do you do it?" I repeated.

He scratched at the cuff of his coat again. "I told you, James. I'm protecting this world from—"

I interrupted, waving off the rest of his explanation. "No, yeah, I heard all that. I want to know why you keep doing it. I saw your face just now. You hate yourself. You hate what it is that you do. So, I ask again: why do you do it?"

He met my eyes again, and this time his eyes were undeniably sad. "Because until now, I've been the only one who can."

He took a step toward me. I tried to step away, but immediately felt an unfamiliar wave of emotions: fear, resentment, and a thirst for revenge. They didn't belong to me. I turned to look behind me at the mass of swirling blue and gold that had taken on a man's shape. I stepped forward again. There was nowhere to go.

Caine put a hand on my shoulder, touching, then withdrawing, and finally resting it on me, as if he weren't sure he should.

"James, you are my son. I had no idea you would inherit my capabilities as an Interstitial. How could I? From a matter of hours after you were born, I thought you were dead. But now, I find you not only alive but an Interstitial like me!" He brought his other hand up onto my other shoulder. Looking into his eyes, I could see something else in them. I wasn't sure what it was.

"You can take up my mantle. You've already proven yourself to have a good heart; Jessica, Steven, and the other two have told me what you did for them. I think, even then, you knew that you had to fight back against the Oppressors, that they had to be stopped and brought down."

I reached up and swept his hands off my shoulders. "You think that I want to become you?" I snorted. "You're a killer! A murderer!" I shook my head, my anger rising once more. "You really think those children that Heretic was protecting deserved to die? What exactly did they do that justified turning them into fuel for your twisted space shuttle?"

Pain crossed his face. I'd struck a nerve, and I pressed on it, harder. "You're just as bad as the Oppressors you claim to be against. And by the way— stop calling them that. They're Mythics, just like you.

And no matter what you keep telling yourself, they deserve just as much ability to choose as everyone else. You're punishing them for something people a long time ago in a galaxy far, far away did to you! You say you're all about people being able to choose for themselves: fine! Let people choose! Let the Mythics choose!"

He looked at me, and there was sadness in his eyes again. He looked at me, and he said nothing for several seconds. I was determined not to speak first. I simply stared back at him, refusing to back down or let him off the hook.

Caine smiled sadly. "Don't you think, in all those lifetimes, that I tried a different way?" He shook his head as he stepped back through the tear between the Folds. I followed him.

"I used to be exactly like you are now, James. Throughout several of the lifetimes, in fact. A number of times over." He pinched the tear closed again, the two sides of it knitting together and going seamlessly back in place until there was nothing to see anymore.

"Each time, I came to regret my decision. And each time after that, it took longer for me to find my hope again." He shook his head again. "I'm afraid I have none left. My actions, though reprehensible, even abominable, are the only means of preventing the repetition of the atrocities of my home world. I witnessed it time and time again. The Oppressor instinct is quite simply too strong."

I'd always been an empathic person. It's what led

me to the career path I'd chosen, where I'd practiced it professionally as a caregiver to young children. I could feel the sadness and devastation that this man, this ageless, nearly immortal man felt over his actions. Why couldn't he connect to that?

Caine closed his eyes, breathing slowly a few times, and the real world was constructed around us in silent white smoke.

"I don't believe that," I countered. "I know plenty of Mythics whose first instinct is to help, to serve, to do good."

"You've been lucky. I've known millions whose impulse was the opposite. Can you honestly say that you can't think of any who betray your own ideals in favor of those that more selfishly serve themselves?"

I hesitated as I recalled the many firesides I'd sat at just a few nights before, listening to the very opinions and attitudes Caine was describing.

Caine's face held no satisfaction as he pointed at mine. "There. You do. You see the terrible truth at the heart of what I speak." He sat heavily on a fallen tree trunk, exhaling. "There's one more thing you need to know." He rubbed his hands against his pants as if trying to dry them. *Is he nervous?*

"There's another price to pay. This one for all of us, Interstitial and Oppressor alike."

"Mythics," I corrected again. He waved me off.

"Anytime we use our power, it steals time off our lives."

"Excuse me?"

"It's true. It's not as noticeable now, because no one uses their power as frequently as they used to. But, it does."

"So, because you have access to your serial killer's gallery, what, you're just immune to that?" I couldn't believe it. *He's such a hypocrite!*

He nodded. "In a word, yes. That is a symptom that we escape. Our curse takes another form." He inhaled and exhaled once as if he were a physician preparing to drop a terminal diagnosis on a patient. "Interstitials, because we live unnaturally long lives, our powers take something else: our memories."

I snorted. "Are you telling me you have Alzheimer's?"

Again, he shook his head. "It's not like that. The more we use our powers, the less we remember of who we used to be. It begins with our earliest memories."

"Then how do you remember what life was like on your home planet?"

"We use a record, a journal, essentially. Within my corner of the Fold, I maintain a library that spans hundreds of thousands of years. It reminds me of where I came from, of what I'm preventing from happening here on Earth."

"Wait! So, you don't even actually remember your home world? You're just going on what you read about it in your journal?" I couldn't believe what I was hearing.

"It's more than that. It's not just a journal. The

closest thing I can compare it to would be a virtual reality simulator. A way to relive the past."

It was my turn to shake my head. "What are you hoping for from this conversation, exactly?"

Caine stood again, recovering some of his old confidence. "I want you to join me, James. I want you to allow me to teach you how to fully use your powers, to become the next defender of Earth!"

I swore. "You gave yourself a title? You're unbelievable!"

He smiled slightly. "Well, it was never official..."

I groaned.

"It would be so simple, James. All you need to do is sweep the contents of your part of the Fold between Deliverance and Translation; all of those you have would be Translated in an instant. It would be painless. They wouldn't even realize what was happening!"

My jaw dropped, and my blood boiled. "You realize that you're casually encouraging me to commit mass murder?!"

"All I'm saying—"

I didn't hear all of what he was saying. I hit him with a blast that sent him tumbling back over the log he'd been sitting on, and I ran. I turned around and sent another blast shooting behind me to keep him off-balance.

I ran until I couldn't run anymore. Then I hid, waiting for several minutes until I was sure I wasn't being followed.

I'd learned a lot, but most importantly, I'd learned for certain that Caine was a madman, and I wanted nothing to do with him. He had captured Heretic, Vasily, and who knew how many of the other Mythics from the camp. I needed backup. I didn't think I could do this on my own. More importantly, I didn't want to.

It was time to take on the United States Military.

Chapter 28

I retraced my steps after several hours and found my way back to where I'd stashed the pack with Heretic and Vasily. I realized that I needed to get myself to a place where I could see what was going on in the camp. I spent most of the night climbing a peak I could remember seeing from the lodge. From there, I would be high enough to see down into the valley and the lodge. I could have attempted to teleport there, but I was still nervous about it after my demonstration from Caine.

When I finally reached the peak, I couldn't suck air fast enough, and my legs were jelly. I had no doubt that this was the highest elevation I'd ever been to in my life, and it felt like it. Looking across the valleys and seeing several even higher peaks surrounding me, I couldn't imagine being at the height they were at. I made a mental note never to climb Everest. I reached into the pack and removed a pair of heavy binoculars that I'd found the previous day while going through its contents.

I silently blessed Henry Hoover. After fiddling with

several knobs, dials, and switches on the tubes of the binoculars, I was examining the lodge through night vision lenses with adjustable zoom. I could make out the individual faces of those walking back and forth between the lodge and the rest of the camps.

Heretic had been right; there were hundreds of Mythics being held in tight groups around the fires of the camps by rings of soldiers holding rifles. I scanned group after group until I found who I was looking for. I could see Clara, Pat, and Sammy in the second camp from the lodge. I couldn't find Henry until I turned the binoculars on the lit front of the lodge. Through the large front windows, I could see Henry, sitting on one of the couches in the entrance, flanked by armed guards and talking animatedly with what must have been some high-ranking officer.

Digging into the pack again, I pulled out some jerky to chew on and took a swallow of water from a bottle, then settled into the down sleeping bag I also managed to produce. For the second time that night, I thanked Henry Hoover for his foresight and preparedness.

I didn't think the military would keep their prisoners at the lodge for very long. I turned out to be right. After another hour of restless napping, where I only caught a few moments of sleep in between scans of the camp so as not to miss anything, I watched through the binoculars as they began loading Mythics from the camps into armored troop carriers for transport, presumably back to the city. It was harder to make out faces now, as the brightening sky in the east provided enough light to render the night vision less effective, but not enough to see clearly through the regular lenses.

This wasn't going to be pretty. As soon as the first carrier left the shelter of the Brick, I felt certain that the Mythics within would waste no time in using their powers to escape. There had to be a way to communicate between them to coordinate any escape attempt.

Unfortunately, there was no time to think through things and come up with a foolproof, well-informed plan with contingencies. I had to act now. The first carrier had begun moving, making its way down the road a short way. I was in luck; the first one stopped down the road, where it sat waiting for the rest of the convoy. They had ten transport vehicles in all, each pulling a secondary trailer behind it that also carried human cargo. I counted as they loaded the second transport; they piled twelve Mythics along with four armed troops into the main vehicle, with another sixteen Mythics and four troops going into the trailer. That made two hundred and eighty Mythics, all told, if they filled each transport to capacity. Not a bad start to an army if it came to that.

I scrambled to put everything back into the pack except the binoculars, which I left hanging around my neck. Then, I placed my right hand on the pack and it disappeared in a puff of white smoke. I didn't know why I hadn't thought of storing it in my Space—in the Fold—before. Still getting used to it, I guess. I kicked myself, thinking of how easier it would have been to climb the mountain in the dark last night if I hadn't had the huge pack on my back.

I breathed out a long breath, watching it steam out forcefully in front of me and then disappear into the air. The fourth transport pulled forward, filled to capacity. I only had a few minutes left before they'd all be on their way out from under the Brick, and it would be too late to do anything.

I tried to work a plan in my head, backtracking from the hoped-for outcome. I needed them to wait until the last transport had completely left the Brick before anyone made their move. That meant getting a signal of some kind and communicating with those in the front transport. Comms weren't an option, and I couldn't exactly just send an email. My heart started double-tapping in my chest. I was going to have to teleport in somehow. There wasn't any other option.

Closing my eyes, I focused my attention inward, trying to somehow calm my heart and still my lungs. After a moment, the wind tugging at my hair and brushing my skin faded away, and I knew I'd made it into my part of the Fold.

Several loud, shuddering wails forced my eyes open. Several white-haired individuals huddled close together, a few of them fallen to their knees. They were all staring at me as if I had two heads. I peeked over my shoulder to check that they weren't looking at someone or something behind me: nothing.

I was puzzled; none of the people here looked

familiar. Come to think of it, I couldn't even remember having brought so many older Mythics into the Fold.

One of the women who had fallen to her knees had her hands cupped to her face, and I could see she was crying. I took several steps toward the group, intending on helping the woman to stand up. The others didn't look like they were in much better shape than she was.

When I moved toward them, one of the old men stepped in front of her, holding up his hands ready to fight. In a shaky, age-ridden voice, he said, "What the hell happened? You never came back!"

I stopped. My mind raced and plummeted into blank walls over and over again. *What is he talking about?* I took in this man, with his cargo pants and his "Guns N' Roses" tee. The inside of my mouth dried up and I had difficulty swallowing.

"You—I—how long do you think you've been here?" I whispered.

"Think?" the old Tank asked, taking a halting step toward me. Several of the others hissed for him to be quiet.

One of the Mythic women—who looked vaguely familiar now, as I tried to imagine everyone I'd brought in, just older—spoke up from behind a hand she held to her mouth.

"We've been in here for years—decades! It's been impossible for us to know, really, but—" She gestured to herself, then the others, and snorted sarcastically.

Her voice quavered as she fought to hold back the tears that glistened above her lower eyelids. "We gave up hoping that you would ever come back!"

Suddenly I knew how it was that the Danton children strangely all seemed the same age. I only had time to connect these dots before I was forced back into the moment.

"Dozens of us are already dead!" the shaky Tank shouted, breathing hard just with the effort of his outburst.

My head was reeling. *I did this. I'm responsible. More deaths on my hands.*

"I can fix this." The words were a croak in my dusty throat, and I had to clear it to get them out again. "I can fix this!"

"You can't fix dead!" The Tank shouted, and the others in the group shook with tears and sobs.

Part of me was screaming that I had to hurry, that the convoy would be leaving the Brick any second. I had to force myself to remember that time worked very differently in the Fold. Obviously. I needed to get to my Translation Fold.

"Give me just a minute!" I said, closing my eyes and licking my lips to prepare to concentrate.

"We've given you years!" the Tank hissed.

I didn't open my eyes, but his words cut me deeply. The truth does that. I'd made a terrible mistake, and others had paid a terrible price for it.

I stabbed my two fingers into the air in front of me, thinking only of the Translation Fold. I didn't feel anything. No impression of another space. I took a breath and tried again. Still, nothing.

"What is that, yoga?" the old man spat.

"No! Just—Please!" I closed my eyes tighter, clasping my hands over my nose and mouth in desperation, then sliding them together in front of the tip of my nose. I tried to focus on my breathing, counting the breaths in and out. I reached out with one hand, slowly curling in all but the first two fingers. I squeezed those two fingers together, imagining inserting them into a lock in the air in front of me.

There was no warmth, no breath of cold air, no difference to confirm it, but somehow, I knew that it had worked this time. I slowly lowered the hand, imagining pulling down a great zipper through the air in front of me. I opened my eyes. Through a tear, I saw several floating puddles, two of which glowed with the now equally familiar and haunting golden flashes of light.

Ignoring the gasps from the aged Mythics behind me, I stepped through the tear. Suddenly having a thought, I turned back to the opening.

"Don't come through here; you'll die! I'll be out in just a second."

Praying that they would believe me, I turned back to the issue at hand. I walked to the largest of the puddles in the air. Close enough to touch it, I felt a flood of emotions, and the puddle morphed into the outline of Julian Danton once more. The gold flashes crossed the entire silhouette. I pushed my hand deeper into the puddle, moving it into the center of the silhouette's chest, trying not to think about what —who—this mass used to be.

What now? I focused on the gold flashes of light. I remembered the light when I'd shown Foster and his SWAT officers my abilities, how it had responded to my gestures and intentions. Hand still within the puddle, I reached out with my fingers, imagining that I was beckoning the light in.

It took everything in me to not yank my hand out as the lights started swirling concentrically toward the center. I couldn't suppress the shiver and jolt that passed up my spine and over my skin.

Just as they had for Caine, the lights spun faster, the closer they came to the center and my hand. As they consolidated into a single contracting circle, I felt a blossom of warmth around my hand. The circle became a sphere, and I slowly closed my fingers around it, holding it like I would a bird I didn't want to crush or let fly away.

I withdrew my hand carefully, unsure about what would happen next. The sphere of golden light rested in my palm, appearing on the surface still and unmoving. But I knew, somehow, that the lights were swirling faster than they ever had before, the illusion of stillness through rapid motion.

I turned back toward the tear, holding my breath as I watched the golden ball. I walked back through, moving as though I held a cup of water that was filled to the brim and trying not to spill it.

I stepped carefully through the opening, careful not

to move my hand too much. Truthfully, I had no idea if the substance I was holding would react negatively to being jostled or not; it just seemed prudent to take precautions.

"Who's first?" I asked, turning to look at the group of Mythics leaning on each other for support. More had gathered, coming from who-knows-where.

"What is that?" someone asked. I didn't see who had asked the question. I was still focused on the ball of light.

"This will make you young again," I said, carefully raising it up.

The crowd whispered and muttered.

"We trusted you once, and some of us paid for it with our lives! Why would we do it again?" someone yelled.

"Because you're out of allies and options." Caine's words rolled off my tongue before I even realized I was thinking them. I cringed, but I continued to hold out the ball.

No one moved for several moments, then a woman stepped forward. I could remember meeting her with Vasily, promising her safety, then taking her into the Fold. Her gray hair, the wrinkles below the corners of her mouth and around her eyes, and the arthritic curl of her hands stood out like accusations to me. "I'll try it."

I nodded gently, then held out my other hand, palm up, asking for hers. She put one tremoring hand on top of mine. I turned her hand over, sliding my own underneath it and holding it up, then carefully tipped the golden sphere into her cupped palm.

"Now squeeze it," I said, my voice a whisper as I prayed that it would work.

The woman closed her fingers around the sphere, and her hand stopped shaking. Just as it had with Caine, the light dissipated into her hand then up her arm and throughout her body. Watching her closely, I heard her give a small gasp, but her face didn't look like she was in pain.

Slowly, slow enough that I couldn't even pinpoint what was changing, she began to look younger. Her hair wasn't quite as gray, browner. Her face wasn't nearly as wrinkled, and her hands were not nearly so curled and drawn.

The whispers from the group behind her grew louder and more frantic as the moments passed. I simply stood there, watching her in equal parts fascination, amazement, and disbelief. After a minute, I would have guessed her age to be in the early to mid-forties. It had worked.

The woman held up her hands, peering at the palms and backs, then ran them through her hair several times, then over her face, feeling the old familiar contours and curves. She laughed, then reached out and slapped me, hard.

"That's for dumping us here!"

I hadn't even opened my eyes from the slap before I felt her arms around my chest, hugging me tightly.

Muffled from the folds of my bunched shirt, I heard her say through sobs, "This is for coming back!"

I hesitated for just a moment, then returned her hug, holding her as we both wept.

I opened my eyes when the whispering reached a crescendo that I could no longer ignore and someone shouted, "I'm next!" The crowd had grown, but only to about fifty or so. I started to wonder just how many had died since I'd put them in, then shook off the thought. I didn't think I was ready to face it just yet.

"I only have enough for one more," I shouted, then had to raise my voice even louder to be heard over the resulting groans and moans. "But I know where to get more!" To myself, I whispered, "A lot more."

***

I was prepared for booby traps or alarms— something— when I opened a tear into Caine's Translation Fold. I wasn't sure that I would even be able to before pushing apart the sides of the tear and the now-familiar gold light spilled out.

I turned to the crowd of several hundred aged Mythics who had gathered in groups of three to five. I swallowed and took in a long breath, letting it out slowly. The number who'd died must not have been as great as I was afraid of.

"No one can follow me through this..." I hesitated, looking at the tear in the air. "...opening. If you do, you'll die, do you understand?" I looked out at the crowd, trying to make direct eye contact with as many individuals as possible. Those who met my eyes nodded quickly, then looked away, clearly uncomfortable.

I stepped through, the floating light-streaked puddles all around me. I looked behind me, waiting for a moment to be sure that no one would try and follow in misplaced enthusiasm. No one even stepped close enough to the opening for me to see them.

They're afraid of me. I had the thought with a jolt.

I shook my head to clear it. The sooner I resolved this situation, the sooner I could get back to the one I'd left outside the Fold in the military convoy. It was slow going, but I knew that didn't necessarily mean as much in here. I repeated the process mindlessly hundreds of times: insert a hand in a puddle, swirling lights, ball of gold. The crowd of Mythics gradually transitioned from a shuffling throng of old folks to a shifting mob of young people, moving explosively from place to place as they talked among each other. I tried to ignore the variety of looks shot my way. For every one person who thanked me, there were ten who glared continuously, merely grunting or receiving the gold ball in silence.

When the last person had been restored, I closed the tear and then turned to face them, shouting and waving my arms to be heard.

"I need your help!" I called out, then cleared my throat.

"We don't owe you a thing!" a male voice at the back of the group called out.

"You don't give orders anymore!" a female voice shouted in agreement.

I nodded in acceptance. "I'm not giving any orders. I'll return anyone who wants to return to the outside. But let me explain what's going on out there." I shifted nervously. This was the first time I was addressing a group of Mythics like this without Clara or another higher-ranking Safeguard member present. Everything from here on in was on my shoulders. I blew out quickly in preparation.

"There are several hundred Mythics who have been captured by the military. When I entered the Fold," I pointed around us, "they were loading them into several armored transport carriers, probably to take them back to the city for… something." *Trial? Imprisonment?* I had no idea.

I continued my speech. "I can't tell you how sorry I am for what happened here. I wanted to help, and I waded into using powers I'm still only beginning to understand."

Rumbles of angry murmurs rolled over the crowd. "I'll take all accountability for those who passed in here. I never meant for that to happen. But right now, we still all have friends and family who are out there in danger. We don't actually know what will happen to them in government custody. That might be the scariest thing about all of this." I again made direct eye contact across the group. I saw the same fear I felt reflected in numerous sets of eyes. "They need us right now." I still saw more than a few angry faces, but even those were nodding.

"We're out of allies, out of options." It bothered me that Caine's words still resonated so deeply with me. "But if there's one thing I know about Safeguard, it's that when our backs are to the wall, we're able to make it out and manage the situation, even when it seems like an impossible mess!" For the first time, I heard rumbles of assent, mingled with nods.

"How many Tanks do we have here?" Several hands went up.

"How many Thinkers?" Many more hands.

"Techs?" A comparable number of hands were raised across the group.

I nodded a few times, planning.

"All right," I started. "Here's what I'm thinking."

Chapter 29

Through the binoculars, I watched soldiers close the doors of the final vehicle of the convoy and tap on the outside. I couldn't hear it, but I could see the vehicle shudder as the engine started, then bounce and jostle as it started forward. I heard a very faint air horn. It must have been a predetermined signal because the other vehicles in the convoy also shuddered, then began rolling one by one, beginning at the first.

The cab of the first vehicle crossed the border of the Brick, and I closed my eyes. It was getting easier and easier to go into the Fold, each time I did it.

The crowd of Mythics crowded around, arranged in the groups I'd directed them into.

"Group A, ready?" Seven Mythics raised their hands. I stepped over to them. "Two Thinkers, Tech, Tank?" I asked.

They looked at each other, and gradually four hands rose into the air.

"Take hands," I said. The four of them joined hands, leaving a space for me.

I took a deep breath. Now came my difficult part. I put my hands together, then stopped.

"Maybe I'll try this on my own first." I walked several dozen yards away as the crowd looked curiously on. Nothing like trying a new skill with an audience.

I put my hands together in front of me and closed my eyes. *All of Existence, extrapolated from a single atom...*

With my mind, I reached outside the Fold, for a single atom. I felt a weight on the palm of my right hand. I focused on my Translation Fold and felt an answering weight on my left palm. Holding my breath, I pressed the two palms tighter together and felt instant warmth between them.

Opening my eyes, the gold light leaked from my hands, and I cupped them tighter, glancing nervously at the group within shouting distance as I remembered the last time I'd performed this maneuver outside the Fold.

What next? I panicked slightly as I realized I didn't know. I focused my attention on the warmth and light between my hands and tried to remember what Caine had done. I remembered him throwing his hands wide and the lights of the universe scattering into place. I was loath to throw my hands out, though. I could still smell the burning hair, skin, and flesh of the officers closest to my last failed demonstration.

I shook off the unpleasant thought, renewing my focus. There were no other options. I either did this successfully, or we were completely out of options.

This was our only shot at recovering from everything that had happened the last couple of days.

I could feel the reaction in my hands building, energy collecting. It felt a little like holding onto a handful of sand; no matter how hard I tried, I could feel more and more escaping as my hands filled. I focused on the reaction and tried to tune into it as I had just before things had gone so bad with the SWAT team.

I could feel the energy, feel it spinning and revolving in my hands. I panicked, not wanting it to explode again. I couldn't reverse the reaction, but I couldn't bring myself to move forward with it, either. I stood paralyzed, unable to close my hands further, unwilling to let them open. Finally, the reaction decided for itself; my hands blew apart and I flew backward, tumbling in the air.

Without true gravity, it was too disorienting to simply try again with the group above me, standing on the wall, so I oriented myself back with them, planting my feet in the nothing of the floor of the Fold.

There was a flurry of movement and sound from the group of Mythics. My blowing myself up was neither building confidence nor winning me friends. I squared my shoulders and spread my feet. *This has to work.*

Once again, I gathered individual atoms, a normal one from outside, and an antimatter atom from the Translation Fold, and initiated the reaction.

This one blew me backward, but less; I opened my hands earlier in the reaction.

Three more times I attempted to materialize the

star map that Caine had shown me. Once more it blew up in my face, once I accidentally sent the normal atom back outside, and once I did somehow manage to extinguish the reaction. I must have sent the whole thing into the Translation Fold.

The crowd of Mythics was beginning to converge again, the groups gathering together, assumedly to discuss my failure to deliver on my promises.

I closed my eyes, and I simply stood there, breathing. I lost track of how long. Time in the Fold was one resource I had in spades. I decided to make good use of it. I cleared my mind of everything I could, letting myself hear nothing but my breathing, pushing away every insistent thought that tried to push itself in. After my breathing and my heartbeat slowed to slower than I thought possible, I let myself think clearly of one thing, and one thing only: the star map.

Eyes still closed, I raised both my hands out to my sides, calling the now-familiar single opposing atoms necessary for the reaction. I brought my hands together, steady and still. I saw the shapes, the clouds, and the swirling discs of galaxies at every possible stage of formation and dissolution. The warmth filled my hands. Instead of trying to control it, to keep it contained, I set it free, nudging it outward in unfettered expansion and growth. Acting on nothing but pure hope and instinct, I swept my hands apart in the same manner I'd seen Caine use.

Something felt different. Rather than the burst of

an explosion, I had a sensation of spreading warmth, like walking toward a fire on a cold night. I opened my eyes, and the galaxies and formations that had filled my head filled the Fold, motion and life captured in three brilliant gold dimensions. I choked on a laugh that was mostly sobbing, and my eyes burned. *This was going to work!*

The group of Mythics all shared the same wide-eyed, open-mouthed amazement that I'd felt when I'd witnessed Caine show me the map. The map started to shake and falter, so I turned my focus back on it. *How do I know where I am?*

Staring at the endless expanse of the universe, I thought I saw a formation glimmer slightly differently than the others. Reaching out through the air, I tried swiping, as if the entire room were a giant touch screen. Nothing happened. I tried again, with the same result. I reached one hand more tentatively into the air and tried to focus all my attention on the sensation at my fingertips.

As I moved my hand through the air slowly, I felt a subtle variation in the space in front of me. Moving the fingers back, I felt, not with the fingertips themselves, but more so in my soul—it felt like—tiny impressions in the very air, like grooves in the blade of a pocket-knife. Feeling carefully, minutely, and trying my best not to imagine what I looked like to the Mythics shuffling constantly closer, I found a grip with each finger on my right hand and gently applied pressure, drawing it back toward me. The room shifted, visually sliding in the direction I pulled. I heard a retch as someone lost their last meal—*which was what, exactly? Focus!*

I repeated the process several times, getting faster with each draw. The moans behind me had decreased in both volume and frequency. They were either used to it, or they had decided to close their eyes. Finally, the galaxy that had caught my eye was directly in front of my face. As it came closer, the glimmer I'd noticed concentrated on a specific point. I reached up, feeling for impressions, and caught them with both hands within the galaxy. Then, I pulled with my hands, stretching the galaxy apart. In a flash, we were within it, gas clouds, celestial formations, and stars first growing then disappearing beyond my ability to see them. I kept zooming in until a single tiny star caught my attention. Pulling it close, I pulled us in toward it and saw several tiny objects surrounding it. One of the objects gleamed brighter than the others for just a moment.

Earth. Familiar now with both process and mechanics, I zoomed in swiftly, led by the gently pulsing light that was my constant guide. Familiar continents, North America, found the Great Salt Lake, traveled east and pushed in closer and closer. The mountain range, the Uintas, spread from east to west. Forest green blankets materialized and then disappeared as individual trees took their place. A moment later, a huge blank area on the map appeared. The Brick. I was looking closely at the military convoy, the first vehicle frozen in time just inside the border of the area that Caine had cleared with his blast soon after his arrival.

I stared, not quite believing what I was seeing. I expanded the convoy, centering on the lead vehicle. In no time, I was standing inside the vehicle, seeing lit in brilliant gold the six Mythics seated along each wall, the four soldiers standing ready in the aisle, rifles shouldered and pointed at the floor of the vehicle.

I waved to the four Mythics who'd raised their hands to my questions so many minutes—hours? —ago. "Let's go! This is it!" The four of them came to stand by my side, the two Thinkers putting themselves close enough to touch two of the four soldiers each. The Tank went to stand near the rear door of the vehicle. The Tech went to stand in the aisle close to the driver and the soldier riding shotgun. I hadn't realized that the driver was accessible through the rear.

"We need one additional Thinker per vehicle! We need to take care of the driver and the soldier in shotgun." I waved for one additional Mythic to join the group. A woman wearing black plastic-framed glasses and a ponytail jogged over, taking up her place next to the Tech. She nodded at me.

I looked around me, at the mind-boggling display of gold lights recreating every detail of the world outside. I looked at the Mythics, whom I realized were all looking at me. I nodded once, which they returned. "Remember, keep things under control until the last vehicle is out from under the Brick. We get out as many as we can in this single take. Who knows when our next opportunity to rescue folks will be? Everyone clear?"

Every Mythic head nodded. I took a breath. "Okay." Reaching out, I stood in the space between the two Thinkers closest to the front of the vehicle. Each of the Mythics in this group took up hands, careful to avoid touching any lights within the vehicle that represented people or objects.

"Here we go," I whispered, more to myself than anyone else. I took the two Thinkers' hands, closed my eyes, and took a breath. I opened my eyes, exhaled, and the gold lights became skin tones, dull metal, army fatigues, and a dozen puzzled Mythics. "No one do anything!" I shouted into the small confines of the carrier. That was all the time I had. I let go of the two Thinkers' hands, closed my eyes, and went back into the Fold.

I felt winded as if I'd just run a great distance. I felt tired like it, too. Mythics ran to me in groups of several. They'd disbanded again.

"How long have I been gone?" I asked, looking around at the faces. I didn't think they looked noticeably older, but I probably wouldn't notice unless it had been years. I'd only been gone for literally a few seconds in the real world. What did that translate to here?

Several of them shook their heads, and a few shrugged.

"Not really sure. Maybe a few months?"

I swore. How was that even possible?

"Okay, we can handle that. How's everyone doing? Anyone need a pick-me-up?" I looked around the group, checking in on individual faces as much as possible. No one spoke up.

"All right, then next group." I looked around. "I need the two Thinkers and the Tank for the trailer of the first vehicle."

The three Mythics requested stepped forward.

This time, when I pulled up the star map after a few tries, it took only a few seconds to navigate to the convoy.

I cursed again.

The trailer of the first vehicle was only partially protruding from the blank space of the Brick. Inside, there was only a small space where we could fit the four of us in the aisle between the seats along the walls. Only one of the soldiers was visible.

I looked around me at the three Mythic volunteers.

"What do you think? Do we risk it? Or do I go back outside and wait for the trailer to leave the Brick?"

"What, without us? You do realize that we still have to wait, right? It's only seconds for you, but we live weeks in limbo in here?" One of the Mythics in the larger group spoke up.

I flinched. It was true, and I didn't feel good about it, either.

"You're right. But, there's not really anything we can do about it. I can only take out the few that will fit in each vehicle on each jump. I can't take everyone, or I would. I hate that you're all in here just waiting. Any solutions?"

One woman raised her hand. "Why can't we all go out to a safe location and wait there?" Then you can pick us up in the groups that you need, bring us here, then into position in the convoy?"

I hadn't thought of that. It did make sense, except for one thing.

"What if Caine finds you?" I asked.

"How would he?" someone replied. "Surely he couldn't find us in seconds?"

They had a point. It was a good plan. I didn't know why I hadn't thought of it.

"That could work. Definitely be easier for all of you. A little more work for me, but definitely worth it if you all don't have to wait for months and years, right?" I laughed a little. There were a lot of nods. I couldn't blame them.

"Next question is, where to take you all? And that means you'll all have only seconds before it's your turn. You'll need to stand in tight formation, and in order, so I can just transport and bring you into the Fold right away. But that's doable, right?" More nods.

"Okay, how about the middle of nowhere several miles away?"

"Wait, but what if something happens to you?" someone asked.

I paused. Another good point. "Good point. Where, then?" I didn't want to leave them stranded in the middle of nowhere with no idea where they were and no supplies to survive. No one had any quick solutions. I knew one place where there typically weren't many people, and where they'd be safe for a while, at least.

"Everyone take hands. I know where you can go."

Like everything, creating and manipulating the map came easier with each practice. In no time at all, I was looking at a black hole in the middle of the forest in Illinois. Home.

I turned to the group. "This is my house, where Jared and Deby lived, probably where Safeguard was born. You'll be safe here. If I don't come back, you can let yourselves into the house and use this to access all of the secret hidey-holes." I took the wristband out of my pocket and quickly explained where to find all of the Safeguard secrets I knew about. I handed the wristband to the Tank in the Guns N' Roses shirt.

"That's that. I'll either take that back from you on the last trip, or you can use it to get in. Either way, keep it safe, all right?"

The man nodded, putting it in his pocket.

I rubbed my hands together. "All right, well, let's do this, and I'll see you all in a few seconds!" I tried to laugh, and so did a few of the others.

The whole group got into their small squads, then held hands.

"Remember, as soon as I leave you there, everyone drops hands except for the smaller groups. It's gonna happen fast." I gave the two Mythics' hands I held what I hoped was a reassuring squeeze.

The golden lights of the forest at the edge of my property solidified into the greens and greys of trees in full summer foliage and I yelled, "Everyone else let go! Group A trailer, hold tight!" I dropped the hand in my left and kept hold of the one on my right, the first of the group I was after. We popped back into the Fold, the blue-grey mist back in a wave of white smoke.

I dropped the hand, gasping for air and feeling as if I'd just run a marathon. My legs had no strength, and I could no longer stand.

"You okay?" the man whose hand I'd been holding bent down, putting his hand on my back. My arm shook as I raised it, waving him off.

"Fine. Give—Give me a minute." I stayed on my knees for several moments, refusing to look up and check if they were watching me. I didn't want whatever it was they were holding in their eyes for me at that moment.

When I could, I stood up, wiping my nose on the back of a tremoring forearm. I didn't push away or protest the hand that one of the women put out to steady me. I looked at her and smiled. "Boy!" I said, trying to make light of it. "That one really took it out of me!"

The woman managed a grimacing smile in return. *I feel the same way.*

I managed to stand with my knees only slightly shaking. I locked them to try to rein in the movement.

"Okay, let's do this!" I said, trying to fill my voice

with enthusiasm I definitely wasn't feeling at that moment.

It took me more tries this time to get the star map right. I was so tired, I just couldn't quite focus completely on the hand movements I'd been practicing, like trying to tie a shoe when your hands are cold. Finally, the gold light again diffused through the Fold, and my arms sagged as I navigated once more to the mountains and the convoy. This time, the trailer was completely out from under the Brick. When we went inside, it was much easier for the two Thinkers and the Tank to take up their positions.

I straightened up, my arms shaking from supporting my weight on my knees.

"Ready? Remember, incapacitate the soldiers, and prevent an early breakout."

"Yeah, yeah, we know! Do it already!" The Tank in this group was a tough-looking woman wearing a denim jacket vest over a black tank top and thick-soled, tall boots. I decided quickly that she wouldn't look at all out of place astride a chopper motorcycle.

I took in a heave of air and let it out slowly, then took hold of the other woman's hand, who in turn held the other Thinker man's, who held the Tank woman's hand.

At the very end of my breath, the interior of the troop carrier materialized, and I immediately let go of the Thinker woman's hand, letting myself fall back into the Fold.

I just kept falling. I felt a sharp pain in my chest near

my heart, and it felt like I had a bull elephant sitting on my ribcage; no matter how hard I tried, I couldn't draw in a breath. I wasn't sure which was screaming louder in protest, my empty lungs, or my starving brain. Either way, it only lasted a moment before I blacked out, and didn't see or feel anything more.

Chapter 30

I had no idea how long I was out for. Could have been seconds, could have been the equivalent of months. I had no idea. When I finally came to, even the effort of opening my eyes required several tries to muster.

My whole body felt slack, like a bike tube straight out of the box; not just slack, but actively compressed, as if someone had duct-taped the end of a vacuum hose to my mouth and walked away. To my great relief, I noticed that the elephant seemed to have moved from my chest. I was at least breathing.

What do I do? I can't even hardly move! With normal gravity not an obstacle in the Fold, I was able to bring one of my hands up even with my eyes. If I'd been in the real world, collapsed on the floor, I wasn't sure that I'd have been able to fight gravity and the ground to get it there.

Caine's words came back to me in a surge of panic: *"If you were to attempt such a jump, the energy required to do so would consume every cell in your body. There wouldn't even be dust left."*

I guess I'd underestimated how much energy even jumps just here on Earth would require.

With a jolt of nausea, I realized I had only one option. I extended two fingers on the hand in front of my face, and the entire arm quivered and shook with the effort. I'd seen the same movement in elderly folks with Parkinson's. I poked my fingers into the air, feeling for the lock I'd imagined before. I felt the difference and started pulling down. I was only able to make an eight-inch tear before the effort became too much, and the arm simply stopped responding to my signals.

For the next several minutes, all I could do was lay there, staring through the small tear, wondering if I was going to die staring at the solution to my problem. The gold lights were mesmerizing, watching them circle, dive, and race over the surface of the floating blue puddles.

I refuse to die here, staring into the light of the Fold, while the Mythics outside are captured or killed! I managed to push my arm forward just a touch more, sliding it through the opening toward the nearest puddle.

I felt a rush of emotions: love, fear, anger, jealousy, rage. The puddle morphed into the shape of a man wearing some sort of skirt or long dress on his lower half, but a bare top. Then, my fingers were within the puddle, and the gold lights began their characteristic swirl.

A moment later, I pulled my hand back just enough

to expose the golden sphere of light, then squeezed it between the two fingers and my thumb.

Warmth flooded up my fingers. With the warmth came energy. I could feel the rush of life spread over my body. When it reached my head, it brought freedom. I hadn't known how heavy and weighed down I'd felt until that very moment. I felt like a hot air balloon that had just had all its mooring lines cut and its ballast bags dropped. I felt myself shooting upward, free and unfettered, capable of anything. I felt invincible. For a moment, nothing mattered besides just how good I felt at that moment. I felt light, free, and at peace.

When I finally remembered what I was doing in the Fold, I felt no rush, no pressure to perform. I pinched the tear closed, summoned the star map, and easily found the Brick in Illinois and the waiting group of Mythics. I made the jump easily, reached out to grab the closest hand of the next carrier group, and reverted quickly back into the Fold.

After that, the next three sets of transports went quickly and without incident. After every other jump, I would open a tear and take in another golden light orb, and the feeling of freedom, detachment, and pleasure would intensify. *I could go on doing this for eternity!* If this was what immortality felt like, I would gladly do whatever it took to chase that feeling forever. The best part? It was easily within my grasp, as an Interstitial. And I didn't even have to do anything for it. Caine's store was practically limitless.

I had just taken the last group into the final trailer and departed into the Fold. All that was left was for me to transport just outside the convoy and send the signal, a harmless blast in the air that would let the waiting Mythics know that the last vehicle was out of the Brick and time to make our escape.

Everything had gone perfectly. I had executed my part to perfection! Every convoy vehicle: twenty jumps into individual carriers, twenty jumps to Illinois and the group. I manipulated the star map to show the field outside the Brick and jumped to a point maybe a hundred yards away from the road. As the world solidified around me, I prepared to throw the atoms that would make the signal burst.

Before I could, several things happened at once. Several whole trees, roots still trailing huge clumps of earth, came flying from the trees ahead to land across the road in front of the lead vehicle. The moment they hit the ground with a shuddering crash, they burst into searing flame, spontaneously and without explanation.

At the same time, the ground on either side of the road suddenly heaved, huge berms rising up like crashing waves only to freeze at their highest point, effectively locking in place the entire line of transports. They were trapped.

I dropped to the ground, scanning wildly for the Faithful. It didn't take long to find them. They stepped from the trees in a solid line, Caine at the center, walking toward the burning logs, Steven and Mary at either side. Jessica and Elizabeth were on either side of them, Raven beside Jessica. This was the first time I'd seen all of them together, aside from that first day, when they'd been in a tight group behind Caine. I made a quick estimate: this was probably everyone. There had originally been forty-six in the group. This looked to be about that, minus the one man who'd died. They extended in a single line on either side of Caine, headed for the trapped transports.

I panicked. I threw a burst into the air, where it exploded fantastically, then hurled a burst at my feet, launching myself to a height where I could see what was happening inside the berm. I only hoped those inside had enough time to react.

I shouldn't have worried. The moment the echo from my blast died down, every door on every trans-port exploded outward, nearly identical dents warping the metal from the inside. Mythics came streaming out, yelling and shouting, some of them holding the rifles taken from the soldiers inside.

I landed heavily on top of the berm. "Run!" I shouted, praying they would hear me over their own shouts. "Caine!" I pointed in the direction of the ap-proaching line of Caine and the Faithful, which had started running when my blast had broken the still-ness of the sky.

I spotted Clara, Pat, and Sammy near the front of one of the groups leaving their transport. I jumped up and down, frantic, trying to get their attention. I wasn't surprised to see that Clara was holding a rifle and shouting orders to the Mythics around her. I used my hands to create a flare, setting it off right away in my hands to attract their attention. It worked. Several of the groups leaving the carriers looked, and the familiar faces of the Mythics I'd placed in each vehicle started running, calling to others to follow in my direction.

Slowly, other groups noticed their clear direction and followed suit, turning toward me and moving forward. Too slowly. With a cough and a burst of movement, the fire on the tree trunks receded long enough to admit Caine and the Dantons, then rose back up with a vengeance. At the same time, the line of Faithful extended around and began running down each length of the berm. The many Tanks among them picked up huge rocks from the ground and began hurling them over the berm, scattering the group of Mythics funneling in my direction.

It was chaos. I watched as several Mythics lagging at the back of the crowd turned on Caine. Several fired rifles and others ran at him with yells and cries of defiance and fear. None of it mattered. With a single wave of his left hand, they all dissolved into black smoke, which siphoned and spun in a vortex into his palm. *How many?* I tried not to think about it. I had to shut down the feeling part of my brain. There wasn't time to feel things right now. Feeling would get me and countless others killed. I had to act.

The Dantons. Without them, his abilities would be more limited. Without them—With them! They weren't tied to him; they enhanced all the Mythics around them. *Me. They'll enhance me!*

Without thinking, I threw a burst at my feet that sent me flying directly into the fray. On the way in, I looked down, directly into Caine's eyes. It was as if time slowed.

I wasn't sure what he saw, but I saw fear, I saw uncertainty, I saw... Was it disappointment? It was gone in a moment, but suddenly he was yelling and calling to his Faithful, perhaps warning them as they climbed to the tops of the berms on both sides. I felt something new, an additional tingle of my cells as if I'd just touched a small electric fence. The Danton children's effect. I was in range.

I landed on my feet, crumpling to the ground and rolling to absorb some of the impact. I scrambled to my feet, off-balance. Caine was on me, but he had no power, no reaction in his hands. Instead, he caught me with a fist to my jaw that left me reeling, seeing flashes of lights behind my eyelids and tasting blood.

"How dare you?!" He screamed, repeatedly. "My Fold. You steal into *MY* Fold and you steal from me?" He threw another punch, this one at my gut. I barely had time to turn slightly, taking the blow on my side, rather than right to my diaphragm, as he'd no doubt intended.

I pushed off of my back foot, reversing my momentum, and threw an elbow into his sternum. I felt a crack, and he grunted then hissed what I'm pretty sure was a curse in another language.

In the moment it gave me, I looked around, blinking to try and see through the pain in the side of my head where he'd hit me. I found what I was looking for: the line of the Faithful, throwing rocks, some of them holding their hands to their heads doing God only knew what. Looking down the line, I saw Elizabeth and then made direct eye contact with Mary Danton. She stared at me, her face unreadable. I didn't have time for discussions and lengthy reunions.

I looked at the line of the Faithful, and I waved my left hand. Without a sound, no cry of protest or pain, the entire line, shy of Elizabeth and Mary, disintegrated into black dust and rushed toward me, a trail of black smoke.

The avalanche of emotions and sensations that flooded my senses as the horizontal column slapped at my palm was nauseating. This was the first time I'd Translated anyone when I wasn't either an infant or unconscious. The sensation left me vomiting violently, hands on knees, completely incapacitated. The boot that suddenly flung into my limited view of the vomit-spattered ground in front of me laid me flat on my back, a broken nose streaming the taste of heavy blood into the back of my throat.

Caine's words to me were pure vitriol and disgust. "You violated the single most sacred code of my entire culture!" He hissed, and I clearly heard a sickening grinding of bone on bone as he staggered back, clutching his chest. I must have completely fractured his sternum.

He put a boot on my chest, and I felt a change in temperature as the sun disappeared. We were in the Fold. Caine's portion of it. Squinting through the tears brought on by my broken nose, I could make out several shapes. Heretic, Vasily, and my birth mother, Rachel, stood looking on.

"An Interstitial's Translation Fold belongs solely to him! It's the one place in all of Existence that is his alone, and you defiled mine! Only ties of blood even make it possible for one to enter that of another. I would *never* desecrate or profane even my worst enemy in such a manner!"

I tried to respond, but I gagged on the blood in the back of my throat. I spat, and the pain in my nose spread across the rest of my face, hot waves of agony. "I'm not you," I croaked.

I turned onto my belly, pulled my knees under me, and pushed up onto my hands. I worked to clear my throat so that I could breathe. *Please, Heretic, be reading my mind right now! If ever there was a time to be a creepy, eavesdropping, super-powered android, this is it!*

I saw the android shift in my peripheral vision and glanced at him. I had no idea if he could hear me. I saw him nod. I smiled in spite of myself and my situation. *We've got him.*

"Do you find this amusing?!" I'd never seen Caine so mad. I'd seen him dissolve human beings to dust without showing so much as a grimace, and yet here he was, throwing a tantrum that I'd broken into his room.

"Awww, are you afraid I'd read your diary?" I ladled on the sarcasm, hoping to push more buttons.

Caine's eyes went wide. He evidently wasn't used to being spoken to this way.

I pushed myself to stand, wiping blood and tears from my eyes.

I shoved my hands into my pockets, trying to make myself the poster child of "I don't give a damn" attitude. I paced in a semi-circle around Caine, then stopped and turned to face him, my hands still in my pockets.

His voice shook, and his fists were clenched as he stared at me, his eyes wild and wide. "I offered you everything, shared knowledge and understanding to every query you made of me, and this is how you re-pay me? By stealing from me and taking the lives of those who have served faithfully with me for millennia?" He said something in the other language again. "Clearly, I misjudged you."

"Believe it or not, I get that a lot. I'm over it."

I took my hands from my pockets and made a desperate throw at Caine.

He dodged the object I threw, which Heretic caught deftly. In one smooth motion, the android caught hold of Caine's right arm and clamped the c-shaped bracelet into a tight "o" that went right through the middle of my father's forearm. He wouldn't be able to bend it back out of shape on his own. I'd played with that wristband nearly all my life; I'd never been able to bend it, even with both hands.

I couldn't decide if his scream was more outrage or pain. He threw his left hand at Heretic, smacking the android on the chest, but nothing happened. His power was gone.

He fell to his knees, clawing at the piece of metal clamped through his arm. I was afraid for a moment that he would get it out due to sheer ferocity, but the metal didn't bend or budge.

His eyes wild, he stood and ran at me, his hands raised and hooked, intent on my throat. A huge hairy arm caught him from behind, claws grasping the thick coat, then yanked him backward, his feet flying out from under him, and threw him to the misty ground.

The Russian werewolf's toothy grimace hovered inches above Caine's surprised face.

"Give good reason," he growled, teeth snapping together meaningfully.

Caine didn't move.

"James!" Rachel ran toward me, her fingers reaching out but not quite touching my face. "James, I'm so sorry! I had no idea that Joseph—that your father, that he..." She trailed off.

I winced, touching the hot skin around my nose. The bleeding had stopped, miraculously, but the skin was still hot. However, as I stood there, I could feel an uncomfortable tickling and grating deep in the bridge of my nose, then there was an audible click and a flash of pain.

I swore yet again, tears filling my eyes reflexively. I was shocked, though, when the pain immediately and noticeably began to decrease, before disappearing altogether.

"I—I think my nose just unbroke."

Heretic looked at me, cocked his head to one side, and asked, "What *have* you been up to, James Strader?"

I laughed. "Oh, I have lots to show you, Harry."

"You choose them, then?" Caine's voice was barely above a whisper.

I turned to look at him, huddled on the floor, his right arm cradled to his chest, his breathing shallow and accompanied by a wince with each inhalation.

"I *choose* to let them choose for themselves the type of people they're going to be, just like I did."

"And what type of person is that, exactly? The sort who absorbs the souls of his enemies, killing to make a point?" He chuckled quietly. "And here I was thinking that you *didn't* want to be like me."

I didn't answer.

Heretic and Rachel exchanged glances. The android spoke first. "James, what happened? What's going on out there?"

I reached for his and Rachel's hands, nodding toward Vasily. "Grab his hands. We're not out of the woods yet."

Chapter 31

First, I jumped back to my parents' house to drop off Rachel and secure Caine in the makeshift prison cell that had housed the Dantons, Sammy, and Vasily before him. True, Rachel could no longer get into either of the Safeguard bunkers, but she was out of danger, and, worst-case scenario, she could stay in the house if we didn't make it back for some reason.

As I opened up the star map for the second time, Heretic emitted an electronic whistle. "This is extraordinary. Imagine what we could learn out there among the stars."

"Don't count on it," I chuffed. "Caine mentioned something about gravity fields tearing you apart jumping across space like that. I'm not sure it's possible."

The robot raised a finger. "Yet he spoke as someone who has done it."

I paused, then shook his head. *Not the time.*

"We need to get back to that fight."

Vasily growled. "Yes. Let us finish this."

The clearing just outside the Brick once more zoomed into view. I paused for a moment so that we could look the scene over. Outside, only a few seconds had passed since Caine and I left; just long enough to drop off Rachel.

One arm of the Faithful's pincer was gone. I intentionally cut off any feelings about where or how they'd gone. *No time.* It was a lie, but I told it to myself, nonetheless.

At the center of their former line stood the Dantons and Raven, a gap where Caine had been. The other arm still extended forward, the Faithful at various stages of being perched along the berm, some of them, the Tanks, with rocks in hand or just having thrown them. Some of them still had their hands to their heads. I pointed these out to Heretic.

"What are they doing? I'm assuming they're Thinkers, but what are they doing? What capabilities do Thinkers have at a distance? I know Pat talked about how they can manipulate memories and things, and I know he could do stuff to my brain while touching me, but what can you do at a distance?"

Heretic shrugged. "Sew confusion, mostly. As you said, actual manipulation of the nervous system requires physical contact. However, as you seemed to know, a certain level of telepathy is possible. My guess would be that they're simply trying to add to the chaos of the situation, prevent the Mythics from coordinating any effective or coherent opposition."

I nodded. "That makes sense." *What about Tamers?* I scanned the situation and noticed several of the Faithful who seemed less intent on the battle at hand.

Some of them were looking up, others back toward the forest.

"I think we can assume that they have reinforcements from the forest coming at some point. I'm just noticing these," I pointed out the handful of Faithful I'd noticed. "They're probably Tamers."

"I will secure the rear flank." Vasily rumbled, crossing his shaggy arms.

Heretic and I both looked at him.

He shrugged. "Is wrong word?"

I laughed. "Not exactly. Are you ex-military at all?"

He scoffed. "Definitely not. Crime bass have flair for dramatic."

I laughed. "You mean boss?"

He squinted. "What I say?"

"Bass," I said, wiggling my hand in front of me. "Like the fish."

He dismissed it with one wave of a huge, clawed hand. "Bass, boss, same thing; both cold-blooded, scum-sucking bottom-feeders."

I shook my head. "Vasily, we really do need to have a drink sometime." I turned back to the map depicted in front of us. "So, you'll cut off any animal allies they have coming in." I blinked at the phrase, the oddness of it still sticking out to me. "What do we do about the Tanks? We don't have any Con-guns."

Heretic raised a hand. "Why don't we simply have you teleport everyone away? That was the plan originally, was it not? Or you can imprison them along with Caine? It seems such an easily-managed situation, now that Caine isn't a threat. To use an earlier analogy, we now have the biggest gun in the fight; negotiating a surrender should be fairly simple."

I shrugged. "I guess we could. I guess I'm just hoping that, now that we've cut the head off the snake, as it were, we can talk the others down or something."

Heretic put a hand on my shoulder. "A noble intention and sentiment, but don't forget that these people, by all accounts, with the exception of your sister and the Dantons, have been loyal to Caine for countless centuries. I find it highly unlikely that they would suddenly switch sides. Statistically speaking, of course. The sooner they're out of the picture, the better, I should think."

An image sprang unbidden into my head: well over a dozen new blue puddles shot through with gold lights floating in my Translation Fold. I nearly gagged. I pushed the thought away.

Heretic turned me to look at him somewhat. "James, are you all right? Your face just flushed drastically."

I pushed off his arm. "I'm fine. Okay, is that our best course of action, to just get everyone out as quickly as possible? What about the Dantons and Raven? Should I take them, too?"

Heretic shrugged. "It couldn't hurt, I suppose."

I nodded. "All right, that's the goal. I guess we could even put the Faithful in the same place as Caine. Because of the effect of the metal, I don't think any of the Tanks will be able to get that wristband out of his arm. You were only able to because you have freaky robot strength, not Mythic strength."

Heretic stared at me. "Indeed."

"All right, easy enough?" I asked, holding out my fist.

The android stared at it. "What is this?"

I shook it. "A fist bump. It means we're good. Harry, I thought Mom, Dad, and Raven were helping you with all this social cue stuff?"

Heretic shrugged. "We decided it was an inefficient use of energy and processing capability. I maintain control unless the situation explicitly demands it."

"You mean you decided." I grinned.

"I decided." If a robot with no face of his own could smile, I was sure he would have.

He bumped my fist, then I took his hand and reached out for Vasily.

When I jumped back into reality, I didn't go right back to where I'd left it from. I put myself right between the Danton children, where I figured I'd feel their effect strongest. I tried not to think of it as stepping into Caine's shoes. I shook that off.

The real world materialized, bringing with it an assault of noises. Guns were firing, there were screams and yells from both sides, and the Safeguard Mythics were effectively in retreat, despite their greater numbers and weapons. It didn't seem like the Faithful had noticed that Caine was absent yet.

I raised my right hand, intending on taking the

entire remaining flank of the Faithful in a single hand wave. Before I could, an explosion rocked the transport carrier nearest me, mangling the wheels and knocking it up onto its side. Every Mythic head ducked. Where had the blast come from?

I scanned my surroundings, confused. Suddenly, a high-pitched whirring sound caught my ear, and I looked up. A drone, propellers holding it hovering in the air high above us, rotated, trying to get a better angle on something. I didn't know a lot about drones, but I recognized a gun barrel when I saw one, and this one was definitely pointing right at me. I waved a hand, intending to simply absorb it, but it was too far away.

There was a click, then a second rocket-propelled grenade flew toward me. A grenade moves an awful lot slower than a bullet. A second wave of my hand and the projectile disappeared into black smoke long before it got to me.

"Father Caine?! What did you do?" Mary had noticed me, and she was not happy with the surprise that I was not Caine. A car-sized section of the berm suddenly broke away and flew at me. I barely had time to turn and face it before it struck me, and I felt several pops in my chest as a handful of somethings broke or tore before the pain of the experience made sights and sounds irrelevant. I was able to place one hand on the chunk, and it disappeared in white smoke before crushing me beneath it entirely. All things considered, I was lucky, even if my chest didn't see it that way.

This was not going as planned. The pain was already starting to recede, and I could feel bones and tissues realigning and healing, but it was slower than it had been with my nose. The effect of the golden light balls must have already been wearing off.

"Traitor!" It was lower than the last time I'd heard it, but I still recognized Elizabeth's voice. I heard metallic pops and looked up from my back just in time to see a cloud of vapor spill out of the carrier, rapidly condense into water, then rush for my head. Liquid filled my ears, eyes, nose, and mouth. Elizabeth was going to kill me.

My first thought was simply to enter the Fold and escape. The faster my lungs and brain started screaming for oxygen, I knew that wasn't an option. I could see the shape of someone close by through the bubble of water that covered my head. I took a chance and took them with my right hand. Immediately, the water around my face splashed to the ground, and I coughed, spewing from my mouth and nose.

Another grenade went off, and I heard someone scream. Things were now officially out of hand. I sat up, trying to get my bearings and adequate oxygen at the same time. I was looking at Steven's back, several feet away from me. While he was distracted, I waved my right hand, and he collapsed into white smoke. I looked around for Mary and Jessica, hoping to avoid any more near brushes with death. Both young women stood on the edge of the berm, their attention firmly on something back in the direction of the ranch. I stumbled up the berm behind them and waved my hand again, and they, too, joined their brother and sister in the Fold.

I lifted my head up over the berm to see what they'd been looking at. My heart skipped a beat, and I groaned when I did.

Several military assault vehicles roared out of the forest coming from Henry Hoover's ranch. Large machine guns on the roofs of the vehicles spat whistling lead at a terrifying rate. Those Mythics who'd been able to get up and over the berm raced back for the safety of the other side, but many were too late. Scores of them were cut down in a matter of seconds. I checked the crowd, frantic. Where were Pat, Clara, and Sammy?

Pulling myself up over the edge of the berm, I threw a burst in the direction of the lead vehicle. It was too small; the explosion lifted the front of the vehicle and sent it bouncing on its suspension, but it ultimately came rolling on, the man in the tower dealing death every second.

I stood up, and a primal scream ripped through my vocal cords. This time, the entire lead vehicle disappeared in a golden explosion of light that turned orange and gradually stopped rolling end over end, a raging inferno. The other two vehicles broke off, turning and driving perpendicular to our position, spreading out and making a more diverse and difficult target.

I looked back down again for Pat, Clara, and Sammy. I heard the telltale hum and looked up to see easily a dozen more drones speeding over the road toward us from the ranch, almost assuredly armed.

"James, watch out!" I heard someone shout my name and turned around just in time to see a drone drive itself into the ground behind me, its propellers shearing off against the packed earth. I looked up to see Sammy, one hand supporting Pat, the other raised toward the downed drone. Our eyes locked, and she simply nodded. Clara stood on the other side of Pat, still shouting orders. A crowd of Mythics was racing toward us, the remains of the nearly three hundred who had been driven off the ranch.

"Get to me!" I shouted, waving to gather everyone's attention. I was still standing on the top of the berm, my back to the outside. Heretic was suddenly there, standing beside me. I heard, not with my ears, but with my mind, his voice.

"Mythics, come to James! We can get you to safety! This fight is unnecessary. Get to—" Suddenly, the android's head spun to look behind us. "James!" he shouted. He leaped forward and pushed me down the side of the embankment, just before several dozen whistling rounds ripped through him, shredding metal plating, and spitting out torn wires and mangled circuits. He went limp, and oil, fluids, and arcs of electricity poured from his body as it clanked and tumbled down the embankment.

"Heretic!" suddenly Raven was at the robot's side, cradling circuits and the remains of his casing in her hands.

"The Creator." Heretic's voice was distant and tinny as if it came from the bell of a faraway phonograph. "My objective is complete. James is..." The voice trailed off, and one last arc of electricity passed over the android's head, then he went silent.

I turned, my voice cracking with suppressed emotion. "Everyone as close as you can!" I started waving, my right hand trailing white smoke as I pulled people in at every side. Those at the back crowded in as those in the front disappeared, and I took them into the Fold, too. At last, it was only me. I turned as I heard a rough panting, and Vasily came loping up to me, reaching out a hand. I took him in.

I stood in the wreckage, listening to the crackling of several fires, the whine of the drones coming back for another pass, the sound of additional approaching engines, and the shouting voices of troops on the other side of the berm.

I thought of my adoptive mother and father, who had helped in programming and giving Heretic his mission of helping me find my way now lost to me for good with the destruction of Heretic's memory banks. I thought about Heretic himself, who had been instrumental in giving me the space and the information needed to choose who I wanted to be. I thought about the Mythics all around me, Faithful and Safeguard alike, who'd been cut down without mercy, without a trial, without justice. Most of them had done no harm to anyone, aside from upholding the tenets of Safeguard. They weren't perfect.

Yet, they'd been massacred, deemed a threat, and exterminated without another thought. That wasn't right. That wasn't fair. Caine had worked for lifetimes to protect humanity, to keep them safe. He'd dedicated his entire existence to exterminating their competitors, like a gamekeeper on a wildlife preserve. This was the result.

I passed one last look over the twisted and still-smoking remains that had been Heretic, and I decided. If it was a fight that the humans wanted, I'd give it to them. I, and those like me, had every right to exist, to live our lives just the same as any other person on this planet. If that meant that we had to fight to be allowed to do that, then so be it.

I picked up a rock the size of a softball, and I placed my left palm on top of it. The rock began to glow, brighter and brighter. I set the rock on the ground and stepped into the Fold.

The war for Mythic independence had begun.

End of Book Two

The story continues in Book Three of the Strader
Notebooks: Mythic Sovereign

Acknowledgments

I've always wanted to be an author. It's always kind of been like the pipe dream of the child who dreams of becoming an astronaut when they grow up: sure, there are a few who actually do, but most of us settle for much tamer, more run-of-the-mill professions and careers.

Here I am, having completed the second of many books to come, and I still have a difficult time believing it's real. I guess I always thought there would be a bit more pomp to it. Y'know, the whole podium, celebratory medal of official induction into the guild, all that jazz. Instead, the moment between a writer with no books available and an author with multiple books on the market was only separated by countless hours in front of a computer screen, dances of exultation in the shower as a plot hole fills in nicely in my head, only to come crashing to my knees as I realize I didn't write it down and my brain in the shower is nothing more than a fleshy sieve.

That being said, I can't adequately express the appreciation due to those who have brought me to this point. Claire is the silent partner in all of this. She puts up with my brainstorming, suffers through my melodramatic reading of countless drafts as I work out kinks, and is always the final push over the edge telling me, "Just publish it!" Claire, you're incomparable.

The other significant influence at this point is Amy Specker. She's been the first and most devoted among my beta readers, and the one who inevitably reenergizes me in my work, helping me believe that what I've written deserves more than the digital dung heap. Thanks, Amy.

Justin is a nerd. As a child, he tried to read every single book at his local library that had the word "dragon" in the title.

Justin lives in southern Illinois with his wife and children. To learn more about Justin and to follow along with his upcoming projects, follow Justin on Facebook at Author Justin K. Nuckles and join his monthly newsletter to get exclusive behind-the scenes content and updates on upcoming projects that aren't available anywhere else.